The Early Steam Locomotive

by

Robert Badella

authorHOUSE

1663 LIBERTY DRIVE, SUITE 200
BLOOMINGTON, INDIANA 47403
(800) 839-8640
www.authorhouse.com

First published by AuthorHouse 09/17/04

ISBN: 1-4184-7030-9 (e)
ISBN: 1-4184-5323-4 (sc)

Printed in the United States of America
Bloomington, Indiana

This book is printed on acid-free paper.

TABLE OF CONTENTS

CHAPTER ONE

The first piston operating steam engine had been originally developed by Thomas Newcomen of England during 1712. Those distinctive features of the Newcomen engine were a unique combination of one hollow cylinder which was fitted with a round piston. Once that cylinder was filled up with pressurized steam a counter-weighted mechanical device would raise its piston upwards. Then next by spraying cool water onto this exterior surface of the cylinder, vaporous steam was being condensed which had gravely resulted in creating a vacuum. Also, the atmospheric pressure of energetic exertion easily pushed this piston downwards inside of that cylinder, thus causing a pump plunger to be lifted upwards. These valves for admitting steam and condensing water were all manually operated.

In 1757 James Watt being a maker of mathematical instruments opened a shop at Glasgow University along southwestern Scotland. Watt had been repairing a model Newcomen steam engine during 1764, and evidently was impressed by its waste of steam. His reaction had been to preserve and separate that reducible condensation into an enclosed chamber apart from the cylinder, but in connection with movement of its engine. Simultaneously, by keeping this cylinder permanently hot and relatively cold it would not be necessary to heat and cool the cylinder with each stroke of that piston. Watt's separate condenser was famously patented for "A New Invented Method of Lessening the Consumption of Steam and Fuel in Fire Engines" within 1769; and by 1775, the House of Commons extended his patent for twenty-five years.

Oliver Evans was a wagon worker apprentice at the time of 1772, and initially had been first to grasp this primary meaning about steam power within America. During 1784, he built a factory mill outside of Philadelphia, fundamentally to reduce its major industrial problem for grinding grain. Moreover in actual performance on one of his conveyors, power was merely supplied by waterwheels, and labor was only required to set that mill into motion. Grain had to be fed in at one end, and passed by a system of conveyors and chutes through these final stages of milling and refining which then emerged out from the other end as finished flour.

By 1790, Evans was producing a high-pressure steam engine for economical purposes while ardently trying to accommodate both land and water transportation. However, the possibility of that engine for road conveyance was not entirely favorable, and he was incapable to convince certain authorities for allowing this elementary operation of it along the Pennsylvania Turnpike. Within a few years later he had engines performing several other kinds of work which included sowing grain, driving sawmills, and powering a dredge. In June of 1805, Oliver Evans had reasonably constructed his new type of steam-engine scow known as the Orukter Amphibolos, and it measured 30-feet long by 12-feet wide. That contrivance of his steamboat and wagon had realistically been equipped with wheels to run on land as well as on water, and soon became this first powered road vehicle to operate in the United States.

John Fitch was a land surveyor along the Ohio River and became mainly interested about producing steamboats. Fitch had skillfully gained its exclusive rights to conduct and build steamboats shortly after decisively failing to potentially divulge the inevitable permission from distinguishable representatives of these American colonies. However, he willfully had been discouraged in presuming to attain supporters, and was lacking those earnest funds to extend further with his incredible development. During 1787, he built a 45-foot vessel powered by a set of six paddles, and together with that intense action of his steam engine, accomplished a successful run along this Delaware River before a group of delegates to the Constitutional Convention. He also assembled a much larger steamboat for carrying passengers and freight with regularly scheduled trips between Philadelphia and New Jersey, and had been granted a U.S. patent for steamboats on August 26, 1791. Fitch was the first American to achieve some measure of respective esteem and public recognition; however he ignored building and operational costs which adversely ensued in an attemptable failure to affluently demonstrate that economic value of forceful steam impulsion.

More importantly within this intervening period Europe was utterly execrating about its unstable concept of steam power for land and sea functions during the same time when a farm boy of seventeen had gone from Pennsylvania to pursue his wealth in Philadelphia. Robert Fulton was an apprentice to a jeweler, and scrupulously studied art in the evening to become a painter. He also saved four hundred dollars for travel, and continued to properly proceed ahead with his studies under Benjamin West of London by 1787. Valuable to note Fulton had robustly acquired this experience of canal engineering with such conceivable inventions for dredging harbors as well as building locks to support canals, and he particularly presented preliminary plans for a complete system of inland waterways during 1794.

In 1801, Fulton met up with Robert Livingston whom at that time was minister to France, and they both helped to build the submarine Nautilus under an agreeable grant from Napoleon Bonaparte. Fulton and Livingston had efficiently assembled a steamboat which ran on this Seine River at Paris as early as 1803. The two of them returned to America after joining together in a partnership, however Fulton was not fully recognized as its inventor of steam power for the sea. Robert Fulton had carefully taken into consideration all of these inventors prior to his own, and secured a useful and tangible explanation of operating a steamboat. But, he would not have recognizably proven this prosperous success without obtaining its beneficial and financial backing of Livingston. Their pretentious side-wheeler steamboat the Clermont, primarily had been operating along this Hudson River in 1807, and jubilantly completed an experimental trip of 150 miles within thirty-two hours. Worth mentioning was that after making a few valuable improvements, Fulton then renamed the steamboat North River, while it went into regular service between New York and Albany. Ultimately Fulton saw his feasible steamboat in triumphal operation which resulted for him to build the Phoenix so as to claim superior recognition of being its first seagoing steamship.

This noble engineer and ship designer Robert L. Stevens had been a prominent and perceptible figure of naval shipping design. Stevens usually assisted his father in building yachts, sailboats, and schooners. Both Robert and John Stevens had evidently constructed a paddle-wheel steamer which was put into passenger operations between New York, and New Brunswick; New Jersey during 1807. Robert also created a "false bow" for its steamship New Philadelphia in order to strongly increase speed performance so that it would be able to depart from Albany, New York in the early morning, and arrive at New York City before nightfall. Additionally Robert Stevens had built his ferryboat Hoboken within exemplary proportions along modern lines during 1822. As an enthusiastic yachtsman, he diligently designed its 88-foot sailing vessel Maria, which had an auspicious reputation of being known as the fastest yacht around this world for over twenty years.

An English engineer by the name of Charles Vignoles had been accredited with his invention of this inverted T-rail. Apparently, Robert Stevens with his strength and stability cleverly introduced a similar design to that of Vignoles by the 1830's. Stevens had thoroughly discovered that iron rails could be firmly supported under wooden ties, and by applying gravel beneath a solid bottom foundation it would appropriately provide privileges for building a sufficient and permissible railroad. As a matter of fact his rail and roadbed construction had deeply emphasized an overwhelming progression in the United States. He also equipped this front of a locomotive with a metal grilled shape frame, and had significantly increased their number of driving wheels to advantageously permit better traction.

Therefore the locomotive being a separate unit which can independently move from one place to another is dominantly controlled by a skillful source of power. So it is that by understanding a locomotive we are adequately able to perceive this railway system. The tremendous impact of steam locomotives had brought on its railroad into becoming a "railroad" itself. Moreover these twin strips of steel visually allow this capable capacity for a permanent pathway of destination in operating a locomotive train.

* * * * * * * * *

Chiefly that generalized influence of trackage had drastically played an intricate role for developing those systematic railroads.

However, the most greatest aspect upon railroad building was when their final achievement had been prudently conceivable about harnessing steam power, replacing this unstable strength of a horse in substitution for an enduring powerful machine. So by self-intelligence and logical reasoning the railroad fundamentally begins with formal introduction of its locomotive, that famed "iron horse". On the contrary its practical success and usefulness of this Newcomen engine had been modified by James Watt with his separate condenser so as to establish the first basic steam engine.

Eventually those responsible inventors would soon realize that there was more of an indelible interest to this worthwhile production of inventing a locomotive than merely putting an engine on wheels. There had been problems which obviously existed in trying to make it pull, rather than just spinning wheels along their tracks. Also there was the daring perceptibility of assembling together a mechanism that would soundly hold in place while chugging ahead, and be subjugated to road hazards, as an alternative to eagerly supporting locomotives upon a securely well-built structure. And, there was a vital factor of building a dependable engine with enough power in relationship to its weight bulk for moving itself as well as a load.

The many difficulties which steadily had been encountered were so frustrating and intense that nearly twenty years had consequently passed. James Watt's earlier steam engine had admissibly been at work while being widely used around coal mines and factories. By 1789, Richard Trevithick who was a superintendent of mining machinery in Cornwall; England, actually demonstrated his first preferable outcome with steam. Furthermore Trevithick's valuable contribution to the railway system had been ascertained over this process of harnessing steam power for its exact purpose of land transportation.

Richard Trevithick in 1797 had promptly constructed both working models of stationary and locomotive engines which were later on given an exclusive patent. Trevithick was held responsible for designing a full-scale steam engine which was conveniently at work in these ore mines. He also became a mechanical engineer and built his first steam carriage that had been fully tested during 1801. The steam engine which Watt's constituted was a meaningless source of strength in releasing low-pressure steam (five or six pounds to the square inch) by generating its power from a small condenser. This earlier type of steam engine had been excessively heavy and was extremely cumbersome which hardly produced much horsepower at all. Physically that engine had not been strong enough to pull anything, for example to carry an enormous amount of weight along a road or even to provide a necessary and proficient speed requirement.

Its definite and forceful determination of Richard Trevithick had been to create high-pressure steam (fifty pounds to the square inch) whereby in omitting this condenser on Watt's steam engine. His impulsive meaningfulness of removing that condenser would be to increase its amount of flow vapor coming from a boiler where water is heated and circulated. Trevithick's next step was to procure a fire hot enough so as to withstand such pressure, without its need of a heavy blower. As a result, Trevithick had been solely responsible for turning this exhaust steam, coming from these cylinders up through a smokestack, thereby creating an ample draft to burn an immense hot fire inside the boiler.

Specifically much of its critical and inherent requirements for harnessing steam power had favorably begun to sensible influence those valiant inventors as well as superior engineers which were contributing their strenuous and timely undertakings of accomplishment. On Christmas Eve of 1801, Trevithick was trying out this new idea he proposed and it worked, his self-propelled steam carriage expectantly hauled these first passengers ever to be moved by steam propulsion.

Within two years later, Trevithick had been operating a steam omnibus at London, and built his <u>New</u> <u>Castle</u> locomotive during 1804. This locomotive ran on a Welsh tramroad, but its engine had been too heavy for the road, and subsequently was relinquished which Trevithick tolerably anticipated for his desires were to run a steam hammer with that engine. In 1816, Trevithick had willingly entered its service of these Peruvian mines, thus entirely excluding him away from the locomotive scene. More important Trevithick's toilsome distinctive solution by opening a draft, had greatly expanded its future of building an engine of stability which was capable enough to pull itself with any reasonable amount of force.

However this could scarcely be considered a prominent and victorious resolution over their struggling efforts. Although it had been a brief attempt dynamically revealing in which direction to fervently scrutinize. But there was a persistent man already at work who was the person to bring about Trevithick's beginning to financial prosperity; this brilliant engineer working at these Killingworth mines along northern England, learning to read and write at night school, indulging in his imagination of reproducing an iron horse. Furthermore that native of the colliery district near Newcastle upon Tyne and great railroad pioneer was George Stephenson.

Time had substantially elapsed and eight years passed in which Trevithick's demandable task was inevitably attained for neither Stephenson nor other inventors were never able to clearly repeat without much success. By 1812, John Blenkinsop who had been an English inventor built an engine that could essentially pull. Blenkinsop's locomotive was equipped with a vertical two-cylinder engine, and had been driven by two shafts that were geared to a fifth toothed wheel running on a "rack" rail roadway. This British coal miner, inspector William Hedley had constructed his steam locomotive Puffing Billy during 1813, which in effect signified that four evenly positioned wheels rolling along on smooth rails would incidentally exhibit both its supporting and pulling power urgently needed. Moreover Hedley's locomotive had mainly relied upon an intense physical friction, and was very consistent for pulling coal wagons between a mine and wharves.

Nevertheless this uncertain dilemma of harnessing steam power for public and freight transportation was definitely moving closer to a final completion. In addition these engines were accurately conformable and adequately acceptable, but they were potentially lacking its compulsory speed which was strongly required to pull heavier loads. As a matter of fact those Blenkinsop's locomotives remained in service for decades, and later caused extensive competition among other engineers for its release of George Stephenson from London. Lord Ravensworth had been a mine-owner for whom Stephenson worked under, and he would not let those mines which employed Blenkinsop and Hedley move ahead of him. In notable consideration, Ravensworth set aside its indispensable funds for building this engine that Stephenson had insistently intended on producing.

George Stephenson supposedly had a plan of his own by which he wholly proposed to accomplish along with the financial assistance and backing that was bestowed to him. Trevithick had reliably proven how to obtain expedient and resourceful power. Between them, Blenkinsop and Hedley had shrewdly shown how to perceive traction. Hedley's <u>Puffing Billy</u> significantly demonstrated that equally uniform wheels moving on smooth rails, would pull—something which both Trevithick and Blenkinsop had needlessly doubted. It was Stephenson who was to resolve this next problem, imposing that its engine's weight evenly rest upon all wheels in spite of roughness along the track. Otherwise, any unbalanced wheel might have a slight tendency to spin rather than pull.

Stephenson's first engine was the <u>Blucher</u> which had been brought into service during July of 1814, and courageously displayed to be distinctively characteristic. Although in his second attempt, George Stephenson had found that apparent difficulty which was confronting him. While assembling together his wheel framework, he used steam cylinders; and each cylinder draws steam at the same exact pressure from its boiler, so as a result it had kept this boiler weight relatively equalized on their wheels. In fact that type of framework assembly design had prevalently induced its attention of Europe towards Stephenson, and his "Killingworth" style of engine. It also improved upon this pulling power of earlier engines, as well as the possibility to easily reach moderate speeds.

Special attention should be noted that those recently proficient improvements upon its Killingworth engine did not mean achieving an ultimate development while striving to conquer greater efforts. Even though a relatively allowable and dependable engine had been created, it unanimously refused to earnestly reveal if this engine *could pull more economically than horses*. Everybody had been under an evident impression that these engines were uniquely interesting, like novelties, by which Stephenson and a few others could barely accept with much belief. Although it was absolutely certain that when all costs were added together the old trustworthy horse would copiously win without hesitation.

* * * * * * * * *

Meanwhile a period of time had briskly passed at London until July of 1821 when a community of people from Stockton and Darlington, two towns within that region had been under total agreement for projecting to build a Railway System. Accordingly their principal purpose of this railway would be to clearly connect and collectively join together those towns, and also to allegedly employ these services of engineer George Stephenson for completing its ongoing and vigorous task.

A solemn commitment had been firmly issued to this steam locomotive for the first ever indicative performance in history at a general public ceremony. That binding pledge would also accommodate practice trials for the locomotive to imperatively demonstrate their stable endurance among strong rivalry with other strengths of power. Horses would be at the starting line for under its law, this "public way" had to allow any horse and wagon upon advance payment of proper toll. While neither horse nor locomotive could not surpass two rather steep hills during that competition, Stephenson had cleverly emplaced a firm devise acceptable by these civil engineers of the day for applying power to transmission. As a matter of fact this was a "cable railway" whereby stationary engineers had been pulling cars along in a forward direction with ropes which were wrapped around barrel shaped round drums.

On the contrary Europe was beginning to foolishly envision that these competitive workouts would permanently establish which method—horse, steam locomotive, or cable railway—would be the most productive. But, failing results after that upshot of their grand opening on September 27, 1824 had obviously confirmed nothing at all. Undoubtedly, extreme chaos aversely ensued from those varieties of strategies which basically prevented any single classification from presumptuously succeeding within this supportive occurrence.

Although another permissible affair at striking ground, a sounder test had to be thoroughly proven, and one year later this prospective opportunity for it had appropriately arrived at London. Likewise a selective group of individuals had been intimately determined to prosperously create a railroad from Liverpool to Manchester, and in likeness of their Northtyne side friend, they desirably wanted to diligently employ George Stephenson for his tactful capabilities.

However public disturbances quickly erupted over gaining a legitimate and pardonable exemption which had compulsively compelled its rational providers to put Stephenson beyond in comparative approval of these London engineers, George Rennie and John Rennie. They were customarily granted those stringent privileges on May 1, 1826; except when they wouldn't have Stephenson as their resident engineer, George and John Rennie were abruptly rejected, and Stephenson was solidly chosen by this local community.

Perceptibly the board of directors soon saw themselves faced with uncertain destiny between a choice of alternatives which had to be amply decided upon for its Liverpool and Manchester Railway. George and John Rennie, like most civil engineers of London, highly favored a cable railway, and the land grant was actually acquired on its vital understanding that this feasible technique would be suggestively used. Special attention should be made that Stephenson which everyone assumed, would only imaginably conceive to produce locomotives. But if that were his mere intentions, thus assiduously challenging this exemption, what might explicitly occur in heedful observance amongst their directors if those locomotives should speciously fail?

Stephenson at once boldly comprehended the wisdom and expediency which characterized him for being not only a competent engineer, but also a famous promoter as well. Expressively in an eminently renowned memorandum which was dated November 5, 1828 he wrote a rather powerful, imperious, and domineering case for its locomotive. Consequently since these advisable directors were quite hesitant, Stephenson and several others had insistently prepared a program which bitterly would justify putting steam locomotives on the road.

It was a devious scheme in order to emphasize that if a steam locomotive encountering such unique demands could be obtainable then there would be no formal argument for any further procrastination. Henceforth, its infallible directors had been anxiously persuaded to formulate their distinctive requirements into a prize competition. And, on the 20th of April 1829, all of Europe had sensibly been informed that 500 pounds would await this locomotive which on October 1, 1829 among other deeds could especially fulfill the following:

1. Effectually consume its own smoke (the charter had insisted upon this above all else);
2. Draw twenty tons if weighing six tons, and proportionately less if of lighter weight, at 10 miles an hour;
3. Perform these feats with a maximum steam pressure of 50 pounds to the square inch; and
4. Perform better than any competing engine.

These predetermined potential requirements were highly regarded as such a definite implement that one dubious Liverpool gentleman certified himself willing, if they had been possibly attained, to "eat a stewed locomotive wheel for breakfast". But George Stephenson, an enthusiastic engineer who would meet those demanding challenges of that sort, flauntingly felt confident enough about winning.

Throughout his prestigious years of designing and building locomotives, he had vastly donated many important improvements, largely but impressive when added all together. Its quality of steel was improving which instinctively allowed him to use springs rather than steam cylinders for mounting his wheels. Also, Stephenson's shopmen were learning more about better ways of working up alloy metals (this was important in those days, before any scientific tests of metal had been made) so that these moving adaptable parts of a locomotive would adequately function once they had been soundly attained. Although perhaps most indicatively of all, he had a keen agile helper, his son Robert (born 1803) who already had accredited himself as a genuine chip of the old block in mechanical ability.

Instantly within a decisive moment, Robert Stephenson had impulsively decided with pure aspiration to repulsively abolish this "Killingworth" plan type of engine totally—the design with which his father ascribed his reputation—for being bulky and cumbersome. Conceptually those Killingworth details, and every other steam engine during its time had been using a vertical drive from cylinders to wheels, and that kind of structural arrangement had imposingly demanded an abundant amount of weight in movable parts. Robert had ostensibly proposed to lessen this unessential weight by suitably mounting his cylinders in a relatively horizontal line with their wheels. Reasonably its significant determination had been to aptly hold the weight down to nearly four tons. If he was capable enough to ascertain this achievement, then these exerting rules for severe and rigorous competition would justifiably permit the locomotive to run on four wheels instead of six; and practical lengthy experiences had normally guided both George and Robert that by its increments of additional wheels just merely amounts to attracting more difficulty. And, Robert was supporting his arguments by pointing to this recently built <u>Lancaster Witch</u>, a locomotive demonstrating nearly all of those predetermined ideas he wanted to steadily attain which was running nicely on the small Bolton and Leigh Railway.

To all this, father George had prospectively presented his formal objection for Robert's cognitive consideration: That if a locomotive primarily designed as Robert intended, would certainly need an ample and sufficient boiler type of any previously built boiler known. Otherwise, it would not have the power necessarily demanded to carefully initiate its speed requirements. Robert had tolerably planned on carrying out this prudent suggestion which was generously volunteered by Henry Booth who was a distinguishable congenially official of the Liverpool and Manchester Railroad.

All of those earlier steam engines had one or two flues for carrying hot fire in its boiler out to a passage through a smokestack. Moreover with that supportive advice which Booth initially offered was to substantially increase its heating capacity by efficiently installing more tubes. This was the indisputable answer if it could be comparatively accomplished, but would it? Although it was a big concern as both of the Stephenson's knew that this implicit result may have been its virtual solution. However the only problem was that when steam pressure begins to rise in a boiler, these ends would have a natural tendency to swell outwards, and might pull loose from their tubes.

After cautiously evaluating those obvious circumstances, George had willfully determined to utterly deem the boy responsible; and Robert then effortlessly dwelled into that new assignment. When his first boiler bulged as normally anticipated, he energetically employed the use of stay bolts,—installing longer rods inside its boiler, fastening their ends together—and this swelling was readily reduced.

Also, he had been experiencing some troublesome difficulties of unequal expansion within these reddish-brown copper tubes from between its heavy solid iron boiler, at a point of exposing a high temperature heat inside of the firebox. So in order to properly defeat this obstructive trouble a newer kind of tube-fastener had been advantageously considered and which was uniquely installed. Before those days of precision machinery techniques, there were certain problems with fitting pistons and cylinders, as well as designing lighter but yet stronger alternate metal parts.

Being under the shrewd and watchful eye of George, Robert Stephenson had evidently exceeded by solving each of these surfacing mechanical problems which persistently transpired. Seasonally both spring and summer passed, while everyone seemed to have been fairly given an opportunity to earnestly win this Liverpool and Manchester prize. Inquiries and entries were abundantly pouring in from its viable competitors about who would participate in the "Rainhill tests". Likewise there were schemes of all varieties such as sail cars, flesh-and-blood horse on treadmill, as well as boilers that moved along on wheels which had all been taken into immediate and understandable discussion.

* * * * * * * * *

This grand day of their official opening trials took place in London on October 6, 1829. The binding obligation of these directors had been to accurately verify its most qualifying types of power motion available which reluctantly reduced that rival competition to only six entries. Among those six entries of this competitive contest was the <u>Rocket</u>, which had been honorably entered by the Stephenson's. Also, the <u>Novelty</u> which had been built by John Braithwaite and John Ericsson of London was formally listed as an entree. Timothy Hackworth had gainfully obtained its rightful permission to enter his locomotive the <u>Sans Pareil</u>, and additionally three other locomotives which hardly managed to even contend towards that prestigious award. Nonetheless, six machines were fortunately enough to marvelously exhibit an enticing event for these loyal supporters.

The day itself was one of arousing adventure and delightful admiration. There was a stretch of track laid northwest of England and west of Rainhill, near Liverpool—historic name of Rainhill tests—which had been their chosen site for those test trials. Also there were between ten to fifteen thousand people in attendance on opening day, including numerous engineers from every civilized part of this country. Moreover a large band had distinguishably contributed its part in front of colorful waving flags as huge crowds overly exceeded many of these taverns in town.

It was a trembling sound an instantaneous reaction when the <u>Rocket</u>, adoringly decorated in black and yellow paint with a white smokestack began to take starting position. That twenty ton load requirement which was wholly proposed among its mindful directors had been profitably demonstrated by this courageous locomotive at a speed of eighteen miles an hour which set the immense crowd in total amazement. Within a challenging sequence, this detailed copper and blue <u>Novelty</u> had visibly appeared on these tracks to show its paces without any apprehension in front of many goggle-eyed spectators. Expediently, the <u>Novelty</u> had pulled that tonnage load implemented for competing at Rainhill with an audacious incredible speed of twenty-eight miles per hour.

On the contrary those influential directors were seriously and highly favorable of testing their other entries which still

14

endured on the following morning as this day was coming to an end. Principally these intriguing individuals anxiously saw its first trials of locomotive competition in an outburst of thrilled and daunting excitement before they had spontaneously dispersed away. At Liverpool that evening all were in quick sudden agreement over the Novelty for lively chatter was sparkling throughout its towns and taverns. Furthermore the test trials would eventually help as a determinate factor for affluently proving a victorious winner of this contest, and consequently everyone concerned about steam engines had to intensively wait with astonishing anticipation.

That night the Stephenson's had felt terribly worried over its Novelty's speed, and they were somewhat apprehensive about winning this race. Apparently these emulous intentions of George Stephenson were to vehemently excel that first trial run of competition, and to efficiently concentrate more on the locomotion power of his Rocket. Nevertheless this climatic weather on that next day had abruptly postponed its test trials as rain and muddy conditions had persistently prevailed on the 7th. On October 8th, those imperative competitors of this race were defiantly confronted with crucial tests which instantly became dubbed "The Ordeal", taken from their language of its announcement as set forth: "The following is the Ordeal which we have decided that each locomotive shall undergo".

> The Ordeal required that each locomotive
> make enough round trips over the
> course to equal the run from Liverpool
> to Manchester. Also it must maintain
> full speed for an aggregate run of
> thirty miles. Then it would refuel, and
> repeat the performance—if it could!

Critically a desperate protest in awesome disapproval and disappointment had ultimately risen amongst many competitors of this race which then despitefully caused them to be arrogant and clamorous over its test trials. However these watchful directors had been avidly determined for carrying out that explicit meaningfulness of their Ordeal, for stamina was a test of endurance which was of greater importance than speed and pulling power, and they had perfectly demonstrated the right to proceed ahead. This impetuous disagreement had finally ended between those directors and competitors when the Rocket was intently ordered back to its race, and that spirited locomotive had astonishingly shown an achievement of quality and stability. The Stephenson's locomotive occupied an entire day, and two days had relatively past due to inevitable weather conditions until the Novelty was ready to run again.

Currently at the time George Stephenson had been actively proving his engineering experiences and shop skills with its Rocket locomotive. When the Novelty ran a second time it performed well, but unfortunately experienced a broken water pipe, and had to be modestly retired for mechanical repairs. Furthermore for two days of solid uninterrupted delays, other entries in these trials were being tested, except they could not withstand such extreme perseverance of extensive lengthy runs. On October 14th, the Novelty had been back on track again, and deceivingly broke down once more so Ericsson had to significantly withdraw from this competition. The Rocket had drastically remained in contention by competently standing up against that Ordeal, and officially was declared the winner of this race.

Once those Rainhill test trials substantially had been proven and were inherently accomplished, then direct acceptance for the steam locomotive was predominantly recognized. It had been Stephenson's convincing and satisfying victory which imaginably reflected its birth of our early railroad into America, where that essential and prevailing groundwork was prestigiously established with his Rocket. Many of these engineers were easily excitable to witness an effectual locomotive represent its functionary work for a specific resolution of hauling freight uphill, providing passenger service, making race horses look like donkeys, and also to meet its demanding challenge of determination in a worthwhile continuous effort.

Thus, the name Iron Horse has been chiefly associated with bringing on railroads after which Trevithick had solely brought forth over twenty-eight years ago by turning exhaust steam up through this smokestack, and nearly seventy years after Watt's introduction of its first steam engine. Steam power had been definitely available and could be prevalently attainable for a meaningful railroad to be put into operation. Likewise all that potentially existed had been to set up and construct railways with foreseeable contemplation of running locomotives on them for the general purpose of carting goods and carrying passengers.

Although it was a diverse situation which opposed these energetic men who were vigorously waiting with diligent intuitions to build and run railroads throughout the United States. Moreover its essence and fundamental increasing development of new business activities had intimately encouraged righteous creation of a railroad in finding it expedient to permeate this young interchanging commerce. However, prosperity of promoting railroads in order to clearly allow indicative circumstances did not generally evolve upon having good locomotives. Further to feasibly obtain and posses the best possible steam engines, careful consideration for structural expansion was not yet practical unless adverse problems could be solidly resolved. Its biggest problem facing those early engineers had been to conceivably persuade some financial investors that plentiful and bountiful business movement could be securely ascertained to pay a profitable cost for the many quantities of miles and line necessarily on behalf of benefiting their probable opportunities. Consequently, the most particular condition of America's trouble was to proficiently acquire enough available tracks for adequately funding its railway construction rather than trying to purchase expensive and costly locomotives.

As evident railroad building in America had partially gotten off to a gradual start at first because of trackage being an utmost concernment during that time. Even in a surrounding land which was thickly covered with elevated mountains, mighty rivers, and untamed forests, where would such futuristic sums be initially invested with any subsidized prospect of yield? For instance, a 50-mile line might cost anywhere from half a million to a million dollars to constitute and fully complete construction of building a railroad even with the flimsiest of road tracks. These analytical conditions may explain why railroads were so slow to produce locomotives which could advantageously offer prosperous rates for freight and provide passenger service to those growing territories within this country.

CHAPTER TWO

Before any conceivable roads were ever designed upon or planned out in America famous old Indian paths presently had been in existence during the time. Those remaining trails were deliberately blazed along an encompassing region of heavily thicken forests, and vast flat lands that had been prevalently occupied by some native Indians. Many of these reachable trails were primitive pathways inhabited among its Indians, and which had actually opened up possible routes so as to provide better accessible and available roads throughout our rural country.

The Mohawk Trial being an Indian footpath had been precisely turned into an ox road and which became its first interstate toll-free roadway in the United States by 1786. Apparently numerous amounts of migrating settlers and exploring pioneers had been frequently occupying distinct control of that Mohawk Trail. Moreover these early inspirational travelers desperately needed an easier route in which to crossover this Appalachian mountain chain from New York State, so that they could bring about their traveling Westward journeys. During the 18th century, its Mohawk Trail had been greatly improved by an abundant number of additional new turnpikes. Furthermore this Mohawk Trail which primarily travels through much of Massachusetts had strongly remained in current usage until those earlier decades of the 19th century.

Its first ever major paved roadway situated in North America had been the Philadelphia-Lancaster Turnpike which initially opened for providing services by 1794. This spiked barrier turnpike had aptly been serving as a rich and prosperous agricultural region. Also, that remarkable Philadelphia-Lancaster Turnpike had shown an increase of steady and wealthy profits, which considerably paid dividends in as much as fifteen percent to their shareholders. The fundamental construction of this hard-surface, stone, and gravel turnpike was built at a cost of $465,000. Additionally those

18

many miles of turnpike building had been privately constructed in Pennsylvania along a 62-mile length of required specifications with nine tollgates in full operation.

During 1818, the Cumberland Road was engagingly offering transportation of traffic between Cumberland in Maryland, and Wheeling; West Virginia. Most of all lively public demand was beginning to stir up amongst everyone about building a feasible road to the West. In 1806, Congress had crucially voted in approving funds for preliminary surveys of a federally financed highway. Moreover the first 20-mile stretch of its Cumberland Road had been essentially built during 1811. Consequently, within six years this prestigious turnpike road triumphantly advanced another eighty miles to Wheeling, located along its eastern bank of the Ohio River. By 1833, the Cumberland Road had been strategically extended to reach Columbus, Ohio; after which affordable and obtainable finances were appropriately raised by urban land sales for development of that parcel of road.

This exalted period of turnpike composition within America had formatively been its first forty years of that 19th century. In fact those turnpike roads were commonly in frequent usage by heavy traffic and stagecoaches. Likewise tollgates had permanently been prudently established at particular intervals of between six and ten miles. Also a nominal fee of 25-cents was adequately required to be paid for each carriage crossing over these tollgates. As a final result, that costly expensive of building a turnpike road had been sufficiently repaid. Furthermore, the average cost for constituting and construction of a turnpike, had realistically ranged from $5,000 to $10,000 per mile of road surface. However it was not until the glorious opening of this Erie Canal, and its coming of steam locomotives along steel railways, that such turnpike roads with their significant tollgates were plainly appearing in these Eastern States.

At its beginning of this 19th century only 100 miles of navigable canals had been exceptionally built in America. Valuable to note these conventional canals would easily permit an advantageous and practicable waterway system for steamboat navigation along many of those Eastern Rivers. More important this idea of better transportation was truly indeed a demand at that time, and James

Monroe had officially authorized permissible grants of public lands. The Canal Era had relatively provided our early settlers with an access to inland areas, and also aided its farmers for shipping their crops to marketplace. In 1817, John C. Calhoun who was a nationalist leader and helpful sponsor of internal improvements said:

> "We are greatly and rapidly—I was
> about to say fearfully—growing. This
> is our pride, and our danger; our
> weakness and our strength… Let us,
> then, bind the Republic together with a
> perfect system of roads and canals".

DeWitt Clinton who was governor of this State of New York had been held responsible for planning out a presentable proposal of the Erie Canal. Special attention should be made that this governor had effectively persuaded the state legislation to authorize expenditure funds for allowing waterway construction of a canal in attempting to link together those rivers of its Hudson, Delaware, and Potomac along with these Great Lakes via that Mohawk Valley.

At the present time, there were no functional roads existing to prepare and furnish much of their accessible supplies needed as only horse and manpower alone had been all which was reasonably attainable for building a canal. Furthermore a small wilderness village of level terrain situated at Rome, New York; was chosen for its potential site, and also to proceed ahead with that vigorous and toilsome work. Basically this digging of the Erie Canal had formally commenced on July 4, 1817 where an opening by a forest, near an edge of a proposed channel was readily selected and easily cleared away. A ceremony was about to take place at that site, and every last man was elbowing his way through huge crowds which had joyously turned out for this spectacle celebration. When the governor along with a half-dozen notables properly took their places upon a platform floor, a ceremonial shovel was solemnly passed from Clinton to Judge Joshua Hathaway, president of the village; then to Canal Commissioner Young, and next to Judge Richardson a contractor, who promptly caused its shiny blade to spitefully bite into this rich, black forest mold two feet thick while cannons boomed and artillery popped.

These first fifteen miles of this Erie Canal had been acceptably completed by October of 1818. In fact many of those workers were either natives of New York, or recent Irish immigrants which were amply being paid fifty to eighty cents a day, plus rations of food and whiskey. Additionally these workmen tools customarily used for excavation had mainly consisted of spades, picks, axes, and wheelbarrows. However, the ditch digging laborers were quickly supplemented with horse-drawn plow and scraper, which decently resulted in firmer embankments of rigidly keeping and holding back its waters. It had taken seven men and two horses to grub between thirty and forty tree stumps per day with its usage of a huge circular shaped stump puller. Also river streams had to be necessarily crossed by aqueducts, and along several places solid rock was blasted away with black powder charges. On the contrary, waterproof lime was its resourceful material in constant practice for building canal locks, since these Erie's original locks were a combination of wood and stone which had purposely displayed wasteful deterioration.

However, irked by lengthy delays much of its critical excavation work became tediously sluggish along this Big Ditch. During the year of 1819 an increasing number of faithful pioneers had sadly indicated their utter dissatisfaction towards DeWitt Clinton, vividly expressing an outward relentless discontentment. Although sensing that the trouble this might cause, these Commissioners had made an amicable decision to fatally discourage skeptical criticism by holding public ceremonies in an orderly fashion to partially help and sensibly acquaint those people with astonishing marvels which had been studiously concluded.

The valid opening along this first suitably finished section of its canal a strip of area between these places of Rome and Utica was to be appropriately held in October of 1819; just two years and three months after their ceremonial sod breaking which had formally taken place at Rome. Its first voyage ever along that Erie Canal had been a propitious occurrence and political maneuver among those Canal Commissioners. By March of 1823, DeWitt could honestly present to the people of New York State—220 miles of approachable canal from Schenectady to Rochester. Also when each new section of this Erie Canal had been entirely fulfilled an increasing amount of navigable steamboat vessels were pouring into the canal, and tolls had to be taken for proportionally helping to accelerate their final accomplishment of its project. More specifically even some storekeeper merchants of Buffalo had expectantly proclaimed that earnest and strenuous developments from this canal had been reducing its freight charges down from $100 a ton by land in comparison to $10 a ton by canal. As a result, farming products and manufactured goods could flow eastward to New York, and then would return westward, thus giving them predominance over other Atlantic seaboard ports.

This festive celebration of the Erie Canal's final completion had been jubilantly observed on October 26, 1825. There were only five canal boats which had spontaneously departed from Buffalo and New York City that were supposedly scheduled to arrive at Albany. Governor Clinton was onboard the Seneca Chief and had been its lead boat of that small flotilla. Then following alongside this Seneca Chief as part of its official fleet were the Superior, the Commodore Perry, the Buffalo, and Noah's Ark. Beside Governor Clinton there were two brightly painted wooden kegs which were to be liberally released at a ceremony known as the "Wedding of the Waters". Richly being encircled by hundreds of boats, its Seneca Chief cheerfully approached into lower New York harbor, where DeWitt Clinton had prominently ejected a keg of Lake Erie water into the Atlantic Ocean. Most importantly after eight long years of hard labor, and worthwhile costly expenditures of $8 million, despite numerous amounts of troubles, and arduous difficulties the Erie Canal was exclusively declared open to its public. Last of all digging excavation and building efforts of this Erie Canal had been even more of an undertaking and greater achievement than was its laying of the first railroad in which to crossover these western mountains for reaching the Pacific Coast.

Additionally while being such a worthy financial success to these Canal Commissioners, the Erie Canal had radically changed much of its conceptual image of this whole country. At Schenectady, their yearly river and canal boat traffic had unanimously increased from 6,000 boats in 1824; to 23,000 by the year 1834. Moreover the population of New York City as a striking result brought upon by its strong impact of that Erie Canal, had widely risen from 124,000 people during 1820 to 203,000 by 1830. In conclusion this canal had favorably supported New York State in becoming its largest of the Union, and had ultimately given that great migration a tremendous boost for providing an easier and cheaper way of transporting their goods westward.

* * * * * * * * *

Meanwhile the public was beginning to regard turnpikes and canals as State owned, and inasmuch by comparison they had modestly proven to be an unsuccessful method of transportation. As a matter of fact some of those useful canals had brought on considerable and troublesome problems such as water overfilling in these ditches, frozen conditions during its winter months, and maintenance of embankments and locks had all been excessively expensive to their advert supporters. This canal system was a tremendous impact for the inert steamboat; however it had been advantageously anticipated that a much greater source of steam power was soon going to reveal reputable recognition. Many concerned settlers had been confidently determined about finding a better way of continuously carrying their profitable rich lands to market, and thus by 1880, the steam locomotive and accommodating railroad had exceedingly ruled supremacy over internal operations.

On the contrary American railroad builders as well as various intelligent engineers were dynamically seeking to find bearable methods, in addition to superior advancements of railway transportation. An important earlier aspect which these rail lines quickly ascertained had been that influential operation of a steam locomotive would be conceivable only if they could dominantly control all of its traffic moving along their customary lines. As a common carrier, those railroads of America had been assuredly expected to rightfully receive for shipment anything within practical, sensible, and moderate justification. Therefore unlike waterway canals and turnpike roads, the railroad and these railway companies had affluently owned and constantly operated, all of its particular equipment which allowably was functioning along their rail lines.

Some of the first notable railroad improvements had been strictly focused on this foundational structure of that roadbed itself. Moreover their original trackage had been built with wooden rails, and they were capped with iron straps of 20 to 25 feet in length which were laid flat on top of those tracks. However, because of prevailing extensive conditions such as heat, frost, and weight these strap rails would often have a tendency to pull loose and bend upwards, so as to form "snakeheads" which rigorously caused breakage within the floors of their coaches. Also its wooden rails would often show certain indications of rotting out from prolong exposure due to severe and extreme weather temperatures. Principally these spokes of earlier wheels for coaches, and steam engines, had been uniformly structured with wood, and which in effect that when a locomotive train was traveling over those rails at a speed of fifteen miles per hour, had potentially caused this hot dried wood to screech and squeal alarmingly.

Nevertheless that actual thickness of those strap rails could have been comparatively increased in conformity so as to bring under control its occurring problems of snakeheads which many times would either derail an engine or wreck a train. In fact one attributable solution of a newer type of rail was this T-rail, which had been primarily designed by Robert Stevens. Also Stevens was president of the Camden and Amboy Railroad, and he installed that unique railway construction along his New Jersey line. Worth mentioning was that this type of iron T-rail had been essentially imported from England during the late summer of 1831; weighing thirty-six pounds to the yard, and which had been amply rolled in lengths of eighteen feet long. Not only was this T-rail flat bottom strong and safe, but easily could be spiked to their crossties, and soon it became a standardized railway structure among all first-class steam locomotive lines.

Many of these earlier railroad lines in America had purposely displayed rather distant variations of irregular and different trackage. The normal and acceptable standard track gauge for railroads sequentially had followed that English precise gauge of 4 feet 8-

1/2 inches. However, the Erie Railroad as well as trackage for this Ohio and Mississippi Railroad had been using a broader 6-foot gauge, while the Central Ohio Railroad track line had been built explicitly to 4 feet 10 inches during its 1850's. Those inconstant deviations of track gauges were reluctantly causing many delays in both freight and passenger service that the "American Railroad Journal" had been benevolently emphasizing an absolute necessity of rigid and stringent uniformity within railroad track gauge sizes. Consequently, this general concept of trackage gauge was not to be clearly conceived on a national basis until half a century had subsequently elapsed.

In 1828, John Jervis who was chief engineer of the Delaware and Hudson Canal had been strong-mined to virtuously use locomotives for hauling anthracite to these coal mines at Carbondale in Pennsylvania. Jervis at once had willingly decided to urgently dispatch his assistant Horatio Allen to England with desirable intentions of gainfully acquiring rails, and prospectively purchase steam locomotives of the best possible construction. Moreover, Allen had boldly acquired a locomotive known as the Stourbridge Lion which was built along similar plans of Hedley's—Puffing Billy of England. Indubitably this steam locomotive was utterly assembled at an establishment situated near its foot of Beach Street in New York City known as the West Point Foundry Works. There that Stourbridge Lion had idly sat upon elevated blocks for a period of time, only to spin wheels, and delight gazing onlookers. It was then indefinitely released to this canal company on August 8, 1828, and permanently remained on those tracks at Carbondale before being presented for a remarkable experiment.

Horatio Allen was going to be appointed as project engineer, and had been definitely aware of these existing factors about the Stourbridge Lion locomotive. Valuable to note this steam locomotive had forcefully constituted an abundant weight amount of two tons upon all of its wheels. However those rails were intently devised to merely support and restrain only a ton and-a-half. Likewise Allen had been precariously cautious, and keenly kept a sharpen eye on a wooden trestle railroad bridge which was located just outside of town. It was a do or die situation for Horatio who had been strongly determinable to pertinently proceed ahead with his fulfilling development. While Horatio was standing inside of its cab, he began pulling on this steam throttle of the locomotive as crowds began to cheer while a cannon was also being fired. In effect, that trestle bridge had highly withstood its sudden heavy impact of this courageous demonstration which was feasibly attributed with the Stourbridge Lion. Furthermore, after going more than one mile in distance the Stourbridge Lion had safely arrived back to critically acclaim and accomplish this first skillful run of a steam engine locomotive in America.

Jarvis and Allen had both known that these tracks would not solidly tolerate the Lion's weight for any lengthy period of time even after its trestle bridge had proven this strenuous and burdensome suspension of the locomotive. Distinctively that absurd and worthless Stourbridge Lion had been protectively preserved inside an enclosed woodshed, where it stood idle for many years before its boiler was eventually sold to a factory in town. Many of these children at Carbondale often gaped steadily at this brave yellow lion's head which was painted on its front of the locomotive as it gave them chills and shivers. However some of their movable parts were unwillingly detached, and had been taken by souvenir collectors around 1900, although they were justifiably replaced, and now this reconstructed endurable steam locomotive can be evidently visible to visitors at the Smithsonian Institution in Washington.

More importantly the first steam locomotive in America which had ever consistently brought about any recognizable attainment and achievable outcome within conceivable railroading was the Tom Thumb, built by Peter Cooper of New York during 1829. At the age of seventeen, Cooper was an apprentice to a coach maker and after completing his apprenticeship had earnestly been offered a modest loan to enter upon coach making of his own. Although young Cooper was consciously determined to go into its business of manufacturing, and selling machines for shearing cloth. Within a few years, Cooper had feasibly considered an inducible conversion in another industry for supplying these rapidly growing markets with production of glue and isinglass. Also, Cooper had been eminently accredited towards completion of the Canton Iron

Works, which was built on 3,000 acres of land that he owned and occupied at Baltimore, Maryland.

On August 28, 1830 the greatest race of American history had been held in Baltimore. Its specific objective of this competitive race was to provide encouragement and support to the Baltimore and Ohio Railroad company with a satisfactory steam locomotive. There were two pair of tracks which ran in a parallel direction between Baltimore and Ellicott's Mills—a distance of thirteen miles. Moreover this was its site chosen as their setting for the Gray Mare, and Tom Thumb's engine to compete in an intensive and meaningful event. Those bending curves and series of road grades were splendidly achieved at a moderate speed of fifteen to eighteen miles per hour, and without any conflicting difficulties which were being observed by many of some highly spirited spectators. At the starting line this race was even, and away went horse and engine down these tracks. One notable aspect was its return trip from Ellicott's Mills had been terminally completed within fifty-seven minutes.

That Gray Mare did have a slight advantage at the starting point of this race as Cooper's engine had to pause and wait, until rotation of its wheels were moving to set a blower into direct action. When a safety valve on this steam engine was manually lifted upwards, thin blue vapor appeared, and visibly presented an excessive amount of steam while the horse was perhaps a quarter of a mile ahead. Then a blower began to whistle, and steam blew off in vaporous clouds, as its pace had impulsively increased which instantly caused that engine to demandingly gain on the Gray Mare and overtake him. Regrettably this horse was about to give up, when suddenly a band-belt which drives a pulley located on its blower had unfortunately slipped off. Cooper's hand had been harmfully lacerated while obviously attempting to replace that flexible pulley belt back onto its rotating wheel of his steam engine. Immediately the horse drew closer to this Tom Thumb engine, and had exceedingly transcended in front of that locomotive; therefore claiming prosperity as well as winner of its scrupulous race.

Fundamentally the Tom Thumb steam engine had not been powerful enough in providing for regular service. However, it did resourcefully attribute Peter Cooper with prestige and honor of having run the first foremost sequentially American-built locomotive. This engine was no bigger than a handcar, and had been evidently equipped with a small upright boiler. The ostensible satisfaction of this type of boiler was mainly an improvement to effectively maneuver around sharp curves, while also being able to position ample weight upon their driving wheels for better grade climbing. In 1859, Peter Cooper notably founded the Cooper Union which voluntarily offered free courses in science, art, and engineering. Nearly half a century passed after he had built America's first steam locomotive, before Cooper became a political candidate for Presidency of the minority Independent Greenback Party during 1876.

* * * * * * * * *

Since long being solid backers and firm supporters of the steam locomotive, John Jervis and Horatio Allen had been sharply propelling their inspirational engineering projects once more. In a striving effort, Allen had imperatively won a valuable and victorious decision from his board of directors on January 14, 1830 that steam locomotives would be in probable operation along the South Carolina Railway. Allen had been meticulously in full agreement with his financial donator, a powerful person whose name was E.L. Miller. Between the two of them, they had insistently decided to have C.E. Detmold of Charleston, capably plan and accurately design a rail locomotive which was to be known as the Best Friend of Charleston.

Its first commercial steam locomotive which had been built in the United States for regular railway service was the Best Friend of Charleston. That inventive and unique framework of its locomotive was equipped with a vertical boiler, which was rigidly mounted onto a four-wheel carriage so as to give more strength in making rough roads smoother for the Iron Horse. Moreover this earlier type of steam locomotive had been independently manufactured at a cost of $4,000 by a West Point Foundry in New York, where original assembling had taken place for the Stourbridge Lion—imported from England.

Six months later, this <u>Best</u> <u>Friend</u> <u>of</u> <u>Charleston</u> was about to give our American railroad an unpleasant and terrible occurrence in history attribution. The locomotive's fireman had reluctantly been provokingly aggravated by an excessive roar of steam coming out of a safety valve which was mounted onto the engine. As a result, its fireman had intentionally tied down that closure valve which carelessly produced in giving their train riders the first boiler explosion. Consequently, the <u>Best</u> <u>Friend</u> <u>of</u> <u>Charleston</u> had been progressively terminated as a steam locomotive. However other rail trains then began running on the South Carolina Railway, and were hauling flat carloads of cotton between its engine and their cars so as to undoubtedly encourage those tense and apprehensive train passengers. Furthermore the inevitable steam locomotive initially started full operations on Christmas Day in 1830, and these cars easily transported 141 passengers onboard its first ever scheduled train service within America.

Jarvis was beginning to confidently gain and actually acquire acceptable approval of steam locomotives which had sensibly prompted him to build the <u>De</u> <u>Witt</u> <u>Clinton</u> at a foundry in New York. The <u>De</u> <u>Witt</u> <u>Clinton</u> locomotive and engine had been less than seven thousand pounds in weight, while measuring eleven and a half feet long, which was equipped with four wheels, and also a horizontal boiler. In fact a final presentation of skill and power had been held during its winter of 1831. This <u>De</u> <u>Witt</u> <u>Clinton</u> locomotive was pulling along three coaches, and aptly completed that trip in a timely fashion of forty-six minutes. Meanwhile, the horse had been carrying seven coaches, and it took nearly seventy-five minutes before finishing this excursion. As a result the Mohawk and Hudson Railroad had been actively opened in 1831, and that <u>De</u> <u>Witt</u> <u>Clinton</u> engine was attributively put into regular service along a 15-mile railway.

An evident and presentable improvement of continuity had to be consummately entailed over motive power as these foremost first locomotives servicing America were sluggish and awkward while abruptly causing severe malfunctions along steeper grades when carrying heavy loads. In 1830, Matthias Baldwin of Philadelphia had not evidently realized that he would soon become a great locomotive manufacturer within a few years. At the time, Baldwin being in his early forties had peculiarly deviated away from his former business as a jewelry maker into devising machinery for book publishers; and was attempting to put together a steam engine for his factory at Philadelphia. Franklin Beale an owner of a museum at Philadelphia had basically perceived a desirable popular interest towards Stephenson's Rocket, which virtuously gave him an incentive idea of duplicating a miniature reproduction for its stringent purpose in moving around a few people on this floor of his gallery. Baldwin who had been well acquainted with assembling small parts from his past experiences, and possessed by an intelligent knowledge of steam engines would be a wise choice to possibly originate and construct a copy of its Rocket replica.

Matthias Baldwin was starting to regularly establish his reputation as a railroad locomotive builder, and conceptually had built his steam locomotive Old Ironsides. While assembling together this four-ton locomotive, Baldwin had used a horizontal boiler for the engine, and its framework consisted of only four wheels which merely traveled one mile an hour on April 25, 1831. However, some superior and noble changes were to be thoroughly consummated which had greatly increased this speed of Baldwin's locomotive steam engine to twenty-eight miles per hour. During 1832, Baldwin was being instantaneously approached by the Philadelphia and Germantown Railroad which had been in desperate demand for a dependable rail locomotive essentially intended for its Pioneer railway line. These authorities of this Commission were partially responsible for its creation of the Baldwin Locomotive Works, and in operation at his plant, he had productively assembled more than 1,500 locomotives.

Its first British-built locomotive that Jervis prosperously obtained was the John Bull which had been imported from England. Additionally this John Bull locomotive was twelve feet long, and used a combination of upright and horizontal boilers for burning a hot fire. Also those driving wheel axles of that steam locomotive had an overall measurement of four and one-half feet apart, which necessarily resulted in a considerable amount of overhanging weight at each end. Likewise this overhang had distinctly caused plenty of complications as its engine was in constant danger of derailment. Significantly on a rough track the locomotive would have a natural tendency to teeter fore and aft while hammering these rails.

John Jervis had an indispensable resolution and was strongly determined to reliantly solve those conflicting difficulties by rebuilding that engine. On the contrary, he decided to place a swiveling four-wheel platform beneath its engine's front-end, which then in effect would soundly support this overhanging weight problem. And in order to avoid overhang at the rear of that engine, he could take away one pair of these driving wheels, and place its other pair at the back of this firebox. Thus, by having a longer wheelbase, it would restrictively prevent the locomotive from teetering and hammering as well as to lead its engine safely around winding curves along these train tracks.

When that John Bull locomotive engine had been rebuilt within conformance to these required specifications a decent conversion was wholly achieved in contemplation of conquering those perceptibly surfacing annoyances. As a matter of fact its first successful conformable adaptation of the Iron Horse to American tracks had clearly stood as a rewarding accomplishment. Valuable to note was that at some point in time all of these American-built locomotives were going to be properly equipped with "bogies" or the swiveling platform. Furthermore this swiveling bogie platform mechanical device had skillfully improved upon its turning, tracking, and qualities of a locomotive.

Although that steam locomotive was still proving hard and cumbersome on American trackage primarily because of the way power from its cylinders were being applied to their wheels. Those cylinders of Stephenson's Rocket had been solidly mounted outside its line of driving wheels at each end, and used connecting rods which were affixed to its wheels. But this type of structural arrangement, had solely applied power to the extreme ends of its driving wheel axle, and defiantly was causing some locomotives to shimmy along on these railway tracks. It was not until 1833, that John Brandt a mechanical superintendent at the time had brought this problem forward to Coleman Sellers who was owner of a foundry and machine shop at Cardington, Philadelphia. More specifically their only reasonable and sensible solution for resolving that constantly occurring problem was... ***counterbalancing***. Furthermore directly opposite of these connecting-rod fasteners on each wheel, Sellers had cleverly emplaced an offsetting weight which was sufficient enough to tolerably balance much of those disturbing forces that were continuously developing. As a result this newly inventive idea of Coleman Sellers had consistently proven to be a swift technical advancement as counterbalanced outside connectors became a widespread universal factor for the railway locomotive.

* * * * * * * * *

These contentious and anticipated engineers in America had been rather resistant and became earnestly positive to implement more power by building bigger engines as well as using additional pairs of driving wheels for supporting them. Sequentially, when more than one pair of those driving wheels are used along the tracks, one axle and pair of wheels might be moving upwards, while its other was moving down; and so long as each axle had been fastened by their own springs on this frame, these contrary forces would have a natural tendency to rack an engine. Therefore, by attaching any extra driving wheels onto the locomotive would not be likely unless a predictable solution was to be explicitly found for better continuity.

By the year 1839 while working for Garrett & Eastwick, a mechanical shop located in Philadelphia, Joseph Harrison Jr. had brilliantly solved this problem with his "spring-and-beam equalizer" mechanism which consisted of attaching these axles onto its wheel structural framework. Harrison's spring beam equalizer had precisely permitted equal amounts of pressure on each drive wheel even if the track was rough or unsmooth, as well as providing this capacity of adding more additional wheels onto those locomotives. Especially important was that the <u>Gowan and Marx</u> locomotive had been amply equipped with four driving wheels along with these spring mounted beam equalizers which was put into regular railway service on its Philadelphia and Reading Railroad during February of 1840; and as a remarkable result had splendidly astonished other impulsive engineers by forcibly pulling forty times its own weight. After some years of debatable argument spring beam equalizers came into general usage, and were feasibly considered within strict accordance for adapting locomotives to American railroad tracks. Harrison then initially began a partnership with that firm, which later became known as Eastwick & Harrison. Moreover this newly formed firm of Eastwick & Harrison had been given creditable attribution for building the <u>Mercury</u> locomotive that legitimately claimed to be its first passenger locomotive train to resiliently use spring beam equalizers, and which was advantageously purchased by the Baltimore and Ohio Railroad in 1842.

During 1844 the Morse electric telegraph intuitively began with their functional operation which had pretentiously regulated its determinable destinations of dispatching various locomotive trains at a central point location. The electric telegraph was originally created in 1838 by Samuel Morse through which a series of dots and dashes were being combined together in order to factually represent letters of its alphabet for sending out communicational signals. Likewise this valuable contribution and influential impact of that telegraph system had copiously encouraged a large number of railroads to abundantly install telegraph lines along their railways. Additionally, a sudden rapidly pouring inflow of telegraph operators had been showing up repeatedly in almost ever approachable train station. More important telegraphing and dispatching had morally ended many such tedious tie-ups that often were reluctantly caused by late arrival trains. Furthermore this electric telegraph had been a stable systematic service as well as a practical means of central transmittance for locomotive trains in aptly deciding the right-of-way, and also of choosing which train must back-up to its nearest local railway station.

In 1846, William Kelly who was an ironmaster and scientist from Philadelphia had been first to astutely discover and definitely introduce the chief process of manufacturing steel. He also had been impetuously interested with its iron industry while on a buying trip for McShane & Kelly, a dry goods and shipping company which was situated in Kentucky where he eventually became a partner. Kelly had fortunately persuaded his brother to join with him in forming together an iron works firm; and they usefully purchased an iron furnace, in addition to 14,000 acres of timberland and ore deposits, which had prominently brought about its profitable creation of the Eddyville Iron Works. Nevertheless after several attempting failures to absolutely remove impurities from pig iron, Kelly had willfully succeeded in gainfully producing pure iron and steel during the early 1850's.

Henry Bessemer an engineer from London had been fundamentally working in order to capably bring about and institute mass-producing steel. Also Bessemer had intelligently measured an exact amount of mixed carbon compounds into a batch which contained molten iron, and therefore mainly led to the production of inexpensive steel at low costs, before finally being patented in 1856. As a matter of fact another Englishman whose name was Robert Mushet, had proficiently supplied a key discovery of adding an alloy of carbon, manganese, and iron to those already processed materials of Bessemer's foremost experiment. Valuable to note that these supplemental features had conditionally given this finished product enough carbon to substantially constitute steel while bearably preventing retention of raw chemical elements.

Wilson Eddy and William Mason of New England were utterly deemed liable of actually lowering its engine cylinders to a relatively horizontal position in line with their driving wheels, instead of being bolted onto a boiler, and working diagonally downwards. Significantly enough Eddy had been a foreman at this Springfield shop of Boston & Albany, and evidently had made a vital achievement to strongly increase power as his Addison Gilmore locomotive had competitively performed best in the most excellent manner during a "speed pulling" contest which was being stringently held at Lowell, Massachusetts by October of 1851. Worth mentioning was that William Mason conceivably built the James Guthrie for an Indiana railroad at Taunton, Massachusetts before 1852 which subsequently were using horizontal cylinders as this internal improvement and mutual resolution had soon diligently reflected an independently expedient progression for the steam locomotive.

George Pullman of New York had studiously initiated and customarily established construction of his Pioneer which became the first Pullman car of luxury service running along American railways in 1865. Also Pullman had vigorously produced sleeping cars, and insistently operated them under a binding contract with these railroad companies after becoming president of its Pullman Palace Car Company. Additionally those Pullman cars were a grand superior service which offered modestly reserved seats by day, as well as berths at night, and scrupulously culminated to be an essential contribution towards ordinary railroad passenger accommodations. Furthermore these Pullman cars had consequently occupied as many connecting rail lines as necessary, and conveniently provided through local train runs between major cities with first-class service being exclusively provided by their supportive employees of this company.

Evidently the <u>President</u> coach was operating along this Michigan Central line by 1867, and had been their first hotel car characteristically designed by George Pullman. Its coach was a regular sleeping car which was appropriately supplied with a complete kitchen, and hot meals were eloquently served on standing tables that had been set up in these designated sections of this train. Within the next year, Pullman had exquisitely decided to individually separate those two luxurious services of eating and sleeping by an added introduction of his first dining coach car called the <u>Delmonico</u> traveling along a Chicago and Alton line. Moreover this notable accomplishment had zealously and graciously aroused the public's interest which advisably permitted Pullman cars as equably irrevocable equipment within American railroading locomotive cars.

The much worthy adoption of air brakes for locomotive services had been suitably invented by George Westinghouse of New York during 1868. Principally its railway cars of a train had been properly equipped with brakes which pressed against their wheels by rotation of a hand-wheel that was securely mounted on the platforms of passenger coaches as well as on top for freight cars. As a result when the brakeman was applying its brakes, he had to deliberately run from one car to another in order to preferably stop this moving train. However, Westinghouse doubtlessly needed to imperatively devise a method whereby those functional brakes could be entirely set on all train cars at exactly the same precise time.

George Westinghouse was also responsible for activating a brake system by using compressed air as an inevitable source of power. This tactful device used a steam pump which was solidly connected onto the locomotive engine for compressing air, and hollow pipes had been cautiously connected from one car to another with flexible rubber coupling hoses so as to carry its flowing compressible air to their brake-setting mechanism which could be reliably controlled by a brakeman. Moreover, Westinghouse had jointly incorporated a triple-valve air brake design into his apparatus, and was able to set these brakes of fifty coach cars within two seconds on its last car of the train. In fact this type of air brake arrangement was obviously an influential internal betterment which then conceptually occurred in it being widely acceptable, and the Railroad Safety Appliance Act of 1893, had mandatory made air brakes a compulsory requirement for all locomotive railways trains crossing over America.

During 1893 the American Railway Union had been this country's first industrial labor union to be thoroughly inaugurated and which was encouragingly organized by Eugene V. Debs at Terre Haute. Although within the following year that Union became heavily involved with a Pullman strike, which drastically resulted in an unjust and shrewd imprisonment of Debs. However since that time the State of Indiana presumptuously had their indispensable allotments of laborious violence, especially among this steel industry. Likewise a conceptual agreement between the State Chamber of Commerce, and those union leaders had closely reflected an inclined tendency to both lucidly work together along with its state government in favorably helping to maintain an appealing atmosphere for some incentive manufacturing enterprises.

Therefore these 1830's indicatively became known as this decade of experiment, demonstration, and performance for the Railroad Era. By 1840, there equivalently were as many miles of railroads existing at that time entwining America in comparison to miles of waterway canals. More importantly, those enticing problems of complying and adjusting locomotives to their railroad tracks stood firmly resolved and were reasonably justifiable. Also the diverse types of creative innovations and meaningful intentions had ominously given its American iron horse a rapid growth of evolution which was to assuredly meet all further demands for nearly half a century. Furthermore this early elementary development in steam power to run and operate locomotives had been proven to be an indelible fulfillment for prestigious purposes of opening up new territories of expansion as railroad builders and community leaders collectively continued with desirable attempts to have mainlines built throughout their adjoining towns and prosperous cities.

CHAPTER THREE

Since the 19th century State legislation had been primarily represented among most states so as to protect and safeguard its commitment and consignment in actual movement of goods traveling by inland waterway canal, turnpike road, and railway. Between those periods of 1830 to 1840, the State legislation of New York City had actually authorized, and consequently permitted as many as fifty-eight rail charters. Specifically, a charter was issued by granting a written document for chief purposes of transferring these rights, privileges, or exemptions from a sovereign power of the State to its people, or to a group of them reliably organized into a unified company. Much of the earlier rail construction was built and operated under corporate charters which were politically dispersed from State legislators.

As railroad progression was continuing to sequentially grow so did commercial activities, and soon these railroads were being swayed into a doubtful position of operation which had been brought on by public interest and state regulation. Meanwhile state legislative measures of orderly and uniform standards started to realistically develop upon the railway construction for allowing whether to extend permission of a new line to be built, in addition to approval of its fixed location. Also, those legislators were even taking an ever so increasing involvement over its fundamental operation along these rail lines, especially in conjunction with regards to quality measures of safety requirements. Furthermore, state legislators had been grasping about an overwhelming insight into their financial aspect of these railroads, prudently resulting in authorization of its rates and fares, and had largely considered to exercise licensing powers over other railroad mergers.

When some remote methods of ordinance were proven to be unsuccessful at this time, demandable rules for stricter and continuous control had sharply risen. As a conclusive result, an independent regulatory commission was officially formed within those states, and began to operate under current legislature statues. Also its first commissions had been mainly implemented before 1870 which were principally legislative bodies of government, and their major concern was basically with the railroads. These advisory commissions had morally established certain suggestive advice to both state legislatures and railroad companies, under its right of eminent domain for enacting and enforcing railroad safety measurements, and usually served as factual finding groups; however, they actually had no control over regulating railroad rates.

With such vital interest and rigorous entailment of railway development imperative Railroad Acts were absolutely beginning to be adherently passed for careful consideration of signal modes, brakes, trackage and other aspects of railroad operations. Shortly after that onset of this Granger movement within the Midwest—a favorable process which sought state legislation to locally control escalating railroad rates—the first commission with mandatory powers had been essentially organized. Between 1871 and 1874, these states of Illinois, Iowa, Minnesota, and Wisconsin had jointly created commissions with exclusive power to set maximum rates, prevent discrimination, and prohibit mergers of other competing railway lines. While those Granger laws, except in Illinois, were substantially revoked by its end of the 1870's, these licit laws had set a routine systematic pattern by which many other states engagingly followed in mutual accordance.

It was during 1887 when firm action intentionally guided towards compliance of rail transportation had been taken with passage of the Act to Regulate Commerce. Moreover that act was positively made applicable to all common carriers by railway which were typically involved with interstate commerce, and also to other common carriers transporting goods partially by railroad, as well as in part by inland waterway; and even when both were being used under a common control, or arrangement of a continuous carriage. This act also fittingly enabled to publicly promote the Interstate Commerce Commission which was legally conceived and affluently composed by government agency during 1887 in order to adequately and sufficiently regulate these national railroads, and twenty-five states had regulatory commissions at that time. The Interstate Commerce Commission has extensive power to hear complaints against carriers of alleged violations of law, investigate matters in dispute, order carriers to cease and stop from unlawful practices, and determine its amount of probable damages suffered as a result of these conflicting infractions. In addition, it also possesses the ability of rate-making power, however newer aspects of transport have arisen, and older ones have been improved. More importantly this Interstate Commerce Commission (ICC) now has jurisdiction over railroads, pipelines, motor carriers, and carriers by waterway.

The Continental Congress in 1780 had fortunately passed a resolution that called for its colony-states to abandon their vacant and unappropriated public lands which would then be beneficially disposed of, and in effect later become known as the United States of America. Over a period of time, seven of these original thirteen states had inevitably proceeded to comply with this proposal which included New York, Virginia, Massachusetts, Connecticut, South Carolina, North Carolina, and Georgia. Soon these larger regions of land which had been ultimately under surrender necessarily became its principal basis of public domain lands. By 1802, explicit evidence was well ascertained that these western or wilderness lands not privately owned should belong to the Federal Government for their stringent purpose of public disposition. In addition, this conceptual agreement had vigorously continued even after its states had been constituted out of those lands, and were admitted to the Union. That final procurement for the public domain lands from 1802 until 1846 had fully concluded its forsaken acquisition of territories which were obviously expanding this new nation across the North American continent. Furthermore a dedicated series of complicated schemes and pertinent plans for distribution of its national domain had been thoroughly authorized under the Homestead Act of 1862; offering title of 160 acres to individual settlers, subject only to residence for a certain period of time, and in consistent conformance of minimal improvements on their lands thusly obtained.

In the Middle West during this period of 1830 to 1860, many states had been utterly anticipating a needful desire of roads to be built and constructed for future railways. The demandable costs of building its accessible roads were extremely extravagant which had almost bankrupted half of those new states and territories. Then along came supportive financial aid from the federal government for assigning land grants to privately owned companies in finishing up its required work. Consequently, there were more than four hundred corporate railway charters which were appropriately being allocated by legislature to public service companies intending to build railroad lines within its immediate area at that time.

On the contrary, waterway canals were in a declining duration because of frozen conditions during winter, and stagecoaches eventually became its dominant carriers of both freight and passengers. This could be the reason why so many railroad charters had been granted between the 1830's to 1840's, which unfortunately carried along some kind of clause making it impossible to acquire cash subscriptions for its stock to be purchased. Several of these legislative charters which were in circulation during this time had intently contained restrictive provisions that anything earned over ten percent was suppose to be paid back in a rebate to those canals, and apparently the purchasing of stocks had suddenly fallen. Another stipulation limited by these corporate charters for railways had been that if other shorter rail lines were allowed to haul freight, they could only pull it when the canal was not running. Additionally other particular charter requirements included its sole right that at the end of five, ten, or twenty years that the State could willingly take over these rails at their same exact cost. In fact among those towns closest to the Erie Canal definitely had no specific intentions of perceiving railroads to carry freight, while territories along the further off distances desirably wanted its rails for better transportation of freight. As a striking result these canal companies were drastically cutting their rates to the bear minimum with encouraging support from the State, so that its first rails carrying passengers had to charge the same rates—about three cents a mile.

* * * * * * * * *

New York State's first earnest attempt of constructing rails for running steam locomotives had been a rather short sequence of intermediate local lines advancing ahead in a parallel direction beside the Erie Canal. Its strenuous undertaking for this 15-mile stretch of land located between Albany and Schenectady had rationally received a charter on April 27, 1826 for the Mohawk and Hudson roadbed foundation to be built over that ground. Thus, the route from Albany to Schenectady would take about ten hours by waterway canal, instead of traveling along its railway of that Mohawk and Hudson where passengers could safely arrive in only one hour. Some of those indispensable and remarkable various features of their roadway had chiefly consisted of double tracks, heavier iron strap rails, and train depots; however, the railroad company was deviously fined $300 for laying their tracks inside of these Albany city limits. Furthermore, the superintendent for this line was satisfactorily receiving fifteen hundred dollars a year, later raised to twenty-five, while its president and his associate directors of that company never received a dime for their reconcilable services up until 1844. Moreover its definitive and decisive achievement of steam power was thoroughly accomplished along those railway tracks when the De Witt Clinton locomotive had proficiently beaten that steadfast horse in a competitive race of 1831. Also this considerable task would logically serve of establishing grounds for practically proving the steam locomotive, unlikely its sadden and sorrowful ending of the Erie Canal, and as an ultimate result had convincingly provided an intense and preliminary consolidation of what was to become known as the New York Central Railroad.

This next great linking of rail lines in New York had been to potentially connect that city of Utica with Schenectady for a noteworthy distance of seventy-eight miles. Significantly a permissible charter was orderly granted in 1833, and the initial fares on this line were set at four cents a mile for passenger service. However, nothing but baggage was to be transported along these lines as freight except for its carrying of mail. An important improvement along that rail line structure of roadbed had been its use of a heavier piece of iron strap which was spiked onto both rails. This railway was officially opened on August 1, 1836, and which had been a most boastful day in Utica's history with two trains pulling ten coaches each behind the steam locomotive. As a matter of fact this Utica and Schenectady route was first among others to decide upon duties and rules for railroad conductors—work trains must give way to passenger coaches; also rail trains were to run at least ten minutes behind another preceding train, and a brakeman had to be properly situated at its rear of each locomotive. Furthermore these first officers of this line were the president, vice-president, secretary, and treasurer, all of whom bearably served for twenty years without a cent for their services. Likewise the head engineer's yearly salary was twenty-five hundred, and its acting superintendent had been drawing two thousand dollars.

Those building standards of railway trackage for the steam locomotive railroad in reaching Buffalo had been quite similar and which were very consistent with this earlier construction type like the Hudson and Mohawk route as well as the Utica and Schenectady. More important, the Syracuse and Utica Railroad obtained its charter to permit building their rail tracks in 1836, and this line was formally opened on July 3, 1839. Actually that roadway was a total of fifty-three miles in length, and had swiftly passed through an area of marsh and swampy grounds. Moreover long timber beam piles were driven down beneath a soft watery foundation in order to hold, balance, and support those durable and heavy strap iron rails. Also the railroad company was especially letting their passengers ride free of charge for one week so as to noticeably attract public attention of traveling by rails instead of waterway canals or turnpike roads. On the contrary, these railroad charges for passengers rates were agreeably regulated to four cents a mile, while either standing on platforms or getting off and on train cars when being in motion was strictly a forbidden occurrence. This Syracuse and Utica line also drew its close attention of an important factor by which our Supreme Court had slowly recognized. Specifically for instance an apparent running locomotive train could not get off their railway tracks for an intruder. Accordingly, if a farmer was driving cattle along these tracks, or attempts to dash over a railroad crossing before a moving train, then those obvious damages must be on the vagrant, and not against that railway company. Valuable to note, gross earnings for its first six months were ten percent above all operating costs, and revenue returns had been pouring in at an average of six hundred dollars a day.

These malleable railroads with their extending railways were succeeding although capital funding was abundantly lacking and had not been available, so there were no attainable subscribers to purchase this ascribable and obtainable stock. In New York, northwest of Syracuse just situated alongside the Owasco River was a village town of Auburn. Preliminary funds for building a roadway from Syracuse to Auburn along a 26-mile stretch of land could not be amply raised, which then reluctantly led to bad financial troubles mainly because of the fearful panic during 1837. There had been an urgent demand for gold instead of paper currency notes at these banks resulting from this panic of 1837, and European investors were beginning to finance its growth of America. Therefore, no cash on hand was accessible, and drafts that were issued to pay for land surveys and road construction had doubtfully ended up in protest, as many of those subscribers of its stock could not pay for their assessment costs. Critically a great deal of their four hundred thousand dollar stock investment had been wholly absorbed by these railroad directors of the Hudson and Mohawk. However, the State had indulgently managed to proceed ahead with a sizeable loan of one hundred thousand dollars in order to further continue development, and a substantial charge of five cents a mile was justly allowed for all train passengers by 1839.

The district of Rochester was a prosperous flour milling town in 1812, and which was mutually connected up with that Erie Canal. Their extensive privileges of procuring a corporate charter had been aptly established within 1836, while lying of iron strap onto wooden rails from Auburn to Rochester along a seventy-eight mile parcel of land had appropriately commenced. However some provisions that were conditionally contained by this charter had morally permitted its right to carry passengers, but only when those canals were closed, and passenger fares were kept down to three and four cents a mile. This stretch of trackage was truly considered to be the most worst manageable road in that State, as mails were always late, locomotive trains never ran on time, and its roadbed foundation was rocking to every passing train car. Also, it was along this railway where the leg of a lady passenger was severely injured by its snakehead strap coming up through the floor of a coach. Furthermore on this tract of land, the Underground Railroad was exclusively formed—a term relatively used because of its elusive activities with escaped fleeing slaves which had been utterly carried out secretly during darkness, and railroad terms were often used with reference to that system. By 1840, its pay scale of a superintendent and constructional engineer had been three thousand dollars per year each; the conductors six hundred; these freight agents four hundred; its baggage men three hundred; and the locomotive engineer from seven to eight hundred dollars. Consequently in order to persuade and influence investment, nine dollars a share was being paid in 1842 as interest not dividends on stock subscriptions from 1836.

Rochester being a prominent city located in northwestern New York was evidently joined together with the Erie Canal during 1822, and had formerly served these earlier needs of the Seneca Indians after it was founded by 1789. In fact the Rochester and Syracuse line was merely a combined connection of this Auburn and Syracuse route in conjunction with its Auburn and Rochester rail line. Within 1850, a consolidation of these lines (Syracuse, Auburn, and Rochester) had substantially acquired an investment capital of over four million dollars. But, nobody shouted "watered stock" because there had to be more stocks sold so as to severely avoid bankruptcy, and realistically its public only purchased $8,340 worth of stock subscriptions. Although a major factor was that these land surveys and track construction for building this entire roadbed had sizably amounted to over two million dollars, while currency notes which were being given out by this railroad company at the time allegedly ended up going to protest from five dollars up to one hundred thousand dollars for unintentional nonpayment.

Its virtual linking of trackage from Rochester to Tonawanda was securely permitted their land grant charter during 1832. This stretch of area a distance of forty-three miles were running trains by 1837, and which had been its first locomotive coach to distinctly greet Lindbergh's victorious flight across the Atlantic. Nevertheless all of their five hundred thousand dollars of capital stock was earnestly pledged and solemnly subscribed, before this ruthless and sudden panic in that year of 1837. More importantly there were many agricultural farmers along this line that had been big crop shippers of wheat, and they could not be held back by ridiculous regulations with reference to waterways and turnpikes. As its weather climate closer to the Great Lakes had very often rotted out those wooden rails, these railroad companies were slowly changing over to solid iron tracks, and eventually they would be substituted with steel rails. Also its necessary removal and replacement of rails had taught all steam companies that a *railroad is never completed;* and in 1847, the law of this land had authentically required laying iron rails for elementary purposes of operating steam locomotives.

Considerably these many treacherous miles of railways were rapidly forming together while its perceptive engineers and constructional crews had been eminently anticipated to foresee their accomplishable efforts and achievements in bringing this railroad to a successive completion. New York's final and last linkages of rail tracks were to be sufficiently laid from Rochester to Niagara for a distance of thirty-one miles. Additionally, its labor and materials used in roadbed construction had comparatively ranged between five to eight thousand dollars a mile; but then there had been that dreadfully harsh requirement of paying canal tolls even during closed waterway conditions. Palpably this city of Buffalo being western headquarters from New York to these Great Lakes persistently became very aberrant about having rails, and would not tolerably permit a single steam engine inside of their city limits. In fact some railroad rates had been inappropriately scrambled and were inconsistent along the Utica to Buffalo route, for example it was costing six cents a mile between Schenectady and Troy, as opposed to three cents a mile among other remote railway sections. Furthermore by 1851, all of its proper toll charges which were being paid by these railway companies for the profitable and beneficial acquirements of those waterway canals had been usefully abolished.

There had been as many miles of railroads existing in the United States during the year 1840 as there were miles of waterway canals. One important aspect was that this pioneer steel trail exceedingly extends their railroad network over many eastern states while pursuing two meaningful objectives: connecting eastern cities with each other, and linking its leading eastern trade centers with these mighty rivers and Great Lakes. In December of 1851, those eight intricate junction lines within the State of New York were thoroughly amalgamated together, and became circumstantially permitted to merge as one giant railroad conglomeration. Most of all its bargaining process negotiations of this communicable consolidation was splendidly initiated and finally produced on May 17, 1853; while their pertinent and necessary papers had been promptly filed in July of that year to bring about the New York Central into becoming a Railroad. Furthermore Erastus Corning who was a long-time iron merchant and businessman politician acted as president of this Utica and Schenectady line, before retaining position to be its first president of the New York Central, and therefore later on officially served as a distinguishable Democratic congressman for six years.

* * * * * * * * *

Land grants and railway charters had pertinently represented an important part for imaginable expansion of North America, and also with groundwork construction among our early highways and railroads. These regions of both northern and southern New York had been pretentiously promised a great highway to be built with State aid while this Erie Canal was being concisely promoted within the State legislature. However, once the Erie Canal was formally declared open to its public those Canal Commissioners had drastically manifested no such concernment of setting up an alternate competitive route. As many local and nearby communities were urgently demanding with strong desires in advantageously projecting a railroad charter for their counties, they immediately petitioned the Federal Government to competently plan and perform a land survey of this proposed site during 1832. At that time, Andrew Jackson was President of the United States, and he had been kindly lenient to support permitting a land charter, however certain political action which was brought about by its opposing waterway canal business had positively blocked this land survey in preventing it to proceed ahead any further. As a result the road surveying work had to be efficiently acquired by these useful sponsors at a private cost by which they profusely absorbed.

This unique charter which was to be granted for the New York and Erie railway construction project was indispensably issued in 1835, and strictly provided that their rail line must entirely remain within the State of New York. Moreover that charter had also specified not to crossover into those states of New Jersey and Pennsylvania, and was to be started along its western side near the Delaware and Susquehanna tributary rivers, and then it would follow ahead into the Genesee and Allegany valleys moving through western New York, and finally out to its Great Lakes. This 460-mile of roadbed foundation was suppose to be actually constructed at Piermont for an eastern terminal located along the Hudson River, and then sequentially travels onwards to reach Dunkirk alongside Lake Erie, just north of Fredonia. However, the Erie Railroad was continually facing financial troubles, and its inevitable fate had been in these hands of an unskilled group of local investors. Indisputably this New York and Erie railway was using a broad track gauge of six feet; that is the distance between it's inside of their railheads. Valuable to note this track gauge of Stephenson's Rocket locomotive was 4 feet 8-1/2 inches, which is the more commonly acceptable standard gauge of railroad tracks, while other traditional railroads operating within some Southern states were using a suitable gauge of five feet between their rails.

These worrisome difficulties over the Erie Railroad about finances had been minor in comparison to such fierce and brutal anger of unified teamsters, tavern keepers, and turnpike laborers which were all strenuously working between its links of this roadway. Often there were rational disturbances along upper New York State by 1846 of violent gangs tearing up partial sections of railroad tracks, and defiantly ignoring court injunctions concerning deliberate intrusions with their transferring of train passengers. Though these raging battles at railway junctions where links had been coupled and connected together became known as the "Isthmus Wars" which certainly discouraged and annoyingly discomforted rightful privileges of passengers transferring from one train line to another adjoining route. Nevertheless those irritable experiences had been some notable examples of obstructions, detainments, and nuisances which reluctantly precluded the forward progress and crucial development of any further roadbed railway construction.

Living in New York at about this time was Eleazer Lord, a Presbyterian of Princeton from western New Jersey, who had been kept away from entering into the priestly ministry by a slight weakness in both of his eyes. Before he was thirty-five years old, he had absolutely helped to form its first American import and export tariff system, and was also president of the Manhattan Fire Insurance Company. Eleazer presently made his residency in a country home at Piermont alongside the Hudson River, and had frequently traveled to Europe extensively as he knew what these established promotional railways were similarly producing for England. He also became known as its father of this Erie Railroad, before the first spadeful of earth was shoveled and turned over at a construction site which was called Deposit located in New York nearby Lake Erie. However, Eleazer could not securely estimate these precarious circumstances and entailments of building through narrow canyons of solid rock, or criss-crossing over bridges, and this intense action of rushing water streams which filled up with fifty-foot drifts along those wilderness mountain areas during the winter. Mainly brought upon by that Panic of 1837, these backers of the Harlem Railroad had realistically approached Eleazer with an exceptional offer to outright sell its entire project, and all of their rights for ninety thousand dollars. But this proposed offering was contentiously refused by their members of the Erie board of directors as there just was not enough available cash on hand at that time.

On the contrary once after a half million dollars of its former ten million in capital investment had been conditionally subscribed, this railroad company could then certainly begin to feasibly advance in an organized and reliably method to start with new building construction for a roadbed. Likewise stock subscriptions as well as generous donations among many landowners along this route were steadily pouring in from nearby villages and local towns to push ahead with their work performance for its rails to be amply built. Moreover some growing territories close by this roadway site such as Binghampton and Elmira were abundant producers of farming and lumber products, which had been in subtle agreement for constructing this Erie Railroad. Additionally by 1835, over two million dollars worth of stock subscriptions had been significantly conceivable of which $118 thousand dollars was actual cash while its legal issues and matters were being relevantly resolved. Also these prestigious directors of this Erie were utterly determined to break ground at Deposit as their constructional plans for that route were to be laid out within forty-four subsections, and which intricately consisted of twenty-six contractors to officially commence with its workable construction. At sunrise by November of that year, their chief director of the Erie had formally declared within his own prediction that "this beautiful meadow will in a few years present tracks of rails with cars passing and repassing", so after a long emotional interest for a railroad along southern New York a wheelbarrow of dirt was dug up and hauled away.

It appears that there had been a sudden fire in the lower city of New York during December of 1835, and relevant valuable assets of nearly all its Erie's shareholders were tragically destroyed and badly ruined by those engulfing flames. Moreover this legislature at Albany were favoring canals and opposed rails although they had been willing to politely subsidize the Erie Railroad with one dollar for every two dollars of stock subscriptions. However an assessment amount of two dollars and fifty cents had to be technically paid over to these building contractors for monies spent which apparently was long overdue, and its Erie's debts were an overwhelming total of thirteen thousand dollars at that time. While those outstanding deficits for the Erie were liberally accumulating there were about twenty-five miles of trackage which had already been laid that would surely help to rationally settle a sizeable portion of its debts, but reluctantly the Erie Railroad by 1842 was desperately ordered to be sold at a foreclosure sale for forty-one thousand dollars—interest defaulted on debts. As a result, Horatio Allen was being called in as advisor by the board members at a special meeting, and he was officially appointed to be president of their company.

Allen, now residing president for the Erie had aptly decided that if this venture was going to considerably continue, they would insistently need seven million dollars so as to further complete any future railway developments. Also another assessment amount for five dollars a share had to be beneficially paid out because of overdue indebtedness. Valuable to note that over four hundred thousand shares were virtually forfeited for nonpayment of interest which was a possible indication towards poor judgment in its outcome for that Erie Railroad. Nevertheless Allen diffidently felt helpless and was inevitably lacking power which justly concluded in him resigning; however, he was anxiously persuaded to remain and stay on as its director and consulting engineer until his time of death at East Orange in New Jersey, during January 1890 at the age of eighty-eight.

One notably aspect had been that along some places nearby this route way, timber wood was becoming soft and brittle which began rotting away where it had been solidly laid upon these roadway grades although sixty-four miles of trackage were in running condition for the Erie Railroad. Along the Susquehanna territories from its town of Binghampton to Elmira, one hundred miles of pile-driven work had to be scrupulously constructed over a swampy region. More important, a fundamental product contributing to thoroughly create a new energy supply for this steam locomotive was that black solid combustible coal had been tolerably used for its fuel source instead of burning wood. As a matter of fact, half of those best known mechanical devices and useful inventions for these earlier railroads would have come from the Erie and their superior promoters.

When this roadbed route had earnestly arrived at Middletown many local farmers had gladly donated right-of-way passage, and the Erie Railroad fairly paid these others current prices for obtaining accessible land privileges. Also it had been a common practice to pump water at trackside for supplying power to this boiler of the steam engine. However, at some remote places where river streams where not reachable, workmen had to handily pass water pails in furnishing essential fuel to its locomotive engine. Although situated on top of a hillside near Middletown, there was a mountainous stream with a huge reservoir for holding back river waters. Chiefly the owner of this adjacent land being very much in financial need for money because of his mortgage had laid a long narrow connecting pipe downside that hill to fittingly supply passing locomotive engines with water by its use of natural gravity. The Erie Railroad substantially paid him two thousand five hundred dollars for his original scheme, and that was the primary beginning of water tanks for these durable railroads.

Especially significant Eleazer Lord was back in position again for the Erie Railroad as president, however this whole potential affair was being juggled around like a merry-go-round. Likewise its founder of Harper Publishing House was pleasantly offered this position, but had bitterly chosen not to advantageously accept these disputatious responsibilities. Therefore that final proposal of president for the Erie was precariously taken by Benjamin Loder, a conservative businessman of Westchester, New York. Specifically Loder had never asked for a loan amount from any bank or financial institution, and he had some of these most powerful, strongest, and prevalent men in New York backing him as successor.

Near to its crossing by the Delaware River at a town called Port Jervis, there were hills which had been solid walls of hard rock and vigorously required to be blasted away for building this necessary roadway rail construction. Nevertheless a man by the name of George Scranton at a location which was then known as Slocum Hollow had cleverly realized that by combining both coal and iron together, he could independently manufacture and evidently produce T-rails for the Erie Railroad. Also this type of process in constructing T-rails had incredibly reduced their initial costs of rails from eighty-six dollars a ton down to forty-six dollars. As a result, that distinct settlement of Slocum Hollow just situated easterly between these states of Pennsylvania and New York was then indicatively renamed to Scranton honoring this family which effectively created the Lackawanna Iron and Coal Company in 1840. It was perceptible that these nearby farmers of Pennsylvania were becoming less adverse of the Erie, and together with four horse-and-mule teams had deviously carried those heavy iron rails sixty miles to pertinently reach their exact roadway rail designation. Additionally there had been one hundred fifty miles of railway construction ready for its steam locomotive which was presently operating along those western counties of New York. On the contrary once the Erie had finally arrived at these Great Lakes by 1851, it had been its second longest railroad of this world.

Worth mentioning was that when this ingenious task of connecting their final links of its railroad with the Great Lakes it had been partially celebrated by both rail and boat in a delightful celebration from the 14th to the 17th of May during 1851. Valuable to note that some of those many distinguished dignitaries and noble characters which joyously appeared to actually witness their special occasion were President Millard Fillmore, Daniel Webster, Stephen Douglas, governors of the states, mayors, bankers, and president Loder from the Erie Railroad. Meanwhile at New York City, a rather spectacular procession had happily proceeded to march from Battery up Broadway to its Bowery, then down the Bowery in order to reach City Hall where colorful bands along with horse squadrons and military infantry, as well as police on foot were all excitedly gathered among each other. In addition members of the press were relatively showing up casually decorated in evergreens, flags, and flowers which had been merely arriving by steamboats for joining together with those excitable onlookers before an estimated crowd of 50,000 people. Furthermore along every town situated near the Hudson River and even alongside these railways cheerful banners were inscribed "Welcome to the Iron Horse". All of this had been its official aspects of constructional building for the Erie Railroad while a partial run at Port Jervis was being adequately accomplished at almost a mile a minute with this accompanied steam locomotive.

* * * * * * * * *

The city of Baltimore geographically located in this State of Maryland necessarily covers an area of approximately ninety-one square miles with about fourteen percent of it being bodies of water, and its other eighty-six percent basically consisting of public lands. When the Erie Canal was expediently opened by 1825, it had been rapidly taking much of its richer trade along this new Western country, and had strong intentions of precisely capturing the commercial capital wealth. If that city of Baltimore definitely wanted to significantly retain their marketable profits and financial status, they adventurously had to crossover highly elevated mountains in order to reach its likely approach of the Ohio River, and also provide an efficient and reliable method of conveyance as good as the Erie Canal. It soon became quite perceptible that there was not much of a growing interest for these canals, and on the contrary, railroads were exceptionally beginning to attract particular attention of its business commerce around this country.

During the early winter of 1826, some retailer merchants and reputable businessmen of Baltimore critically began their debatable concernments over its curious involvement of establishing railroads. In fact Philip Thomas had profusely resigned from his former position as Maryland commissioner in July of that year, after apparently giving up prior consideration of a projected waterway for the Chesapeake and Ohio Canal. As a result, a group of influential townspeople of Baltimore desiring to further increase a fair share of its Western trade market sensibly held private meetings so as to affluently investigate relevant documents in determining their profitable and worthwhile development of railroads. Thus Philip was lucratively elected chairman by an appointing committee in 1827, and he expressively suggested that turnpike roads and waterway canals were very practicable forms of serviceable transportation. More importantly, conclusive discussions among this appropriate authorized committee had abundant confidence to continue with their continental growth of American population, and they accurately attributed that those railway accomplishments of England were already proving these railroads would eventually supersede canals. Therefore, this committee consisting of seven men had admirably suggested and reasonably recommended its immediate building of a double track railway for crossing over that Allegheny Mountain chain so as to enter onto the Ohio River during February of 1827.

Principally a firm resolution had been relevantly approved in presenting a binding application to the Maryland legislature for an act to incorporate a joint-stock company which was to be expressly named the Baltimore and Ohio Railroad. This committee was strongly determined to seek a corporate charter for their railway which would perpetually allow them a capital stock investment near the sum of $5 million dollars. Also, the person who was primarily responsible towards drafting of its charter for that proposed railroad company was John McMahon of Cumberland, a graduate from Princeton University. By 1827, he was serving his second term with the Maryland House of Delegates, representing a Baltimore district for this State of Maryland. More precisely that charter being issued had sufficiently consisted of twenty-three sections which exceptionally gave the railroad certain rights, including its use of steam locomotives as well as some exemptions from many state taxes. In addition McMahon had correctly molded his charter rather similar to those earlier charters of turnpike companies, and within later years, other railroad charters would follow his acceptable format.

As a matter of fact this supporting corporate charter for that Baltimore and Ohio Railroad was formally presented to the Maryland legislature by McMahon, and its act of incorporation had been wholly passed without much resistance on February 28, 1827. For the most part this leading act had capably provided an investment of capital stock worth $3 million, but its thirteenth section strictly contained measurable provisions that would heedfully allow the president, and his board of directors to later increase their capital stock by an addition of as many new shares which they might deem mandatory. Worth mentioning the Maryland act of incorporation had been generously acknowledged by its State of Virginia on March 8, 1827, and this charter was also agreed upon with the State of Pennsylvania on February 22, 1828. Furthermore these enthusiastic citizens of Baltimore were virtuously astonished by the implied action which was being taken by those merchants, bankers, and businessmen of that city, in addition to acquiring its railroad charter which was officially granted under the Maryland legislation at this time.

Special attention should be made that a major issue for this railroad was to securely obtain reliable data and relevant facts for building a possible roadway to the West, and also to prepare a preliminary land survey along that terrain from Baltimore westward towards the Potomac River, and even beyond past these range of rising elevated mountains. For their achievable task surveyor engineers had to be acquired and the Military Academy at West Point was its only school of engineering in this country at that time. A key feature was that a General Survey Act was being mainly composed and had been convincingly passed by the United States Congress in 1824, which legally permitted this President to reasonably extend conforming authorization of surveying and inspecting undeveloped land regions. During 1825 to 1827, the U.S. Congress had shown a satisfying concernment about railroads, and the President had been willing to actually grant Army engineers its proper permission of suitably preparing routine land surveys with accordance to this Act of 1824. Accordingly the B&O board of directors liberally presented a formal petition to the local government in seeking federal assistance for its modest purpose of constructing a railway over to the Ohio Valley. In mid-June of 1827, the government had intently notified their acting president of its Baltimore and Ohio Railroad that these considerable costs of developing a land survey would be inclusively assumed, since this forceful project was potentially believed to be of national importance for our country.

Valuable to note this customary survey which had been extensively conducted by these government engineers was a partial route starting from Baltimore and arriving at Washington along a vicinity of the Potomac River Valley, some fifty to sixty miles southwest of Baltimore. Then once having been able to reach the Potomac River, that route would follow alongside a valley going westward into its Allegheny Mountains near Cumberland, and from there travel across a crest to arrive at Wheeling in Ohio. However, this parcel of land just located between those areas of Baltimore and Cumberland had regularly consisted of a series of sharp curves and low road grades. Nevertheless these surveying Army engineers were in cautious agreement that their roadway surface grades should be only limited to no more than 0.6 percent, otherwise any steeper grades would have to be carefully accomplished with this practical use of inclined planes.

In November of 1827, Philip Thomas who was president of the Baltimore and Ohio Railroad had promisingly made public a bid invitation for constructional materials consisting of stone, timber, and iron rails all of which had to be timely delivered to its railroad president at Baltimore on or before July 1, 1828. Also, the Maryland legislation had diligently passed an act which consequently provided that their State should subscribe to 5,000 shares or $500,000 worth of railroad stock, and its operational finances of the B&O began to soar and grow resilient as a result. In fact counting vote tallies for subscription of these stocks were forty-five to twenty-three in this House of Delegates, and eight to three with the Senate. Moreover that state legislature had been gainfully in mutual consent of having a railroad which was helpfully guided with its principal assistance and powerful motivation from John McMahon, this state legislator who had earlier written and sponsored their charter for the Baltimore and Ohio Railroad.

By late spring of 1828, that board of directors for the Baltimore and Ohio Railroad had wisely indicated that enough progress had been thoroughly accomplished for them to openly present an official celebration of their railroad. Also those company directors of the B&O were in serious commitment that its railroad should have a memorable cornerstone, and it could be laid by selective representatives from its Masonic Lodge of Baltimore. Furthermore, it had been virtually decided upon that Charles Carroll this only sole surviving signer of the Declaration of Independence some fifty-two years before, would proudly turn over the first bit of earth for a new railway. Last of all an actual commencement ritual was observantly scheduled to be held on July 4, 1828 at a place called Mount Clare situated alongside its outer western edge of this city.

There were jubilant sounds of cheerfulness and happiness passing throughout their local district on that Friday morning of July 4th, for it was to be a very special Independence Day at Baltimore. In fact many hundreds of country and town folks had been waiting outside which were immensely crowded onto platform balconies, and also along its hard pavement as this exciting parade was beginning to promptly start at eight o'clock that day. Additionally stagecoaches and farm wagons had brought with them large crowds of spectators to excitedly witness such a magnificent and colorful parade; while railroad officials, military units, floats, and bands were all steadily pouring into that region for a joyous celebration. After a short solemn pray and some distinct introduction speeches had been essentially conducted, Charles Carroll easily pushed his spade deep into its ground while turning over this first sod of earth for the Baltimore and Ohio Railroad. More importantly specific intentions of acquiring their railroad charter had certainly proven to be a meaningful determination for the B&O so as to ultimately continue with further development of its westward trade, and also to allowably permit advancement for other joining urban communities of that expanding new American frontier.

When their first rails were laid at Baltimore, dependable horses had been pulling train cars along these tracks as the steam locomotive was not yet in fundamental operation until summer of 1830. Thusly this enticing news of that victorious win of the Stephenson's Rocket locomotive during those Rainhill trials competition at England had seem to have relevantly restored confidence and expectations to consider running steam locomotives within America. Worth mentioning was that when Horatio Allen, resident engineer of the Delaware and Hudson Canal & Railroad had substantially tested its English-built Stourbridge Lion locomotive on his roadbed in 1829, he soon learnt this engine would be too heavy and burdensome for usage on American tracks. Finally the advocating acceptance of steam power for justifiably operating locomotives came to this Baltimore and Ohio when Peter Cooper built his Tom Thumb engine, and had that famous race with a gray mare horse on a return trip from Ellicott's Mills, which had reassuringly concluded president Philip Thomas to reliably put into service steam locomotives for their railroad expectation.

Although strong disagreement and general resentment of planning a railway had often caused severe hardships in obtaining their necessary and available funds of early track construction for the B&O Railroad. As a matter of fact, many individual shareholders were harshly objecting when they had been boldly asked for additional payments in cash money. However its constructional work for these rail tracks shortly began after lying of their cornerstone, in spite of various problems and caustic resentments. On the contrary, formal announcements were beginning to visually appear in published advertisements which were confidently asking for engineering proposals and material bids to be scrupulously submitted for road and railway construction of the first 13-miles of trackage from Baltimore to Ellicott's Mills.

The first part of their rails was robustly built during October of 1829, and several methods of track design had been alternately used. As an example some of its train tracks were basically composed of wrought iron strap which securely held itself upon stone sills, while other sections had this strap rail solidly connected to wooden stringers resting on top of stone blocks. And, a third type of method consisted of those strap rails being placed on wooden stringers that were laid onto wooden crossties which were positioned about four feet apart in distance. However, before long all trackage of its roadbed was being attached with wood rather than stone for sustaining support underneath these rails.

By the end of 1829, there were almost three miles of railway tracks which had been entirely finished for the B&O Railroad although they had been laid out in several different locations along its route. For instance the first section of these roadway tracks ran west and south of Baltimore starting from Pratt Street, and going towards this stone built Carrollton Viaduct which was closely adjacent to Relay House. In addition, two other rather smaller portions of trackage were fully being constructed—one near the Patterson Viaduct that was situated halfway between Relay House and Ellicott's Mills, while its other rail line merely followed alongside the Patapsco River to Ellicott's Mills, directly west of that town. Near the end of May 1830, those roadbed tracks for its railway had been comparatively connected together between Pratt Street and Ellicott's Mills for a considerable distance of thirteen miles. As a result, passenger service for railroad operations along that recently developed route was ready, and within its pages of *Niles' Register* had been a printed train schedule of departures and returns for this Baltimore and Ohio Railroad. Furthermore, railway train tickets were amply costing seventy-five cents per person for a combined round trip of twenty-six miles, and the Davis-built Grasshopper type steam locomotive was fittingly able to maneuver around these sharp curves along its tracks.

During 1830-31 this invigorative construction work for their trackage stretching west of Ellicott's Mills rapidly continued along much quicker than had been normally anticipated. Likewise a partial section of its railway tracks had favorably followed these winding banks along the Patapsco River to notably arrive at its foot of Parr's Spring Ridge located about forty miles westerly of Baltimore. Although at this base of a long and narrow summit ridge, much of the upward slope steepness had by far exceeded their grade requirements of 0.6 percent; so as a result two incline planes had to be built along its downward west side of that sloping ridge. Moreover directly west of Parr's Spring Ridge their route aptly passed over Buck Creek in order to crossover the Monocacy River, then it had proceeded ahead further towards Point of Rocks alongside the Potomac River, in addition to a 3-1/2 mile branch line extending northwards to reach this town of Frederick.

At a very short distance away from that town of Frederick, many of these nearby citizens were appreciable and pleasant about having a railroad serve its vicinity. Also once this section of its roadway rail construction work had been satisfactorily concluded, that sixty-one mile railway route line west of Baltimore was in total operation for providing public transportation services on December 1, 1831. In addition a special train began running along those newly constructed railroad tracks with coach cars that were diligently carrying the governor of Maryland, the mayor of Baltimore, and railroad officials to Frederick from the city of Baltimore. As a matter of fact in June of 1833, Andrew Jackson had contentiously given up riding the stagecoach for railway service, and he became its first American president to ever travel by steam locomotive train along these B&O tracks between Baltimore and Ellicott's Mills.

Meanwhile the Baltimore City Council by mid-1831 had tactfully expressed their permissive acceptance to this railroad company for determination of constructing and laying rail tracks from Mount Clare Station along Pratt Street to its harbor shore approximately located one mile eastward of this city. Also, the City Council formally granted a tract of land near its waterfront for terminal operations, and the Baltimore and Ohio Railroad had proficiently built a train depot at Pratt and Charles Streets. Toward that western end of those B&O train tracks, its railway line stretching to Point of Rocks alongside the Potomac River had been successfully accomplished on April 1, 1832. Furthermore with that growing branch line to Frederick this had prodigiously provided the B&O

an actual progressive accumulation of 130 miles of trackage for the renowned steam locomotive.

Its continuous advancement of that rail line beyond Point of Rocks was a bit slower to actively construct because of some intense hostility with this Chesapeake and Ohio Canal Company. In these earlier stages of planning, both the canal and railroad had resolutely considered following along its north bank of that Potomac River in order to safely arrive at Cumberland. Although just situated in position at Point of Rocks there was an eastern wall of a mountain which had been located extremely close to its waters edge of the Potomac River embankment. And, upriver from this Potomac area there were tight and narrow spots along a twelve-mile route leading out to Harpers Ferry. Especially significant was that this canal company implicitly obtained an injunction which was drastically brought against the B&O Railroad, and ultimately the Maryland legislature had rationally forced a mutual compromise of accordance between both of these respective parties. Most importantly was that a concurrent agreement had carefully stipulated that a rather narrow ledge beside the Potomac River was to be widely shared; but with certain limitations, and the B&O Railroad had been strictly confined to a twenty foot length of single track right-of-way. Additionally, the Chesapeake and Ohio Canal Company had to feasibly build a roadbed for this railroad company within three of its most hardest and difficult places and those absorbent costs were to be paid for by the B&O. Consequently the Baltimore and Ohio Railroad would be adherently required to leave by its north side of that Potomac River onto the waterway canal which was in operation upstream from Harpers Ferry.

The railway line traveling to that Maryland side of this Potomac River just opposite from Harpers Ferry was conveniently completed on December 1, 1834. In fact a six span 800-foot wooden bridge was being constructed across the Potomac River at Harpers Ferry, and which was wide enough to easily accommodate a single pair of railroad tracks. However, while building a bridge across the Potomac River at Harpers Ferry had actually taken much longer than their entire construction work of those twelve miles of trackage from Point of Rocks. Furthermore that bridge was officially declared open for providing rail transportation in January 1837, and as a result, the B&O railway was soon interchanging freight with the Winchester and Potomac Railroad which was indeed servicing a lower valley of its Shenandoah region.

While many months of disputable discussions and conflicting rival disagreements over the Point of Rocks railway line running out to Harpers Ferry continued, a branch line southward to reach this nation's capital was under immediate consideration. Since its initial beginning there had been some railroad developers at Baltimore who were insistently emphatic of a rail line extension south to Washington City—as it was then often called. By end of 1832, land surveying work was being moderately prepared for a thirty-two mile route from Relay House, going slightly east of the Baltimore and Washington Turnpike. Particularly the route of this railway construction was a superior one with minimal low grades and slightly easy curves, and throughout numerous years had productively permitted high speeds with low operating and maintenance costs.

The State of Maryland had conditionally chartered a railway route to Washington which was known as its Washington branch line for that Baltimore and Ohio Railroad on March 9, 1833. Also its construction work for building this rail line began in October of 1833, and their roadbed was being evenly graded including all cuts for double tracks, but only a single track had been evidently constructed to run between Relay House and Washington. A key feature was that no stone or strap rail was to be used for this trackage, instead "T" rails, a type of rail earlier implemented by Robert L. Stevens had been placed on top of those supporting wooden crossties. Furthermore, the iron which was used in its manufacturing to produce these rails had a unique combined total weight of forty pounds to the yard, and those T-rails were being imported by boat from Europe to America.

Probably one of their greatest constructional works along this Washington branch line was the Thomas Viaduct which was fervently named after its B&O president. That huge stone like bridge structure was elaborately designed by Benjamin Latrobe, a civil engineer working for the Baltimore and Ohio, and this viaduct traditionally followed those winding railway tracks over its Patapsco River from Relay House to Elk Ridge. Moreover Casper

Weaver was their construction supervisor in charge at the time for precisely building this gigantic bridge which was over 600 feet in length, and was realistically composed of eight elegant sixty-foot arches consisting of solid hard granite. On the contrary that railway line traveling to Washington was formally opened on August 25, 1835; while four special trains from Baltimore were being pulled by their Grasshopper engines—the Thomas Jefferson, James Madison, James Monroe, J.Q. Adams—all built for this new railroad service by Phineas Davis, a watchmaker who turned inventor-machinist of York, Pennsylvania. In addition, a newly constructed Washington depot was amply situated at Pennsylvania Avenue and Second Street just west of the capitol, and passenger service from Baltimore to Washington was costing $2.50 a person per trip for a train ticket.

* * * * * * * * *

By 1836, this board of directors for the Baltimore and Ohio Railroad had unanimously decided to officially appoint Benjamin Latrobe to be in superior charge of land surveying an area for probable consideration of a proposed extension line which would travel west to Cumberland. While preliminary land surveys were being primarily conducted and intensively studied for its route westerly of Harpers Ferry towards Cumberland, both those sites of Pittsburgh and Wheeling alongside that upper Ohio River had keenly perceived a substantial interest of being joined together with the city of Cumberland by railway. During this time their current revenues of the B&O Railroad were not sufficient enough to possibly finance the nearly approximated worthwhile expenses of $4,500,000 for its major accomplishment of constructing a ninety-seven mile branch line going westward. However the Baltimore and Ohio had morally been obligated to eagerly proceed ahead in asking both the State of Maryland, and its city of Baltimore for financial assistance so as to assuredly obtain these costly funds in helping this railroad accelerate to achieve their reputed railway construction development.

That city of Wheeling which is located alongside the Ohio River had solemnly promised and liberally pledged their resourceful support to the Baltimore and Ohio Railroad for land surveying and construction work to proceed forward with these tracks for this railroad. Although the State of Pennsylvania had later unwillingly decided to refuse permission of the B&O for building its trackage to Pittsburgh, or even in crossing over their state boundary line while on its way to Wheeling. Since this original Virginia charter of 1827 had restrictedly required that any trackage construction work within that State must be thoroughly completed before 1838, newly established legislation was being adopted to make it acceptable so their roadway could be readily connected to Cumberland. Although in 1838, that State of Virginia after some moderate and debatable misconceptions had legitimately passed and approved legislation for granting the Baltimore and Ohio certain privileges of an additional five years to further exceed completion with its trackage construction work. Meanwhile the State of Virginia had firmly demanded that this route from Harpers Ferry to Cumberland in Maryland must entirely remain and stay within Virginia only up to a point of just five or six miles below Cumberland.

Within the many consecutive months of legislative legal involvements as well as financial business activities, Benjamin Latrobe along with his surveying crews had sensibly planned out several exceptional alternate routes for their railroad between Harpers Ferry and Cumberland. Even though that action which was being taken by the State of Virginia had decidedly meant that nearly all of its line would be located south of the Potomac River in Virginia. Consequently, its most practical route which was finally selected by Benjamin had prevalently departed from this Potomac Valley at Harpers Ferry, and continuously proceeded ahead in a rather northwesterly direction to reach Martinsburg for about thirty miles, where it again had crossed over the Potomac Valley—ten miles downstream from Hancock. In addition, that route then enduringly remained along its southern side of Virginia until within five or six miles east of Cumberland where it then travels across this Potomac River into Maryland.

Much of its natural terrain along the territorial areas located just easterly of Martinsburg leading into Cumberland were troublesome and pragmatic in comparison to those regions west of Cumberland. However at a site between Harpers Ferry and east of Cumberland known as Doe Gulley, three tunnels had to be unavoidably constructed for that railway which mainly consisted of two short tunnels of 90 and 250 feet, and a longer 1,200-foot tunnel which was being bored. Its maximum allowable grade within this ninety-seven mile road was less than 1.0 percent, even though one set of tracks were to be laid, the roadbed was consistently graded and had been built to the width of double tracks. Likewise this entire route of its roadway had manifestly included ten wooden bridges plus one bridge of stone, for a combined length of 3,690 feet; all of which was substantially required for their line extension in making it to arrive at Cumberland.

It was imperative that Benjamin Latrobe had to choose and decide upon an approvable route for another adjoining line departing out of Harpers Ferry in order to continue westward so as to accordingly reach Cumberland. Likewise Benjamin had conclusively determined that this best possible route would be to follow alongside its south shore of that Potomac River stretching through a parcel of land situated at an arsenal site just outside of Harpers Ferry which was conceivably owned by the government. Although one fatal detail of improvement which had to be effectively accomplished by Latrobe was to skillfully build a junction switch track for carrying those railroad tracks across a trestle bridge positioned alongside of that arsenal property. As a matter of fact the B&O had alertly issued and sent out reconcilable building contracts to beneficially commence with this ongoing project, and construction work westward outside of Harpers Ferry was subsequently started in late 1839.

A chief factor was that their roadbed foundation which was regularly constructed had ultimately consisted of iron T-rail weighing fifty-one pounds to the yard, and was being placed upon wooden crossties which solidly rested along a bed of broken stone that was sunken one foot deep beneath its ground. Moreover its nearly 8,000 tons of iron which were necessarily required for its single track construction route to Cumberland had been imported from England, and expectantly arrived by cargo ships at these loading docks in Baltimore. During June of 1842, this railway foundation was partially finished to a place within Virginia located across the Potomac River from Hancock, Maryland; only forty-one miles away from Harpers Ferry, and 122 miles westerly of Baltimore. Constructional work for track laying rapidly increased during those summer and fall months of 1842, and as a result the Baltimore and Ohio Railroad was officially declared open to Cumberland about fifty-six miles west of Hancock on November 5, 1842. Nevertheless it had taken about 1,500 men and more than 450 horses for that immense railway construction project to be exclusively completed as Cumberland was a total distance of 178 miles west of Baltimore. Furthermore, the Baltimore and Ohio was leniently able to take over much of its active wagon and stagecoach traffic running along this National Road as rail service was quicker, faster, and smoother than the turnpike coach at Cumberland.

During these six years after track completion of the Baltimore and Ohio Railroad to Cumberland, not much had effortlessly been achieved to vigorously push ahead this roadway any further westward towards Ohio. On the contrary, many of its legal problems which were in vital concernment over their route line for arriving at Ohio had been reassuringly worked out amongst those states of Virginia and Pennsylvania, while a sequential series of letters favoring that expendable connection had remarkably appeared within the *Baltimore Patriot*. In fact several times during the mid-1840's, a Baltimore and Ohio bill was significantly passed by its Virginia legislature; however each time this bill had potentially included difficult restrictions, limitations, and qualifications for vital railway construction. Apparently, it almost inevitably seemed that those Virginia lawmakers still had some bitter feelings over a pertinent point about the B&O literally serving Baltimore along its upper Potomac, rather than this Virginia capital of Richmond, and the James River Valley.

Near spring of 1845, its surveying teams of Benjamin Latrobe had influentially deemed that their most probable route from Cumberland going out to this Ohio River would be to move westward up towards the Potomac River into Virginia, and then northwesterly to Wheeling. During late winter of 1846-47, these Virginia legislators had critically passed a bill which was legitimately tolerable for this Baltimore and Ohio Railroad. By that Act of 1847, the State of Virginia had particularly given this B&O Railroad a prolong extension of twelve more years, or until March 6, 1859 for which to fully facilitate its railway route across Virginia to the Ohio. Also this act undoubtedly designated Wheeling as being a western terminal site which was obviously planned upon at Ohio, and persistently insisted that their rail line should be able to finally arrive at the Ohio River no further south than its mouth of Fish Creek, a place located just several miles downstream from Wheeling. Even after transitional passage from its Virginia legislation within spring of 1847, that board of directors for the B&O Railroad was not agilely pushing ahead much trackage construction work onto Wheeling.

In 1849, Thomas Swann then president of its Baltimore and Ohio Railroad had fundamentally estimated that those predictable expenditures anticipated for building a 200-mile extension route from Cumberland to properly reach this Ohio River would indispensably cost approximately $6 million dollars. Swann then had initially spoken to his board of directors about its considerable importance of this westward branch line, and urgently emphasized that the B&O should build their entire road as one whole segment, rather than a part of its line which was originally conceived. However, there was one existing fact which had to be relatively resolved with this Chesapeake and Ohio Canal regarding its north bank of that Potomac River upstream from Cumberland, and Swann later worked out an agreeable compromise with the C&O Canal for a permanent location site to begin railway work. Principally, Swann was having some stringent problems in financing those 200 miles of strenuous roadway construction between Cumberland and Wheeling, and virtuously proposed that the Baltimore and Ohio competently issue a series of certificate bonds which would be liberal enough for supporting these prudent expenses fortunately concerned with along this new western extension line.

Thomas Swann and Benjamin Latrobe had both voluntarily deemed to release constructional contracts for these remaining 103 miles of roadway surface between Cumberland and its Ohio River during that year of 1849. For the most part Latrobe had earlier anticipated that an allowable maximum grade along this 200-mile route passing through those states of Maryland and Virginia should be no greater than 2.2 percent per mile. Additionally included in that mileage were eleven tunnels with a combined total length of

11,156 feet while the three longest being—4,100 feet; 2,350 feet; and 1,250 feet respectively. Appropriately it had essentially taken over two years for final completion of that 4,100-foot tunnel (Kingwood Tunnel) which was adequately positioned about 260 miles west of Baltimore at an elevation height of approximately 1,800 feet.

It was conceptually estimated that some 3,500 men and more than 700 horses had been busy working the roadway up and down over an immediate area of 167 miles for building this railway extension line by late summer of 1850. Iron T-rail was being laid down along its eastern part of that new route, and trackage was in full operation to their Piedmont Station, just twenty-eight miles southwest of Cumberland by early July of 1851. At Piedmont that surveyed route had initially departed from the North Potomac Valley, and then continuously stretches westerly towards a rather long seventeen mile steady upwards ascent to reach a 2,626-foot narrow summit situated close to Altamont. Especially significant was that elevated ridge by Altamont distinctly divides this watershed of the Potomac River from that of its Ohio River. In addition, these constructional crews working near Piedmont had built a sixteen-stall engine house for those steam locomotives which would be pulling B&O trains up its long elevated and graded roadway.

Once over this steep ridge at Altamont, their railway further endures onward going through western Maryland until it crosses into Virginia at a place called Corinth. Next that winding route moving out to the west precedes to crossover a joining sequence of ridges and streams alongside its Potomac River. Just located only 101 miles westerly of Cumberland at a place known as Grafton, this rail line begins turning northwest and crosses the Monongahela River at a site named Fairmont. In addition that route line at Fairmont further travels down its southwestern corner of Pennsylvania, and eventually descends into Grave Creek Valley at Moundsville along the Ohio River, only eleven miles downstream from Wheeling.

By fall of 1851 up to 5,000 men and 1,250 horses had constantly been engaged to insistently push ahead this working proficient progress towards final completion. Moreover those monthly construction payrolls often ranged to amounts of $200,000 and generally its working crews were paid promptly, but sometimes they were not in certain instances. Basically, Benjamin Latrobe had always managed to steadily work out in the field so that he could keep up with their workers schedule, and also to help in supporting its morale of these tracking crews. Valuable to note that 200 miles of railway line construction west of Cumberland plus their needed trackage, sidings, and yardage had profusely required 22,000 tons of iron rail for building its roadbed foundation.

A major element was that this railway line had been entirely finished in order to arrive at Fairmont alongside the Monongahela River just within 124 miles west of Cumberland, and seventy-seven miles away from Wheeling on June 22, 1852. As a result, its regular operation of steam locomotive trains traveling to Cumberland and Baltimore were productively started at once along that route. More importantly President Swann of the Baltimore and Ohio had faithfully promised these proud and earnest citizens of Wheeling that its roadway would be positively in operational condition by New Year's Day of 1853. In conclusion those last iron rails were being permanently laid down into position, and the final spike driven for this railroad was chiefly accomplished on Christmas Eve of 1852, nearby a slender narrow valley located within eighteen miles southeast of Wheeling at a place called Roseby's Rock.

Even before this rail line was fully accommodative for providing passenger service the Baltimore and Ohio Railroad had been using its partially completed route to indeed compete with other rivalry traffic towards that Ohio River and even beyond past it. At Grafton, a total distance of 279 miles west of Baltimore where that roadway turns northward towards the direction of Wheeling, connecting passenger stagecoach lines were running west to Parkersburg. By summer of 1852, futuristic plans were being purposely made at Wheeling for this Union Line of steamboats to evidently operate from Wheeling to Louisville with railroad services to begin commencing once their line had solely entered upon Wheeling, Ohio. Meanwhile back at these company shops around Baltimore, many of their occupational workers had been extremely busy constructing iron bridges so as to effectively crossover those rushing river streams between Fairmont and Wheeling, while other workmen were strongly building newer steam locomotives and train cars for an expected anticipation of further growth within railway development.

During early January of 1853, a commemorative celebration was significantly going to be held at Wheeling for the Baltimore and Ohio Railroad upon recent completion of their western expansion to safely reach the Ohio River. More than 500 townspeople of Baltimore had perpetually tuned out for this special expected train excursion traveling westward to Wheeling along a 379-mile route which had been successfully performed by the steam locomotive in around eighteen hours. Additionally there were appropriate and proper dignitary speeches being prepared and spoken during this festive ceremony by President Swann, Benjamin Latrobe, and the governors of Maryland and Virginia which then afterwards was graciously followed by a grand main banquet. It was about time for an eventful observance since nearly twenty-six years had immensely elapsed when these prominent leading men of Baltimore were enthusiastically planning to build a railroad over to that Ohio territory.

On the other hand with their railway construction finally being finished to Wheeling, Thomas Swann had incidentally decided that he deservingly desired a peaceful rest from its strenuous life as a railroad president. At the April 1853 board of director's annual meeting, Swann deliberately resigned his presidency position with the Baltimore and Ohio, and had been willfully succeeded by William Harrison who was a Baltimore merchant and member of this board for only one year. Nevertheless shortly after his pungent resignation Swann then traveled abroad on a pleasure trip to Europe and upon his return, he became president of the Northwestern Virginia Railroad for three years before going into politics. In summary, Swann was an important political servant to both his city and state, but perhaps one of his most greatest contributions had been its overall completion for that Baltimore and Ohio Railroad to feasibly accomplish their tactful and determinable fulfillment of bearably arriving at the Ohio River.

* * * * * * * * *

The State of Pennsylvania was rather apathetic and quite hesitant at its beginning in starting with their utmost and initial efforts to build a sufficient railroad for this steam locomotive. Here was that city of Baltimore in the south which had already built a railroad to rigorously climb over those lofty mountains onto the Ohio River. Also, the State of New York along its northern side had sturdily proceeded ahead and diligently accomplished building their railroad over this Albany-Schenectady treacherous and difficult peak for reaching westwards to Buffalo. And in spite of the fact that this Erie Railroad marginally struggled through their financial problems they had been able to reach Lake Erie along New York's southern counties. More important, these reputable merchants of Philadelphia were utterly anxious of retaining their valuable commerce and had earnestly decided upon having a railroad for its business community.

It was during 1823 when Colonel John Stevens of Hoboken, New Jersey had been prosperous to presumably obtain a permissible charter to originally commence with building a railway line alongside the Susquehanna River in Pennsylvania. However, this charter was only limited to a fixed period of ten years by law, and Stevens had not been able to further produce subsequent plans for any potential track construction of a roadway. As a result, by 1829 the State had compulsively taken away that charter from Stevens, and it predominantly became the first to eagerly have a state-owned rail line within this country. Accordingly, a seventy-five mile long State railroad was being built and constructed to arrive at Columbia along the Susquehanna River, which had been actually completed in 1834 with part of its route being double tracked near this riverside. Meanwhile, shorter duration rail lines from Philadelphia to Baltimore, and Philadelphia to Germantown had insistently moved ahead, but were intermittently standing still under independent small private business ventures.

By spring of 1846, a railroad bill had been doubtlessly passed by its seventieth session of the Pennsylvania legislature at a public meeting which was officially being held in Harrisburg. On the contrary a relevant group of private businessmen from Philadelphia, under their normal assumption that they could later be able to realistically purchase these usable rail sections of the Main Line works, advisedly secured a charter from its legislation of this State signed by Governor

Francis Shunk on April 13, 1846. In addition, that newly created railway line would be capable to use the State's own rail system east of Harrisburg, then attempt in building a suitable route so as to crossover these Alleghenies westward to Pittsburgh. Moreover, Governor Shunk had seriously issued a formal proclamation of virtually ending those limiting rights to the Baltimore and Ohio for extending their trackage onto Pittsburgh, thus twenty years after Baltimore had a prior agreement with this Pennsylvania legislature to determinedly reach that city under an observant specified time period.

Perhaps some of these especially anachronous and rather most compelling railroads within Pennsylvania were being built so as to intentionally replace those waterway canals in their actual shipments for its coal trade industry. In fact much of that southern business and trade products of this State were moving towards Baltimore while its northern marketable commodities went ahead to New York, and it was these anthracite coal manufactures of eastern Pennsylvania who were in abundant anticipation of shipping their products to New York and New England. Valuable to note horse-drawn railroads were among the earliest at Pennsylvania to be put into regular service such as the Camden & Amboy Railroad which had confidently connected and linked together its major tidewater towns along an area obviously adjacent to Philadelphia and New York. Furthermore, a few of these more prestigious known railroads in American history had prudently become recognized as the Philadelphia and Reading, Delaware and Hudson, Delaware and Lackawanna, and the Lehigh Valley Railroad.

On the contrary that State of Philadelphia had been first among other states to carefully conceive in this conceptual idea of "portage railways", which thoroughly consisted of a stationary engine and winch being in position at its forward section of an inclined plane, and could even pull boats mounted on railway train cars over the most toughest terrain. Nevertheless Canvass White, who was a civil engineer and had formally assisted with the Erie Canal project, was presently put in direct charge of supervising rail construction work for the Portage Railroad to crossover those Allegheny Mountains between Hollidaysburg and Johnstown during 1827. Additionally this route being a thirty-five mile long railway line had advantageously crossed over its nearly 2,300-foot summit of mountains with an essential combining series of ascending and descending inclined planes. Moreover horses could effectively drag these locomotive coach cars along its level surfaces while a motorized cable system would have to be alternately used for those slightly higher elevated slopes. As a matter of fact the Portage Railroad had been plentifully attained in 1828, and two years later this western section along its Main Line Canal from Johnstown to Pittsburgh was notably opened for services.

While it had been relatively ascertained that these steam power locomotives would be able to ascend road grades of twenty feet to the mile, Philadelphia's best possible route for a rail line to arrive at Pittsburgh was not tolerably considerate enough in making its attempt to a steep crest positioned near Hollidaysburg with any such order of consistency. First of all a sudden uphill climb just immediately situated to the west of Philadelphia was inevitably required to clearly reach its rolling land plateau which had to be fundamentally achieved. Next at this point, a sharp downward descent from that plateau would have to be necessarily needed at Columbia so as to safely approach a uniform level area of the Susquehanna territory. Then their route could follow alongside its Susquehanna River where it would substantially join up with that Juniata River, and appropriately continue upstream alongside the river towards this vicinity of Hollidaysburg. Last of all another sharp uphill climb would have to be equally confronted thereafter accordingly succeeded by an abrupt bold decline to a site location close to Johnstown where then those two rivers could be moderately followed out to the Ohio as well as to Pittsburgh.

In April 1828, the State of Pennsylvania indicatively started to build a cable railway so as to precisely reach this western plateau, and afterwards an iron track railway for locomotives had to be severely constructed to vitally pass over that plateau. In addition another cable railway was basically built at Columbia, and then operation of a waterway canal could be in existence at that time along these rivers of the Susquehanna and Juniata. Also, cable railways were frequently used again to overcome its crest at Hollidaysburg, this very summit of which had to be forcefully tunneled. On the contrary the inland canals would be able to further extend completion of its line to Pittsburgh as that entire system had potently absorbed more than $10 million and was fully accomplished by 1834.

During the spring of 1847 this Pennsylvania Railroad had advisably elected Samuel Merrick who had been a Yankee from Maine, and producer of fire engines to be its first president of their rail line. That president of the Pennsylvania Railroad then preferably designated J. Edgar Thomson who had former extensive experience with developing railroads in those states of New Jersey and Georgia as its chief engineer for their railroad. More importantly J. Edgar Thomson had also been responsible for most of its organizing, planning, and supervision of construction work along a 248-mile route from Harrisburg to Pittsburgh. In early December of 1852, Thomson reasonably secured the current position of president for this railroad company, and had propitiously concluded the Pennsylvania Railroad to Pittsburgh, but was still apparently using its inclined planes of that Portage Railroad for crossing over those higher mountainous ridges between Hollidaysburg and Johnstown.

Although within two years later these inclined planes were no longer in active services, and this entire 355-mile line from Philadelphia to Pittsburgh was being capably made by efficient steam locomotive trains. Thus the Pennsylvania Central which was its existing parent of the present Pennsylvania Railroad had been brought into railway operation, and became the first train ever to use its own rails between Harrisburg and Pittsburgh which exceptionally ran along that route on February 15, 1854. Significantly this rail line extension to reach Philadelphia was expediently implemented and persistently ensured until four years later by lucratively purchasing and gainfully acquiring the old State system. Moreover an all-rail locomotive train service was deservingly provided across that State of Pennsylvania which had legitimately commenced with their railroad operations on July 18, 1858. Furthermore the Pennsylvania Railroad had nine hundred miles of rails by 1850, and strategically held its longest statistical record for continuous dividends within the United States at this time.

CHAPTER FOUR

During its first half of this nineteenth century there were many different types of numberless railroads commonly being formed in America, and had suddenly moved ahead with their use of horses for supplying traction power in order to forcefully pull along coach cars. One of those most distinguishable and notable rail lines had been located at Quincy in the State of Massachusetts which was originally constructed during 1826 with wooden rails for private functions. The Granite Railway was a 3-mile line built by a Yankee builder named Gridley Bryant with limited exceptions and meaningful intentions to haul granite from these excavation quarries at Quincy and Charleston for its memorial building construction of the Bunker Hill Monument which was located in that State. This railway could be substantially considered as America's first railroad which had been remarkably constructed as an experimental line within a surrounding vicinity where eagerness and regional development for better transportation was in serious demand at that time. However, the earliest known railway which had presently existed at Boston was predominantly conceded by 1759, for a specific purpose of transporting heavy bricks from one place to another. Likewise, the town of Boston being an important seashore port had gainfully observed that prudent and accomplished achievement of this steam locomotive at these Rainhill trials in England, and willfully determined that a railroad would be reasonably supportive to feasibly provide their commonwealth community for carrying its commerce across those rugged Berkshire Hills onto Albany in New York.

The city of Boston had not been entirely in favorable agreement to have waterway canals for expanding with commercial production of goods and textiles to reach its Middle West, and was ready to mutually accept the railroad as a transportation medium for practical competition. Valuable to note this nearby Granite Railway operation was proving efficient for reducing their shipping costs of bulky goods—and evident news from England about the Liverpool and Manchester Railroad had been convincingly consummated in their achievable prospects with its rapidly increasing involvement of passenger service. In 1830 these railroad promoters and influential merchants of Boston were rather reluctant about subscribing to stock purchases of railways, due to the countless railroad charters which were subsequently granted at alternate sections of ten to twenty miles of trackage. Many loyal supporting groups of citizens were not especially buying railroad stock, merely because of its rewardable profits which had only been strictly limited to ten percent, and anything above ten percent went directly back to the State of Massachusetts. Moreover nearly all of those state charters being issued had conveniently assumed that after a period of twenty or thirty years, this State could compulsively take over the rails at its own fair valuation of their railway. Apparently these primitive state legislation charter laws of Massachusetts definitely had to be reputedly modified, otherwise its opulent individuals and business investors would not purchase neither stock nor bonds unless at least some tolerable outcome of prospective and suitable financial benefits could be more securely obtainable.

After such various indubitable investigations were cautiously examined strategic measures and organizational plans had earnestly been attempted for indicative preparation to make Massachusetts railroads an essential public works task although all of their sensible undertakings had needlessly failed with discouraging efforts. However, it was this extremely massive accumulation of private capital, partly combined with an equal amount of State guaranteed bonds which had brilliantly projected most of those rather important early steam railroads within the State of Massachusetts. Moreover, Boston was planning to eventually ascertain a portion of its Erie Canal activities in freight transportation at Albany which had logically taken form by February 25, 1825. And on this same date the Massachusetts legislature had definitely procured studies of a waterway project for building a significant connecting canal through even before that Erie Canal was fully operational.

These railway construction crews thoroughly began with their steady and fundamental advancement of railroad growth at Boston by preferably building train tracks of shorter distances. Then after a section of this track had amply paid for their services provided by its railroad company, another partial segment was dependently tied together as the roadway sequentially continued onwards in reaching for a predetermined location. Also, when one line was not able to adequately retain a potential investment return, their railroad foreman along with his workers would merge that weaker link between two strong links, and thus justifiably making its main chain pay for those unsteady loops along the railway. Nevertheless there would be no further requirement of mentioning these numerous names of rail lines as they are often sometimes confusing to the mind. Although some of Boston's most reliable and dependable railroad track lines which were consistently developed within this State of Massachusetts had effectively become what were known as the Boston & Albany Railroad and the New Haven & Hartford Railroad. Furthermore, both of these two obvious railroads had confidently illustrated that by sheer means of firm and solid consolidation of their weaker roadways with those generally stronger lines, definitely demonstrated the best solution for solely creating this explicit term "through lines" among railroad transportation.

The Massachusetts legislature accordingly chartered a rail line in 1830 from Boston to Lowell, and also had given their perpetual concurrence to its particular supporters which were justly asking for a monopoly of this business for several years. Then during a June session of that following year, the State legislation had approvingly granted charters for two more railways with one of them beginning from Boston going south to Providence, a route that for countless years had infinitely carried a heavy turnpike traffic, and this other line was pertinently started at Boston and ensued westerly to Worcester. The Lowell rail line ran for a distance of twenty-six miles which traditionally followed its usual route of the Middlesex Canal, and was customarily opened for railway freight and passenger services on June 27, 1835. In addition, cotton spinning and fabric weaving exceptionally begun on an admirable gamut along that textile city of Lowell, just downstream from the Merrimack River near its end of this canal, and these productive manufactures saw sufficient interest for a railroad to further escalate with their immediate access to reach distant marketplaces. Valuable to note was that the Boston and Lowell line ran northward, and had affluently served its quickly growing cotton industry of that State, which consequently resulted in entirely putting the Middlesex Canal operation out of business.

The Boston and Lowell Railroad was formally organized by Patrick Tracy Jackson, and other members of its Boston Associates as an added supplement to that Middlesex Canal. As a matter of fact their worthwhile capital investment had been in an initial sum of $1.2 million dollars which was available almost instantaneously for roadbed building, and railway construction was vitally accomplished until completion in April of 1835. Their layout arrangement for its route strategically planned was that one set of rails had to be laid for this double embankment, while a double-track set of train tracks were largely provided in order to accommodate available passengers for the railroad. Also, it was comparably decided upon to use granite crossties for reinforcement beneath these rails along with a firm bottom composed of rubble stone which had been sunken three feet deep into this ground. Furthermore, the Boston and Lowell line was a resolute example of its susceptible capableness to import goods from abroad, and had utterly made it economical for transporting marketable products into those adjacent inland regions away from this port city.

* * * * * * * * *

The Boston and Providence line was proportionally located within an area which had extensively anticipated heavy traffic consumption as this railway would definitely provide a crucial shortcut passage running along a recognized water route that existed between two important major cities. William G. McNeill who was a famous pioneer of American railroad building had critically been in charge of land surveying its predictable route which was wholly proposed during 1832. In his final survey report for practical roadway grade concentration, McNeill had reputably summarized that every railway line where urgent goods are being transported in both directions should be primarily designed as one continuous plane alignment, or laid out over a succession of level components within this subdivided area. After an accurate and precise evaluation of certain factual data, that preferably recommended course for the Boston and Providence line had to efficiently surmount a slight road grade elevation of 16.50 feet along some marshlands nearby a rather narrow valley leading into the Neponsett River so as to heedfully reach its height of a Dividing Ridge situated between these two points.

Especially significant was that these conformable directors of this Boston and Providence line being under general guidance by McNeill had carefully chosen their most direct route with minimum surface grade reduction, and least curvature for trackage construction of building a railway. Essentially a double-width embankment was to be built, but only one set of rail tracks had been laid onto wooden crossties instead of stone blocks in order to support a solid foundation under its rails. In addition those railway tracks ran immediately just south outside of Boston passing across a place called Sharon for a combined distance of fifty-three miles in length, and usefully had linked together these two prestigious cities of Boston and Providence. As a result, the Boston and Providence Railroad was its first through rail line service within this State which had fortunately operated their first locomotive train over a newly finished section of tracks on June 2, 1835. Furthermore, distant travelers who were on a journey could swiftly ride its railroad overnight from Boston to Providence, and then Commodore Vanderbilt's new speedy steamer the Lexington would be able to competently put them in New York City that following evening.

On the contrary this railway route which was stretching westward had been of common conspicuous concernment among many Boston merchants as they began to perspectively foresee their steady increase of resourceful products which had been abundantly flowing into its port from New York once the Erie Canal was coincidentally opened in 1825. Unfortunately, due to those treacherous and highly elevated uplands of Massachusetts it was deemed virtuously necessary for only attempting to undertake its eastern end of their route towards this interior of that State, a section of forty-five miles from Worcester to Boston. In addition among several extreme findings which were consistently contained within a few enticing reports for the Boston and Worcester line had definitely made certain redundant references of its exceeding amounts of occurring traffic along that inland town, and also with this great Massachusetts port. Likewise preliminary proposals were actually being compellingly prepared for building an entrenchment tunnel under a western ridge of these Berkshire Hills, however construction work of this project lay far beyond their skillful engineering abilities which were stringently available at that time. Although both the chief engineer and its railroad directors of this Worcester road were rather presumptuous that passenger traffic would be of any meaningful subsistence for their company, but astonishingly enough that line had generously created a passenger service which relatively brought some adjacent towns westerly of Boston into historical city suburbs. More important wage salaries of America at this time had been severely high while in comparison railroad fares were exclusively low which had gradually permitted an increase of steady volume for daily commuting by railway train as early as the 1840's.

Basically that Boston and Worcester line was soon going to be beneficially joined together with the Western Railroad of Massachusetts which would thoroughly enable many New England Colonies to commonly share much of its richer Western trade with New York State. Moreover the Worcester line stretching eastward towards Boston was advertently advantageous in providing locomotive services to a vast popular progressive community for these perspective railroad investors. However, that potential and inevitable construction for building a rail route west of Worcester was becoming rather doubtful to those zealous railway developers as its Central uplands of Massachusetts had been prevalently fixed within a region of steep slopes with gravel soils. Special attention should be noted that knowledgeable and inspiring circumstances for evolution of this prosperous Western Railroad of Massachusetts had been keenly recognized as a prominent developmental line from its initial early beginning stages.

A key feature was that its route of the Boston and Worcester Railroad had to choose a pretentious path for tolerably crossing over those repetitious hills located alongside this Merrimack River and Narragansett Bay. Moreover, the accumulative length of this rail line from their train depot positioned at Boston to its center of town in Worcester was approximately forty-three miles in distance. Therefore, its final conclusive findings of a prepared land survey for this roadbed had distinctively shown that sixteen miles of their route had been almost level, while fourteen miles of ascending or descending summits obviously existed, and the other remaining thirteen miles mainly displayed incline slopes. Consequently, that board of directors had accordingly projected on adapting their railway with steam locomotive engines of durable power and rapid speed which could safely be allowed to run along its railroad tracks.

Principally these winding track curves and variant road grades for this railway of Boston and Worcester were relevantly smooth along its rolling countryside, and redundant grade levels were minimum on most parts of that route which had to crossover three individually separate dividing boundaries. Apparently, failing efforts decisively occurred within its current trackage construction as a rather slender compressed subgrade was being built twenty-four feet wide, while only a single line had been laid down although it was later double-tracked by 1838. Most of all, the roadbed foundation was being fully constructed with iron rails which rested upon wooden crossties, after conducive observations along their Boston and Lowell route had deliberately shown rapid deterioration of a stone structure. Nevertheless it had been evident from this assuring data collected that an appropriate estimation was made to wisely obtain a realistic compromise of immoderate construction spending in comparison with those progressive costs of railroad operation.

One important detail of consideration was pertinently trying to find a suitable site in building a railroad station for this Boston and Worcester Railroad inside such a large metropolis city. Moreover from past experiences, railways often came before such towns were built, however at Boston these railroads had to publicly contend about a feasible location as possible for an acceptable train station which would aptly serve all entering and departing rail lines. The probable choices had alternately varied from placing a depot at an edge of this town, nearby to where tangible companies began their daily operations, or by carrying its line directly through the center of an existing town alongside an established route. However, upon examination on a number of different options that railroad company had diligently decided to bring the line to Brighton—farther south and partially crossing over Mill Basin in order for them to enter into this city. Also, for their favorable selection of a south side terminal site those imperative directors had fundamentally planned on building its line onto newly filled land which broadly extended outwards towards that shoreline of this town closer to navigable waters. Finally, that achieving success of South Station in Boston became the busiest passenger train service which had voluminously represented its profitable value of having a terminal at such a central and practicable location as permissible so as to better serve these growing territories of the land.

That Boston and Worcester line although it's last of those three extension railways situated within this State had proficiently attained their "first service" honors with passenger trains commencing in train operations extending between Boston and Newton at Massachusetts on April 4, 1834. Moreover, the first locomotive train going from Boston to Worcester began running on July 3, 1835; and a formal opening of this railway line was delightfully celebrated on the 6th of that month which had proven to be a valuable accomplishment. By 1837, this Boston and Worcester Railroad had an operating ratio of 47 percent with respectful appraisal to net income, total receipts, and carried over surplus. Also, as can be expected, these railroad developers fervently demonstrated to further reduce their expenditures and finances of railway construction, and to pragmatically continue with disbursement capital for all future investments of building roadways. Furthermore, it was perceptively understood that several general reasons for extraordinary locomotive expenses were due largely because of low minimal costs within trackage construction, and that railroad fares had been somewhat higher in the State of Massachusetts.

Much of its financial prosperity along the Worcester line had vigorously inspired a lot of New England promoters to prospectively devise on completing a railway which would steadily arrive at Albany where a joining connection could then be met with the Erie Canal. This elementary expressive creation for the Western Railroad of Massachusetts had taken more than six years to clearly finish construction of their rail line to Albany, and was the longest railroad ever built in America by an individual corporation. On the contrary these other three existent railroads operating from Boston to Lowell, Providence, and Worcester had modestly acquired their financial funds without too many harshly restraining troubles, however those capitalist investors were alarmingly apprehensive about this influent flow of mercantile trading westerly of Worcester. Moreover, its progressive movement of textile production among many New England ports had been southward towards Hartford, Connecticut and also further westward along the Hudson River in New York.

Chiefly this surveying area that was sensibly prepared for the Western Railroad of Massachusetts had prevalently indicated its highest summit which had not yet been physically reached by a railway, and contingent difficulties at selling stock subscriptions were rather unsuccessful at the beginning. Therefore, its board of directors for that Western Railroad of Massachusetts had to fortunately respond to the only available source of capital by which profit had not been an important issue, they deliriously reputed to this Treasury of the State. Also within a consecutive series of court appeals to the General Court of Massachusetts during 1836, that State had tenaciously granted a sizable loan in an amount of $4 million to its Western Railroad of Massachusetts. Valuable to note, even though four members of those directors were selectively appointed by the State, this Western Railroad became a state commitment although legally it had wholly remained as a private corporation.

The Western Railroad of Massachusetts had been boastfully recognized as being one of its first ever American rail lines to realistically crossover these Appalachians, and by their trackage design and roadway construction those standardized essential preparations of national railroad evolution was handily achieved and recognizably accessible within the United States. Likewise many dedicated merchants and devoted businessmen of Boston were anxiously seeking to gainfully obtain an allowable route to the West, and also its equally intelligent engineers had to cleverly accomplish an enduring task of crossing into two different main sections of this Appalachian Mountain regional system. Although once across those rugged and strenuous Appalachians it was fortunately assumed that their constructional engineers had to readily understand of there being no passageway out of New England except through New York. In addition there had to be worthwhile cooperation from the State legislature of New York as that sovereign body of democracy had determinedly shown restrainable and discernible intentions to voluntarily provide with their helpful solution towards this controversy affair. Furthermore, it had been practical judgment by the State legislation to explicitly expedite legal authorization for granting an extension line to this Western Railroad of Massachusetts in solely acquiring ten miles of attainable land which had intervened along its western boundary and the Hudson River.

At Boston the Western Railroad of Massachusetts had been pretentiously contemplated as being a true Appalachian railway after its vital construction. And these raised mountains, rolling hills, and river streams had cordially reflected upon those original qualities of their rail line. Especially significant the Western Railroad had a combined total of only seven miles of level trackage with its maximum length at eighty-three feet, and there were one hundred and seven miles of excessively higher grades than that of the Boston and Worcester line. Basically the roadbed layout had mainly consisted of deep cuts, great embankments, and sharp curvature within this trackage, while road grades were built slightly steeper when that route was actually constructed as it had been necessary to rather build these grades taller and above those turbulent streams which were being fully anticipated. Subsequently, the first part of this land survey that was under study and investigation for building a roadway had drastically divided these waters of the Blackstone River where this village of Worcester lies, and those of its Chickopee River which actively flows into the Connecticut River.

Westerly of Connecticut that land terrain had been even somewhat higher and which was broken up into numerous ridges and ravens along its western chain of those Appalachian Mountains known as the Berkshire Hills. Likewise this road alignment descends outwards into the Berkshire Valley, and then precedes ahead in extending towards a town called Pittsfield, before passing through Canaan Gap of these Taconic Range Mountains in order to safely reach some lower plateau regions just located westerly of its main chain Appalachian Mountains. Although progress improvement was gradually slow along that section because constructional costs were supposedly high and currency was limited, but this board of directors for the Worcester line had vigilantly incorporated its Western Railroad of Massachusetts to construct building a railway west so as to arrive at that town of Pittsfield on March 15, 1833. Additionally, by 1839 the Western Railroad of Massachusetts upon securance of state loans to their railway company were in liberal agreement to undertake further construction for this western section of its Connecticut River within an agreeable time frame.

During 1840 an appointed committee of directors had prominently traveled to Albany in presumable efforts to sensibly begin stern negotiations with this State of New York for a partial subsidy on its construction work of their Western Railroad extension line into New York. On the contrary, Albany's interests had bearably started building east, and these two lines were modestly joined and later combined together on December 21, 1841 before a grand celebration from Boston and Albany had taken place among them. Substantially, there were a consecutive series of local shorter lines that ran in conjunction at Springfield, Hartford, and New Haven; and had reputably attained a rail merger connection with the Boston to New York line in 1848, during at which time the New York and New Haven had mainly entered upon New York City. Furthermore, by 1855 that Western Railroad of Massachusetts and those Albany lines were bountifully consolidated together in accordance so as to bring into current existence its present formation of the Boston and Albany Railroad.

This Appalachian Mountain range expands over a broader and much vaster area along northern New England than farther south of that region, and are more severely covered with frozen ice accumulations north of the St. Lawrence River territory. However those higher Appalachians have been solidly breached by deep valleys which surprisingly rise up to over four thousand feet in Vermont, and six thousand feet at New Hampshire, while there are an increasing number of less impeding obstructive barriers to cross rather than that of these Berkshire's in western Massachusetts. Additionally, this Boston and Lowell Railroad had plausibly provided for a principal route out of town, and was its linking connection from Boston's harbor in order to reach the main stream of that Merrimack River along north central New England. Nevertheless further acceleration of railway road construction was relatively minimal, but had intently continued along the Merrimack River to arrive at this town of Concord in New Hampshire for a total distance of seventy miles which was thoroughly finished by 1842. More importantly the New England legislation was rather apprehensive at first with regards to steam locomotives although railroad advancement along its region as well as within other New England States were simply former developments of these earlier Boston lines, and had been built specifically in conformable relationship with that systematic representation.

While this Lowell line was being solidly built to proceed outwards towards the Vermont State boundary line by an integral combination of smaller merging connection lines, other meaningful aspects had been under pursuit to tentatively reinforce their capable promotion of Boston's trading opportunities. As both the Worcester and Western Railroad routes had widely passed across that southern part of Massachusetts, there was similar interest among those anxious promoters of adequately building a rail line going over its northern section, from Fitchburg to Boston for a distance of about forty-five miles in length. Appropriately, a permissible corporate charter had been providently authorized and was obligingly issued by the State legislation during 1842, while railroad construction regularly continued ahead upon completion until 1845 for its Fitchburg Railroad, and also some conscious efforts were being accomplished for a projected extension line to arrive at the town of Greenfield in that State of Connecticut before 1850. Likewise it was inevitably understood when building this railway of the Fitchburg Railroad that it had been built as an expectation to their railroad company, and would purely be an initial onset for a railroad to possibly enhance those mercantile growth efforts of Boston.

The Deerfield River which is geographically positioned within west central Massachusetts continuously rises near its western crest of these Berkshire Hills, and has naturally cut out openings for

New England alongside a deep valley of about two thousand feet, it then descends downstream to mutually join up with the Connecticut River just south of Greenfield. Moreover, from this town of Greenfield westward to Deerfield River an adjoining route going over these steep elevated high hills would be easily accessible except sometimes may be tormenting along its way. Especially located by a western edge of Greenfield close to an uneroded section of that Appalachian Mountain chain—stands Hoosac Mountain which had perceivably remained uncut by any streams, and yet to the west of it only five miles away lies Berkshire Valley. Additionally, the obvious assumption among their railroad directors were if theoretically Hoosac Mountain could be carefully tunneled out, it would then undeniably provide for a much quicker and far better route across the State of Massachusetts than customarily obtainable during its present time by the Western Railroad. In summary, economic values and explicit advantages for a lesser graded route was conceivable to these impulsive promoters as the Fitchburg Railroad mainly a freight route railway had an utterly profitable amount of capital investment.

That fundamental significance of initiating the Fitchburg Railroad which intermediately runs adjacent to its Lowell and Worcester lines had been literally their first step to feasibly prepare upon an adaptable railway of later reaching Montreal in Canada. An important factor about their constructional spending to build this rail line was that it had been mostly financed through the sale of stock subscriptions among some dependable merchants residing at Fitchburg or near its route, and those financial expenditure contributions from Boston were almost minor in comparison. Moreover, by intentional endurance of linear branching and sequential railway extensions these Vermont and Massachusetts railroads were uniquely contracted and later fortunately leased out by the Fitchburg line during 1874, while subsequently that route moving along its northern country had properly reached Brattleboro at Vermont within 1849. In addition, this primary building of its Fitchburg line had been mainly a direct conception to visually imagine two possible future routes; one from Greenfield through

Deerfield Valley to Hoosac Mountain, and another from Brattleboro north and northwestward to Canada and the Great Lakes.

With considerable reflection of this Deerfield River route, these earnest railroad promoters had perpetually managed to advantageously construct and lay down a railway line to Albany for accommodating better capabilities of building their tracks from Greenfield to Troy alongside the Hudson River. By 1848, the legislation had explicably granted a charter for construction of a rail line to be built at Troy going to Greenfield, and it was absolutely likeable and evidently perceptible that this route would have to forcefully tunnel through Hoosac Mountain as a capital investment of $2 million had been concisely presumed ample enough for funding of this total project. Although after meticulous review of their prepared engineering location report, its Troy and Greenfield supportive directors had justly appealed to the State for seeking financial assistance, and after legitimate and legislative hearings were boldly conducted a permissible loan was eventually allocated so that railway work could begin at once. Also, those constructional contracts to accomplish tunneling excavation of Hoosac Mountain were contingently given out for its ongoing task in 1855 and 1856, however because of such hostile and impending conflicts over some necessary required building specifications trackage construction was strictly halted and had to be terminally suspended during 1861.

Alvah Crocker who was a veracious promoter of this Fitchburg Railroad in 1856 had been preferably chosen by the State to be vigorously put in charge of supervision work for its tunnel project, and most of their essential equipment which was currently engaged with on that Hoosac Mountain had either been invented or manufactured at Fitchburg. More importantly, this State of Massachusetts by 1863 had voluntarily taken over its principal property which was presently involved with for the Troy and Greenfield venture, and reasonably began to virtually proceed forward with drilling and digging on their own accordance. That provisional excavation work of its east portal through Hoosac Mountain was sluggishly indolent at times which had strenuously resulted in many restraining detainments. Although along with technical advancement of compressed air-drilling, and the substitution of nitroglycerin for black powder blasting had aptly made it extremely diligent to conscientiously improve their progressive development of this purposeful work task.

The rail line from Greenfield to that tunnels east portal had been poorly constructed thus severely causing bridges to drastically collapse, and there was excessive curvature along its trackage construction. Also a cross-section of this tunnel was built at only 14-feet wide and 18-feet high which had reluctantly fallen short in an energetically attempt to meet the State's original requirements of 22-feet wide at its base with a maximum width of 24-feet before finally closing within an archway. In fact gradual progression for erecting these top headings had been realistically slow at times, and along its western part of this monstrous rock structure like tunnel there were huge amounts of water accumulations with massive mineral deposits that had even further delayed their ultimate accomplishment. Nevertheless, after twenty-four years of exhausting excavation and laborious construction work that Hoosac tunnel undertaking was totally completed by 1875; though only four and three-quarter miles in distance and 760 feet above sea level. Furthermore, the Fitchburg Railroad was loyally responsible for creating the Hoosac tunnel route which had infinitely provided this State of Massachusetts with an exceptional qualified freight line traveling across its northwestern section of those Appalachian Mountains.

* * * * * * * * *

Railroad building and proportional rail line expansion in this State of Massachusetts during 1830 to 1846 was vitally regarded to be an experimental era for its tremendous impact upon the steam locomotive. However some of their most typical problems with those early pioneer railroads of Boston had been its wide choices of track gauge sizes, and also the laying of solid rock for crossties. Moreover after building a roadbed foundation with granite ties these obvious engineers soon came to realize that such hard heavy tracks often caused bouncing of carriages, and had even torn coaches and engines into fragments as they noisily rattled along its rails when turning and going around curves. Then of course, Massachusetts had to practically retain rail rate charges that were more or less equally similar in conformance to stagecoach and canal rates at which time were between three to four cents a mile.

Massachusetts had been the first State to potentially release into train service heavier steam engines along their railways, and there were many different sizes of trackage gauge being constantly used for running locomotives. For example, there would be one section of railroad tracks which were six feet across from wheel to wheel, followed by another link of narrower gauge, and then an additional line of track that had been of an even wider gauge size. As a result, worthwhile replacement charges and terrific expenses of modifying the various track gauges to its commonly acceptable size of four feet eight and one-half inches had enormously increased their major costs of building its extension line from Boston to Albany. In addition, changing of their wheel width on steam engine locomotives and train cars had to be strongly resolved so as to proportionately proceed ahead with any further expansion of rail lines by way of Connecticut from Boston to New York.

On the contrary these relatively smaller locomotive steam engines of eleven tons in weight had been amply costing around seven thousand dollars which was about twice its amount that this Baltimore and Ohio were formerly paying for their own steam engines. Likewise those vastly large expenses of purchasing locomotive engines were severely raising intensified doubts amongst some private investors of whether they could efficiently earn their original cost as well as continued maintenance. Being the first of this type, these Boston and Lowell railway trains and many of some New England reproductive replicas were moderately greater advanced and far superior than other railroads elsewhere in the Union. More importantly those railroad promoters of New England had accordingly comprehended its valuable concept that their railroads would influentially depend upon regional trading markets for business commerce, and they accurately made sure about probabilities of interchanging freight with them by selectively choosing this same standardized trackage gauge for all of its steam power locomotives.

Especially imperative were that these railway lines of Massachusetts had to densely acquire this inspiring intelligence of learning to become highly informative about railroad rates varying by different amounts depending upon exact location of territory and seasons of the year. Worth mentioning was that operational costs for running a steam locomotive during winter seasons were comparatively more expensive than operating a locomotive during its summer season. Also it had been critically established proof for many railroad builders and train operators that during the winter season there had been no such direct competition of stagecoaches, rivers, and canals in providing passenger service and freight transportation. Eventually, those steam locomotives of Boston had unfortunately lowered its respectful rates for the summer, and also had to reduce their charges for shorter train excursions. On the contrary, Boston was even cutting rates on their passenger services down to two cents a mile for particular privileges of attracting additional train commuters. Furthermore, by 1843 the Boston and Albany line had been lucratively productive and was significantly acquiring more business traffic than both of its combined rivers and canals within the United States.

Valuable to note that the State of Massachusetts were increasing their transportational activities by promoting parallel branch lines traveling up to Maine, and then which rapidly endured on through these hills of New Hampshire. In addition, some serviceable rail lines advantageously extended northwards into this State of Vermont so as to decidedly take sufficient advantages of traffic transportation moving up to Montreal in Canada. Moreover, linking railway routes were also being vibrantly constructed through those Berkshire Hills along the Connecticut border in order to capture and trap any freight shipments which were going to New York by way of that Hudson River. On the other hand, Boston was hurt least by this sudden panic of 1837, largely because locomotive trains were bringing in profitable dividends so as to actually subsidize for their railroads. Nevertheless within many railways of Boston's expansion lines there had been an abundantly steady growth of industrial manufacturing factories to exceptionally purchase and desirably sell its marketable goods and imported articles.

At first this State of New Hampshire was uneasy and rather unsure about building railways partially because by an influential impact of State law which had repulsively compelled these railroads to proficiently pay local farmers for their own assumable value in obtaining right-of-way land passage permission. As a result the meaningless action taken on behalf of that State law was crucial to all railway construction along New Hampshire from 1830 to 1844, while Vermont had cautiously preceded forth with its rapid development of shorter duration rails, and even had effectively built recognizable establishments around them which justifiably conceded in repealing against that ambiguous insensible law. This was one contributing example of how railways for locomotives have to marginally ignore and refuse to take certain notice of state, national, and political incompatible conflicts. Although by 1845, Boston was capably acquiring much of Canada's half yearly traffic transportation especially when frozen ice conditions intensely forced closure along its only available route line running up and down alongside the St. Lawrence River.

Meanwhile New England's expectable pursuit of gaining an essential Northwest Passage had originally constituted from a combination of short lines which had adequately met the demanding necessities, and mutually consolidated its secondary branches into one or two more mainlines for a substantial and profitable system. Although these New Hampshire and Vermont extension lines were often independent of Boston, they contingently became the metropolitan railroads that further progressed ahead to build newer railways, and which were distinctively destined to currently assume stern control by means of trackage realignment along their rural routes. The Boston and Lowell Railroad was perhaps unsteady in departing away from some stipulated boundary agreements, but had been a positive sign towards that consecutive continuity of branching lines from Boston going to Wells River and White River Junction in this State of Vermont. However, an ideal concept to achieve promotional activities for a magnitude of regional territory along northern New England had been to ascertain its traffic transportation of Montreal, and this vibrant importance of solely organizing the Grand Trunk Railroad which was originally established in Portland, Maine; and with its neighboring Canadian ally, the St. Lawrence and Atlantic Railroad during 1845.

The Grand Trunk Railroad of New England was rather indeed a dependable supplement and reliant substitution for this first railroad which had been constructed to reach across its Canadian border known as the Atlantic and St. Lawrence Railroad. And on the other hand, this St. Lawrence and Atlantic railway had been primarily created to transitionally junction instantaneous at the U.S. border, and which was basically finished by 1853; while yet being another trans-Appalachian route to prestigiously improve upon its future advancement of Canada's territorial chief interests and principal concernments at that time. In addition this route from Portland to Montreal was spontaneously serving as its only key passageway out towards Canada, and had fortunately permitted those British shipping vessels to dock at Portland, Maine. As a matter of fact this convenient enabled connection at Portland was then only a two-day trip closer to Europe by steamship than New York, and even half a day closer than Boston.

Both of these reputable railroads the Atlantic & St. Lawrence as well as the St. Lawrence & Atlantic had efficiently adopted and competently utilized a track gauge size of respectfully five feet six inches so as to strictly keep their transportation of goods safe from attracting any special attention to that significantly growing Boston network of lines which were traditionally built to the normal standard acceptable track gauge. Additionally this Portland and Montreal route had advantageously made useful practice of its surrounding territories alongside the Androscoggin River Valley to crossover these Appalachians in order to reach an eastern range of slopes near the White Mountains at Milan in New Hampshire. After traveling across that mountain range with minimal road grade reductions for about five miles, its route descends downward to a tributary stream of the Connecticut River located at Vermont. Next, it then gradually follows along a planed surface lying just north beyond those Appalachian Mountains where a merger juncture adjacently meets at this Canadian borderline situated about 149 miles away from Portland.

Specifically that rail line departing from Portland going to Montreal was exceptionally opened along a 292-mile railway during 1853, and realistically became Canada's foremost route stretching out towards the ocean sea. However a newly formed railroad company which was known as the Grand Trunk Railway of Canada had been recently organized and consequently took over a new lease along that Portland and Montreal line in 1856, while widely extending it to upper Canada, and then finally onto Chicago. Furthermore once that Grand Trunk Railway had prodigiously changed their rail tracks over to the common standard gauge before 1874, it gradually began to broaden their trackage connections over most of New England, and in 1885 this railroad had securely held half the present stock of its line which was greatly increased to two-thirds during 1898.

Although by 1850, New England had prudently occupied and economically attained almost three thousand miles of strategic railways which were being circumstantially generated outside of Boston. Valuable to note these Boston rails had approximately seventy million dollars worth of private capital in its financial investment of steam power, rails, and locomotives. Moreover this railway line moving out of Boston going to Lowell between 1831 to 1837 was easily costing about $56,000 per mile to build, and by the time some unavoidable mistakes were fatally resolved and finally corrected it had risen to a cost of $88,000 a mile. More importantly those railroad tracks were conceivably built with definite limitations and purposeful intentions of taxing its users and investors, but yet all of these States in the Union had been thrifty spending millions of dollars a year to eagerly build public transportational roads. Furthermore, there were in the United States before 1929, almost six hundred thousand miles of state highways of which relatively eighty thousand miles of it had been soundly paved flat as a floor.

One of the most immeasurable circumstances which Boston had to intelligently give up were railroads had not been free accessible highways for anyone choosing to optionally use them as a desirous and potential passageway. In fact locomotive railways were not a generalized roadway in this particular sense of turnpike wagon roads. On the contrary those triumphantly constructed railways had been the essential property of potently powerful men which possessed its available cash to build them, and were open to the public upon payment of a considerable fare in equal return for reputable services provided for by their railroad companies. Last of all the anticipative railroads were pertinently built by fair taxation among all citizens within that locality who tolerantly have entree to use these roadways strictly for its necessary privileges of interchangeable transportation and evidential conveyances.

CHAPTER FIVE

The first reliant locomotive to ever principally haul passengers by forceful steam impulsion on a regular schedule must properly belong to the <u>Best</u> <u>Friend</u> <u>of</u> <u>Charleston</u>, and which was under conductible operation by the Charleston and Hamburg Railroad. Robert Y. Hayne who had been a Senator from South Carolina earnestly began his timely and strenuous efforts to liberally propel the South into its symbolic economic developments. Moreover, Hayne was undeniable one of its leading promoters of this Charleston and Hamburg Railway, which had been purely destined to primarily connect that exceptional harbor situated on the Atlantic Coast near Charleston with the mighty Mississippi River port of Memphis. Valuable to note was that this South Carolina Railway was actually started in February of 1829, departing from Charleston to reach Hamburg along its Savannah River just opposite of Augusta within the State of Georgia. When that Charleston line had finally arrived at Hamburg by 1833, it was the longest railroad in this world under only one management, and collectively entailed one hundred and thirty-seven miles of continuous trackage.

Alexander Black was the State Representative of Charleston during 1827 and had proficiently proposed a bill to the state legislation for incorporating a railroad to be built from Charleston to Hamburg. Although as a meaningful result, subscription books were tenaciously opened in 1828 for helping to substantially cover its allowable costs of satisfactorily performing a land survey located along those areas of Charleston and Augusta. As a matter of fact the preliminary survey which was in effect being carefully performed by Colonel Blanding had drastically shown that its highest part of a summit intervening between these two places had been 375-feet above Hamburg, and also was 545-feet above this city boundary of Charleston. In addition, the summit was distantly located 123 miles away from Charleston by public road and seventeen miles out of Hamburg.

It was easily understood that this sloping terrain perpetually positioned at its Hamburg side had brought about some concerning problems and difficulties. Although the Colonel avidly felt that he could possibly accomplished a practical solution by several different methods, depending upon its mode of power which would be technically applied between steam locomotives or dependable horses. However if a locomotive train was going to be running along this route, then an inclined plane together with a stationary engine would have to be necessarily required while in general retrospect of horse power they could be eventually eliminated. More importantly since steam had been precisely selected for its reliable source of power, then this incline plane had been definitely an added requirement among these anxious supporters and encouraging railroad promoters for its roadway work of their rail line to be put under construction.

Colonel Blanding had inevitably performed various land surveys for a feasible road in planning out this trackage construction and railway building for its route. Also an area of ground along the terrain to be reached had mostly contained sand on that top surface, although soils beneath this river bottom largely consisted of a dark rich loam. Their rail line beginning at the Charleston peninsula was to run regularly through an appropriately planned route up to a town called Summerville just south of the Edisto River for thirty miles. In addition that route apparently followed a relatively gentle surface to a dividing ridge summit which was situated 510-feet above tidewater, and 119 miles out of Charleston. On the contrary no roadbed grade was ever over thirty feet per mile, and only sixteen miles away from that summit and Hamburg a 3,800-foot long inclined plane with a moderate road grade descending downwards to Augusta Bridge had to be sufficiently constructed.

Most of this necessary and essential railway work had been built upon timber piles rather than surface roadway grading for allowing to adequately crossover these smaller rivers and flowing streams emplaced in South Carolina. Though that track gauge of five feet was considerably selected and justly decided upon among three other similar gauge sizes, and soon it became to be the characteristic

"Southern gauge" for some early steam locomotives. Likewise the rail line was vastly constructed with wooden stringers onto which had been spiked a strap of iron measuring two and a half inches wide and half an inch in thickness. Also, it was rather more economical to build that railroad within an area such as those Carolina coastal plains where pine forests were abundant and easily obtainable at trackside. Furthermore the South Carolina Railroad as it came to be recognized had strictly used original plans and designs in addition to having American built steam engines operating throughout all of its entire elementary and final stages for building.

One of their directors, E.L. Miller from the South Carolina Railroad and Canal Company had obviously been present during its initial opening of the Liverpool and Manchester Railway in London. After cautiously witnessing and watching this capable performance being consummated by Stephenson's Rocket locomotive, he had decisively assembled his own steam engine which was known as the Best Friend of Charleston at a West Point Foundry located near New York City. Meanwhile, Horatio Allen was diligently going to be officially appointed as their chief engineer on the Charleston and Hamburg line after usefully proving to many encouraging authorities about his logical and reasonable demonstration of the Stourbridge Lion. Nevertheless Allen's supportive success in running the first steam locomotive ever along American tracks on August 9, 1829 greatly had qualified him for that amenable position when he indeed arrived at Charleston to take up his duties and responsibilities during September of 1829.

Horatio who was in acceptable agreement to use steam power for applying traction had vivaciously explained his desirous and reputable recommendations to these significant directors of this railroad company. Moreover contained within his bearably findings report, traction was being aptly based upon its worthwhile assumption that within the near future there would be no logical explanation to expect any material improvement among those breed of horses, and who knew what the scope of locomotives were going to place at their command. This formal resolution to evidently adopt locomotive traction was voted on unanimously by all of their directors, and also had been the first act by any corporate body to convincingly permit the steam locomotive as traction power along a railroad for stringent purposes of general passenger and freight transportation. Implicitly the South had no rich merchants or bankers like Boston, New York, and Philadelphia for financial support of their ongoing railway projects.

This Charleston and Hamburg line had been preferably built rather quickly and tolerably due to much of its plentiful surrounding area that once off the Charleston peninsula their route was nearly straight and mainly level for ninety-odd miles to a summit which was situated sixteen miles away from Hamburg. However, it was only along this inclined plane region where these railroad builders had alarmingly encountered some difficulty of its constructional project. More importantly the existing operation of an inclined plane had been disgustingly proving costly and also utterly exorbitant, chiefly because of there being several individual separate slopes lying within a three-thousand foot section. Although in 1835, this incline plane was crucially shortened to twenty-seven hundred feet, and as a result was being made into one continuous and steady single slope. Furthermore most of their roadway construction work was heedfully performed by inexperience apprentices, and they had only become skilled laborers once that railway was finally completed.

Once the South Carolina Railroad was prosperously open for train service operations during 1833, it had pertinently displayed to be a minimal involvement as maintenance and operating costs were greater than had been normally anticipated. Additionally, there were no through service connection lines at Augusta, even though this State of Georgia had conceivably begun with trackage construction of the Georgia Railroad between that city and what became known as Atlanta. More importantly their actual revenues of total receipts were fifty-eight dollars a day, and by 1834, they had generously been increased to one thousand dollars a day. Likewise within ten more years that Charleston road would be able to substantially pay yielding dividends of ten percent to all of its rightful shareholders who held stock along this rail line.

In the meantime there were definitely strong desires and special intentions growing over vital concernment among many railroad promoters for a presentable proposal of planning and building a railway line from Charleston to an opposite terminus location at Cincinnati, Ohio. During 1836, this South Carolina legislature had proficiently appropriated enough financial funds to especially have an accurate land survey suitably prepared for a railway route going across these southern Appalachian Mountains. As a matter of fact their survey findings which had been reported by July 1836, noticeably indicated that there were two mountain barriers which stood in current existence across this geography between those two cities of Charleston and Cincinnati. Nevertheless its names of these two mountain barriers were the Blue Ridge Mountains located just alongside the North and South Carolina boundary, and also the Cumberland Mountains which had been situated on the Virginia, Tennessee, and Kentucky boundary whereby this region could all be accessible and sensibly approached by a rail line. Moreover that western slope of those Blue Ridge Mountains easily could be passed by using this level valley of the French Broad River which was near to its vicinity of Asheville in North Carolina, then proceeds onward towards the Tennessee Valley east of Knoxville. In conclusion, its Cumberland Mountains could be prudently achievable and theoretically accomplished at Cumberland Gap, where only a narrow ridge less than a mile in length divides and separates those distinguishable open valleys of the Tennessee from that of Cumberland.

Generally with the gradual evolution of this economy as well as its expandable railroad network of the South in 1836, had been too early for any type of desirable tasks among their precarious promoters and railroad builders. Furthermore any potential routes originating out of South Carolina to crossover these Appalachian Mountains would have to silently remain idle until after the Civil War. However during the 1870's there was a resourceful involvement within that Blue Ridge route, and prevalently the Asheville and Spartanburg Railroad was indicatively created, which had built their line to safely cross into its eastern front of those Blue Ridge Mountains. Valuable to note was the Asheville and Spartanburg rail line was officially declared opened for train operations by the 1880's, while this railway had distinctively included a section of their route that became famous among enthusiastic railroaders

99

which was known as Saluda Hill, and had been its steepest division of a mainline railroad within the United States at that time. Also the South Carolina Railroad was entirely responsible for attainable advancement to reach the West, but only after many branching lines in the Northeast as well as other Middle Atlantic states had gainfully acquired further access into that remote hinterland.

* * * * * * * * *

When this noteworthy railroad had passed swiftly across the South during those 1830's, both Georgia and South Carolina were its only two states amply comprised of harbor ports within these slower moving rivers of its eastern coastal region. Additionally along that invariable route of this South Carolina railway much of its land terrain traveling over by the railroad had been nearly wilderness except for some recently occupied villages and small towns which were eventually being confronted. However, it was at Georgia where its original and unique representation of this developmental American railroad had been laid out and which was presumably and profitably fulfilled. In fact much of those southern trade products had abundantly consisted of cotton, rice, and tobacco which could be capable of flowing down its headwaters of the Savannah River. Furthermore, the most important valuable commodity that was being transported among their railroads of the South was cotton which later had been bailed for export to many coastal ports where it would then be sent to England or New England.

Both the Central Railroad of Georgia and the South Carolina Railroad had apparently sought to prestigiously divert away from that natural flow of cotton which was continually moving ahead down those river streams. Although it was a growing concern and ongoing persistence of these Savannah merchants and investors who were literally responsible for bringing into customary existence this Central Railroad of Georgia. Moreover the Central Railroad of Georgia had robustly built a rail line from Savannah in order to reach that town of Macon located within its central part of this State alongside the Ocmulgee River at its plateau fall line. Likewise its tremendous railroad boom at Georgia was strongly brought about by final completion of the Charleston and Hamburg line, which had insistently perceived toward future projects being under vital promotion. One important task had been a partial extension of the South Carolina Railroad within this Piedmont Province of Georgia so as to sufficiently build its rail line from Augusta to Athens near an adjacent site of two prosperous cotton mills. Also another major undertaking was to feasibly establish a divisional branch line from the Altamaha Valley for safely entering into Savannah, and continuance of that line from their proposed terminus at Macon to a farther destination inland towards a mountainous range of this Piedmont Province. Furthermore additional discussion was also fittingly introduced for a railway line to be built across the hilly Appalachians, but no such private investor could be even found to risk his capital in its fatal sustainment.

The Central Railroad of Georgia was strictly considered to be a coastal plain rail line and had enticingly benefited from its gentle terrain along this surrounding area. Moreover for the first hundred miles of rails which were consistently being constructed west of Savannah, its steepest road grade was only ten feet per mile. Also at an edge of the Piedmont Province where that route had to ascend over some watersheds separating these various rivers, roadway grades could be easily held down to no more than twenty-five feet per mile. On the contrary, this curvature of their trackage was kindly manageable to many dedicated railroad workers which were shrewdly speculative about any curtailing and frugal conditions for accomplishing railway construction.

By 1836 railway work stupendously began at that site of Savannah for building a line of 190.5 miles in length and which was fully completed to arrive at Macon during 1843. Much of their consummative expenses involved with laying down these rails had been sharply reduced by using a rather skimpy strap rail of 1-1/2 by 5/8 inches, and it was being laid upon mud sills of pine wood which were cut among a vastly amount of trees that had been within this immediate vicinity. Valuable to note that those mindful investors were critically confronted with a shortage deficiency of capital rather than conflicts against roadway design and railway expansion. Additionally in an airy attempt to harshly struggle over their inadequate lack of funds, the State of Georgia had willingly allowed to officially grant a bank charter for this railroad as well as two other lines under special consideration and conversation which were the Georgia Railroad and the Monroe Railroad.

It was virtuously imperative to understand that this city of Macon had been currently dwelling for only some twelve years while its line was being rapidly built along a projected route. Also the noble belief of building a railway through a bountiful agricultural area could be greatly advanced only because of nominal constructional costs. In a modest offering this city of Savannah had generously donated five acres of their land for a railroad terminal to be valuably constructed, and that transformed structure had significantly remained in honorable presence as perhaps one of its finest early nineteenth century railway train stations. More importantly that rail line to Macon was possibly costing $13,000 per mile, about half the American average during this period merely because of indispensable level ground over which the steam locomotive passed and lightness of their rails. Therefore, including materials and equipment the Central Railroad of Georgia had evidently absorbed about $2.5 million which was positively rather a low sum by comparable expenses for a railroad line of 190 miles in length.

This swift and growing development of the Georgia Railroad had copiously built a line westwards from Augusta which was simultaneously used as a branch extension of the South Carolina Railroad. In addition these railway builders miraculously moved forward with their track construction onto the Piedmont Province so as to definitely ascertain those many navigable rivers situated within its coastal plains region. Moreover, the Georgia Railroad which was beneficially being issued an appropriate charter during 1833 had been intentionally authorized to construct a line beginning at Augusta for carrying trunk lines onto Athens, Madison, and Eatonton along this Piedmont Province. Also a major concernment was that the railroad company did not have enough financial funds available for extending their Athens branch line to the Tennessee River, but had solely gained some powerful support from many of these surrounding towns nearby that Piedmont Province area.

Their intense route which was feasibly planned and surveyed, advantageously was laid out by the Georgia Railroad from Augusta to Athens, and had carefully and precisely followed an anticipated pleasant rolling ridge for 105 miles in total length. Valuable to note the construction of trackage work which began within 1835 was further advanced to arrive at Athens by 1841, and adherently traveled downwards into both the Savannah Valley and Oconee Valley. However as early as 1836, the State of Georgia had considerably engaged in creating and promoting a rail line from Augusta going west so as to remotely come upon the Tennessee River. In addition, this Georgia Railroad had extensively expanded its Madison branch line moving westward along an incline slope of the Piedmont Province largely to encompass their destination for arriving at that city of Atlanta which was formerly known as Terminus. On the contrary, this 170-mile railway line running from Augusta to its joining connection with the State railroad was aptly finished in September of 1845, just a month before the Central Railroad of Georgia had built their extension line from Macon which had initially been started out as the Monroe Railroad during 1836, and was securely completed along a 103-mile line to Terminus.

Mostly all of these railway lines being skillfully constructed within the South had proven to be reasonably productive, and were certainly wise and useful investments. But more importantly those lines were originally formed and wrought by their respective communities, and which steadily prevailed entirely independent for nearly 150 years. Relatively some easy to approach branching lines had promptly expanded with continual heavy usage for rail transportation of cotton moving to Savannah and Charleston. Especially prominent was there had been an abundant amount of distribution merchants which were bringing food back with them from the Middle West to some plantation areas of this Piedmont Province once the State railroad was thoroughly in full operation. Although special attention should be made that not many prosperous and widely improvement lines were ever built in America than those which were substantially organized and formally originated within the South.

These maneuverable forces and circumstantial capabilities of the Central Railroad of Georgia were admirably revealed once this State had diversely rotated its devastated determination of it being a truly mountainous range type of rail route. During November of 1836 a railroad convention was stringently held at the town of Macon so as to strongly examine the State's ability for them to effectively start constructional work of building a railway so that it could eventually gain access into this Tennessee territory. Thus, its final outcome of their conference deliberations had strategically recommended that the State undertake construction for a rail line not to exceed over 130 miles in length beginning from within eight miles of this Chattahoochee River to reach Ross Landing alongside the Tennessee River. Last of all, the State legislature had fundamentally chosen to solidly adopt a bill in 1838 that would permissively allow a State commission to sufficiently supervise work construction of an acceptable railway, and which was to be paid for by its Public Treasury.

Its elemental railway project had begun almost immediately for planning a 138-mile line to Ross Landing which was soon to become the city of Chattanooga. In fact while building its roadbed foundation for a rail line most of that terrain along the route was fortunately regarded as extremely cooperative even though it was an actual extension of these Appalachian Mountains. Additionally trackage alignment was kept rather simple and cautiously proceeded ahead rather smoothly except for an obvious area just west of Dalton, where a quarter-mile long tunnel had to be dug and excavated under Tunnel Hill. Likewise this State railway which came to be known as the Western and Atlantic Railroad had frequently used the Allatoona Pass for reaching over to its lower southern portions of Blue Ridge. During May of 1851, their railway was commendably opened, and the first steam locomotive train was running between Terminus and Chattanooga. Most importantly, that variant track gauge size of five feet was being commonly utilized for railway construction in both South Carolina and Georgia which continuously stretched westward of these mountains while the South had gradually experienced its reflective approach so as to copiously reach those expanding territories located along the Mississippi Valley. Principally, less than one-third of its encompassing combined total railroad mileage by 1860 was merely assembled and modestly integrated within the South.

* * * * * * * * *

Almost every community which primarily existed east of that Mississippi territory had proudly and sensibly observed this characteristic arrival of the Iron Horse in the 1830's after following its distinctive organization of the Baltimore and Ohio Railroad as well as other influential railroads. Moreover the Louisville and Nashville Railroad was confidently granted a corporate charter on March 5, 1850 for this prestigious purpose of building and operating a railroad which would progress forward in reaching over to its Tennessee state boundary. Nevertheless an estimation was made that some 7,000 persons had annually traveled by stagecoach lines between these two cities of Louisville and Nashville, and which had been costing them anywhere from twelve to eighteen dollars per trip. However some unavoidable difficulties seemed almost inevitable about the Louisville and Nashville for confidently starting with their constructional work which were a potential procurement of vital finances to accomplish this roadway construction project, and also determining a most practical route for an adequate railway.

There were two surveying parties which were being sent out along an area of land to plan upon its essential proposed line for that Louisville and Nashville Railroad during August of 1851. Likewise conscious and concise efforts were additionally made to properly acquire these obtainable and necessary funds as subscription booklets had to be unfortunately opened at the offices of Guthrie and Tyler at Louisville in September of that year. Consequently after about one year of severe and intensive land surveying work over 2,000 miles of tolerable territory had been consistently covered for building this new rail line. Also following its approvable selection of a feasible route for the Louisville and Nashville Railroad these survey teams meticulously completed their tactful task by spring 1853.

In January of 1853 a measurable presentation was accurately prepared and afterwards had been submitted by Morton, Seymour, and Company to the Louisville and Nashville board of directors for commencing with railway construction work. Moreover this current proposal was wholly agreeable and therefore under its terms of that stipulated contract they were to furnish labor and materials while their work had to be sequentially implemented within specific accordance of particular instructions which were given out by these directors of the company. However its construction work was temporarily delayed in May of 1854 because of some troubling financial problems which nearly lasted for a solid year. Although about thirty miles of roadway surface grade as well as some bridgework had been made readily available for the line running out of Louisville. Likewise, roadbed grading work along this Lebanon branch line which basically extended from their mainline to the town of Lebanon in Kentucky for a distance of thirty-seven miles had been amazingly fulfilled.

Its first imminent laying of this railway officially began by July of 1855 as the roadbed was being evenly graded while also permissive consent to start with railroad track construction was under consideration. In fact some new crossties were cut to its specifications firmly pronounced by the chief engineer, and had been laid two feet apart from center to center. Apparently, this track gauge of five feet was regularly selected as it was the normal standardized size by most of those railroads which were presently operating within these Southern states. By August of that year, trackage construction work slowly moved ahead eight miles throughout this rugged country just south of Broadway in Louisville, and was further advanced twelve more miles from that city. As a result excursion trains which were carrying some press gentlemen and distinguishable citizens had made that trip to the end of its line in about twenty-seven minutes.

The original contract which was courageously obtained by Morton, Seymour, and Company had been reluctantly canceled during October of 1855, and much of its road grading for this route was proficiently performed under a binding contract with some nearby farmers that were living along the line. Moreover under designated discussion among many aspiring railroad directors were to authentically allow their constructional work within several portions of the rail route out on contract to perspective local contractors for favorable attempts to employ its use of skillful labor. By 1856, most of that timeless work along bridges and trestles were under careful construction, and about twenty-six miles of roadway were fully operational for the Louisville and Nashville Railroad. During June of 1856 a mixed freight and passenger train had been making a round trip journey each day between Louisville and Lebanon Junction for a total distance of thirty miles. In addition that Lebanon branch line had been reasonably increased to not further than sixty-seven miles from Louisville in November of 1857; and also steam locomotive trains were not actually permitted to operate on this newly built route until March 1858. Nevertheless there were locomotive trains at Kentucky which had been already running along their first division of its mainline as far south to within seven miles of Elizabethtown by the latter part of 1857. Theoretically it had been later on obviously projected that these rail tracks should be able to reach Munfordville which was situated seventy-three miles away from Louisville until not later than the middle of September 1858.

As a matter of fact a train depot exquisitely consisting of six tracks along with three platforms was vigorously located at 9th and Broadway in Louisville, and which had amply cost this railroad company more than $34,000 dollars to build and construct. Specifically considerable routine land surveys were being thoroughly conducted for a proposed branch line near that vicinity of Bowling Green at Kentucky for an adaptable connection to its state line with other adjoining routes which were traveling north from Memphis, Tennessee. Likewise a major concernment were that the board of directors had taken compulsory steps in order to appropriately secure this completion of their branch line, and also to diligently affect its safe operation of through train service between Louisville and Memphis. Early during November of 1858, some prominent citizens of Louisville had deservingly approved and admirably supported an ordinance which was accordingly allowed by the City Council of acquiring stock subscriptions of $300,000 in esteem attention to begin with railway construction for that Memphis branch. Most of all it was reputably estimated that an approximated cost to construct this Memphis branch route would be moderately in the sum of one million dollars, and its city of Louisville could be rationally supplemented by those various counties serving the railway line.

In 1858 construction work along their mainline of the Louisville and Nashville Railroad was steadily pushed forward, and these rails were gradually being laid on top of those crossties as this gap between its roadbed had been rapidly narrowing together. Significantly an acceptable contract was conclusively in prior authorization to undertake that primary operation of transporting the U.S. mails at a substantially reduced flat rate per mile. Furthermore in addition to a notably train station being located at Louisville, the L. & N. had even advantageously established similar like structures at Edgefield, Elizabethtown, and Gallatin all of which were nearing their final achievements. More importantly was this outright purchase by its Louisville and Nashville Railroad for inevitably acquiring the Kentucky Locomotive Works which had been manufacturing a much higher grade of rolling stock.

On June 15, 1858 the first steam locomotive train running to Elizabethtown at Kentucky had been in serviceable operation, and tunnel digging of Muldraugh's Hill was alertly being equally concluded. By the end of 1858, sixty-two miles of railway tracks were laid just south of Louisville, and their Lebanon branch line was swiftly being completed to its town. Especially relevant at this time was that the Louisville and Nashville Railroad had rightfully owned ten steam locomotives, seven passenger cars, three baggage cars, and thirty-two boxcars. Moreover that railway was officially open from Nashville to Bowling Green on August 10, 1859 with a special locomotive train purposely making the preliminary run as a formal celebration was also being held at Nashville.

It was common practice during that time to take a worthwhile journey with these useful services of both stagecoach and Iron Horse as most distant gallant travelers could undoubtedly pursue this trip between Louisville and Nashville in about sixteen hours. Valuable to note there was a printed list of arrival and departure schedules which had been commonly appearing in some daily newspapers with an emphasis to the fact that this trip could be reliably made with only thirty miles of stagecoach riding. Also, a five-span deck bridge at Green River nearby this vicinity of Munfordville was being resolutely finished by July 1859, and had certainly removed any potential doubts about their vital operation of train services. As that roadway was growing closer to final completion during 1859, elegant plans were astutely adopted and further concluded for practical performance of its first through locomotive train along this rail route.

The first successful run ever prosperously accomplished by railway between Louisville and Nashville was observantly conducted on October 27, 1859 and which had uniquely consisted of a railway train and several coaches. However, that tunnel at Muldraugh's Hill was not yet underway and temporary tracks were being used until its final attainment on the first of January 1860. Valuable to note, regularly scheduled trains were not operating along this 185-mile route of the Louisville and Nashville Railroad until after October 31, 1859. Also as a result it took over nine hours for a passenger train to efficiently make that trip while a freight train had considerably taken approximately eighteen hours of running time.

* * * * * * * * *

As late as 1890 no such railroad company had ever sparsely ventured into this remote wilderness area along these banks of the Elk River which was situated in West Virginia. Their principal resources of that region were lumber and coal which had alertly drawn its close attention of proficient businessmen and railroad promoters. Moreover, the Chesapeake and Ohio Railroad had decently built a line through Charleston onto the Ohio River before 1873, which productively afforded a reasonable motive for a major development of its vicinity. Impressively enough was that the total population of Charleston located within West Virginia was 3,162 in 1870; and which later had been greatly increased to 6,742 during 1890 once this town became its state capital by 1885.

One of the first early known railroads to affluently devise a route along this Elk River territory was the Potomac and Ohio Railroad during 1878. Likewise these railroad organizers had ambitious desires of building a double track mainline from the Potomac River near Fredericksburg to its mouth of the Kanawha

River at Ohio. In fact an evident routine survey of its land terrain was accurately prepared by Major Albert H. Campbell, and ground breaking construction for this new road began during the winter of 1878-79. Additionally a prudent decision had been expectantly made that their allowable maximum surface road grade should not exceed over 60-feet per mile while excavation digging and railway work for twenty miles of this roadbed was being initially started for a route. More importantly many of these communities close by which had been existing along its locality for a newly proposed rail line were being constantly in mutual assumption to favorably have the railroad as a pertinent means of useful transportation. However, those total expenditures of both materials and constructional costs for building a line were slightly over $27 million dollars, and this entire project had remained stagnate before it was undeniably terminated by the railroad company.

Two more regular land surveys were normally planned out along the Elk River during 1881 although nothing was ever clearly established by those opulent railroad promoters. The Elk Railroad was granted a charter by this State in February of 1884 to build a narrow gauge line starting at Charleston, and traveling to enter upon that town of Sutton. Moreover its recommendable proposal for that Elk Railroad was being bearably supported by Donald Cameron who had been a dignified Senator from Pennsylvania, and he rightfully owned extremely large tracts of land along the projected route way. Although of major concernment at this time were that these citizens of Charleston had not been hardly much desirable about subscribing to stock subscriptions in support of instituting and creating a railroad so consequently no further work was ever basically consummated except for some marginal land terrain surveying which had been originally started by 1884.

Special attention should be noted that with its continual decline of these failing efforts to firmly penetrate this Elk River Valley, those nearby communities within the area had approvingly scheduled an appropriate meeting on May 11, 1891 to tolerably discuss crucial plans for organizing their own railroad company. More importantly a corporate charter was indicatively issued to the Charleston, Clendennin, and Sutton Railroad for building a new rail line during May of 1891. Especially noteworthy had been that the West Virginia Central and Pittsburgh Railroad were running some locomotive trains from Cumberland, Maryland going over to Elkins in West Virginia. On the contrary adequate funds could be equally raised around those surrounding counties to specifically provide backing and funding for construction of a railway line originating out of Charleston to reach Clendennin, and it was seriously projected that many local landowners would satisfactorily contribute enough costs to finish up its roadway in order to achieve these invincible intentions of arriving at Sutton.

In the meantime those railroad promoters and directors had fortunately appointed Charles K. McDermott to act as their chief engineer of the Charleston, Clendennin, and Sutton Railroad while some land surveying work for its first six miles of trackage had been thoroughly concluded during the middle of October 1891. By December of that year many local newspapers had kindly printed an advertisement calling for constructional bid building proposals on railway construction work to commence for the first twenty miles, and which would be continuously received by them up until February 20, 1892. Conceivably this roadway and trackage work for building its rail line had begun within an immediate vicinity of Mill Creek just six miles away from Charleston, and by July, further completion of ten and a half miles of road surface had been primarily graded, while two and a half miles of railroad tracks were aptly being laid onto their crossties. Moreover by June of 1893 that route traveling to Clendennin was finally reached and it was taking approximately one hour and forty minutes for the 20-mile journey by steam locomotive train.

During July of 1894 a surveying party was permissibly reported to have been vigorously working towards that town of Sutton for the Charleston, Clendennin, and Sutton Railroad. Also an agreeable contract was relevantly issued to the reputable construction firm of Drake and Stratton for building a road to embark upon Sutton near its end of 1894. Likewise constructional work along the rail line route began at Clendennin during October of 1894, and a new brick structural depot was accommodatingly being built at Charleston. These railroad construction crews had been able to relatively arrive at Queen Shoals located about four miles above Clendennin, and twenty-four miles beyond Charleston in December of 1894. And within that month of February 1895, engineering survey reports had finally been conclusive for its stipulated destination to arrive at Sutton, and additionally ten more miles of new road grading and track lying were being finished to Shelley Junction only thirty-five miles away from Charleston. Furthermore an acceptable contract for a partial section of this route from Birch Run to Buffalo Creek which was situated just above Clay Court House was shortly going to be immediately released.

It was reasonably contemplated that near the end of April 1895, locomotive trains would be running along this road to Queen Shoals as their railroad tracks had been laid to within five miles of Clay Court House. Moreover roadway grading had intensely reached Sycamore Creek by mid-September, and passenger trains started traveling to that area on October 7, 1895. By November the rail tracks were further extended to Clay Court House, and steam locomotives had been amply projected to begin with railway operations to this town in December for a total distance of fifty miles out of Charleston. It was also lucratively suggested that a building contract would be explicitly awarded on December 14th so as to initiate further advancement of their rail line towards Sutton, and by end of 1895 much of the roadway grading preparation for its railway was being extensively lengthen to Buffalo Creek. Meanwhile, Governor William A. MacCorkle had copiously reported that in June of 1895 substantial land requirements had been securely purchased for building train terminal facilities at Sutton; and that the Charleston, Clendennin, and Sutton Railroad would confidently be able to reach that town by June 1896. However during July of 1896 an influential order was reluctantly declared in strict compliance to immediately stop all further construction work, and which nearly lasted for five years. These various reasons for this sudden detainment had mainly included certain restrainable opposition imposed upon by that Baltimore and Ohio Railroad as well as continual refusal of some potential landowners to help with expanding obtainable lands which would eventually produce freight revenues for its railroad.

Meanwhile torrential rainfalls had constantly begun to simultaneously occur by the end of November 1896 which had swiftly resulted in massive landslides in addition to having locomotive trains to be suddenly stuck and blocked. Also some of those construction crews had been sent out to where many railroad cars were awkwardly trapped, and much of its numerous remains had to be dug out with shovels by the railway workers. However more slides persistently continued in February of 1897, which severely permitted closure of this road, and these consistent and prolonged heavy rainfalls were causing many problems with other railroads within southern West Virginia. Moreover extreme flooding soon began along the Elk River during June 1897, and had harshly washed out some bridges as railway service was dangerously forced to be temporary cancelled. As a result it was not until 1901 before any such activity had gainfully resumed again for the Charleston, Clendennin, and Sutton Railroad when a conditional binding contract was allegedly released for twelve miles of construction work in order to reach that town of Otter. Although it had taken approximately ten years to physically construct sixty miles of roadway, and their imminent privileges of having a terminus at Sutton was only thirty-five miles away. One most notable aspect and worth mentioning was that this Charleston, Clendennin, and Sutton Railroad had been exceptionally responsible of opening up the Elk River Valley for greater production of its coal and lumber industry.

On the other hand after stringent and devious negotiations were fully conducted a confirming resolution was ultimately agreed upon and had been officially signed for in its relinquishing sale of the West Virginia Central Railroad on January 4, 1902 to this reputable Fuller Syndicate party. In fact Henry G. Davis was president of the West Virginia Central, and as a stipulated supplemental agreement which was authentically effective had given Davis some exclusive rights to buy back any of those three branches of its railroad that had extended from Elkins. Davis also diligently purchased considerable acreage of coal lands along West Virginia so that he could capably plan on his own dependable railroad to resiliently arrive at these recently acquired new coal fields. Moreover one of his first major steps was to have J.W. Moore Jr. an engineer for the Coal and Iron

Railway (a branch line of the West Virginia Central) to suitably report on all feasible and possible routes running west from that town of Elkins. Additionally Moore was later instructed by Davis to obviously plan on a route for the Roaring Creek and Charleston Railroad going over to this Middle Fork River. Valuable to note was that the Roaring Creek and Charleston Railroad had moderately connected up with its West Virginia Central here at Roaring Creek Junction.

Davis had longtime been surely interested about the Roaring Creek coal fields and righteously decided on buying both its coal lands and railroad from this respective owner. In February of 1902, Davis had willingly signed a vital agreement with E.J. Berwind to rightfully purchase all of its Roaring Creek properties. Likewise an important concern was that this worthy compliance had appropriately entitled Davis to operate the railroad, and soon prosperously became his fundamental move in thusly acquiring an essential railroad empire. Davis was finally ready to begin making these plans officially known, and had critically filed for incorporation of the Coal and Coke Railway Company on May 6, while later being granted a corporate charter for that recently developed company on May 14th from the State legislation.

Its preliminary work of this new railway construction had been initially started on April 17th, and W.H. Bower was advisably informed by Henry G. Davis that he would become general manager for the Coal and Coke Railway. Specifically a contract was distinctly manifested and then signed upon on May 1st with Moorman and Nance to install some masonry for tunneling work along a section of that line from Roaring Creek Junction to Leiter, where also a few houses had been amicably obtained for living accommodations. Likewise another binding contract was being allocated in concurrence with Rosser, Coleman, and Hodge who had earlier completed a tunnel for the Coal and Iron Railroad in helping to supply a compressor to be used for digging and excavation work. Furthermore while performing their land surveying route within this vicinity of Sand Run which was actually located sixteen miles away from Roaring Creek, J.W. Moore Jr. had allegedly reported visual signs of another party of surveyors within that immediate area who were working for N.T. Arnold of the Wabash Railroad.

There were over 370 men collectively involved at work during May of 1902 for that Coal and Coke Railway as a second lodging camp was being built near Loop situated about two miles away from Leiter, and also a notably start had realistically been made on the first tunnel at Kingsville. By its middle of July, Henry G. Davis and W.H. Bower rode together on horseback over this route to a place called Sago for a distance of 30.8 miles from Elkins along the Buckhannon River. However at the beginning of August some persistent troubles were occurring when outside labor contractors had violently attacked its workforce, and seventy men had been lost in that conflicting melee. Valuable to note large scrapers were being put to use alongside this roadbed which had absolutely resulted by lifting the terrain up clear from its ground to provide for an adequate roadway, and their total amount of railway expenditures for constructional costs in August sternly surmounted to over $34,000 dollars.

In October of 1902, Henry G. Davis had written a rather private and confidential letter to his influential attorney for pertinent information concerning the Charleston, Clendennin, and Sutton Railroad. Davis was also deeply and vibrantly conceivable in knowing about who controlled this road, the length of its finished line, indebtedness, and any other relevant data available which could be reasonably incurred. Moreover, Davis had definite intentions on purchasing its stock of the Charleston, Clendennin, and Sutton while requesting that this whole attributable matter be kept rather anonymous. Most important Davis had positively decided that on November 19th to securely proceed forth with procurement of this railroad, and at the time its railway route was sixty-four miles long, and had remarkably embarked upon the site of Otter that previous year. Special attention should be noted that their expense for passenger rates were four cents per mile, and buying a train ticket from Charleston to Otter was costing $2.25 for this entire journey.

Principally for the Coal and Coke Railway there had been 650 feet of tunnel work crucially finished and its right-of-way for their next tunnel was being cleared, except for some tree stumps which surely needed to be grubbed away. Once this was thoroughly accomplished these scrapers would be put back to work in helping to clear its roadbed for final preparation. In fact the first order of 70-lb. rails for construction work had been promptly placed during May of 1902 with the Pennsylvania Steel Company. Additionally six flat cars for that new road were particularly purchased from the South Baltimore Steel Car and Foundry as well as an indispensable order of 500 wooden boxcars.

Although much of their construction work along this roadway was to encouragingly continue at the start of 1903 for that Coal and Coke Railway as masonry for tunnel portals were cut, however before installation could begin, time was certainly needed to wait for better weather conditions. Nevertheless some basic land surveys had been carefully prepared for the Charleston, Clendennin, and Sutton Railroad by Charles K. McDermott for its persevering thirty-five miles of line from Otter to Sutton. At the beginning of February, W.H. Bower was able to reliably indicate that trackage had been laid from Leiter to Loop which was a distance of 12.6 miles from Elkins. Furthermore Bower urgently pointed out to Davis about his strenuous responsibilities which were tenaciously involved with in trying to justifiably organize these two railroads, and also of building its rail line connection link.

During February of 1903, Davis had distinctively instructed Charles McDermott their acting superintendent for the Charleston, Clendennin, and Sutton to tolerantly prepare and precisely plan out their first twenty-five miles beyond Otter so that constructional contracts could be dependably awarded to experience and qualified contractors. The meaningful determination of Davis had been to possibly connect together its Coal and Coke Railway with the Charleston, Clendennin, and Sutton Railroad although he did not plan on going up along this Elk River any further than Sutton. Towards the end of February, land surveying work consistently continued and was literally completed to Sand Run, approximately eleven miles from Loop as this railway work could be considerably contracted out to start with roadway building. During March of 1903 the first four miles of trackage were being laid with 70-lb. rails which had forcefully extended through tunnels and over bridges. Also, these necessary constructional bids were opened and a binding contract was appropriately awarded during April to MacArthur Brothers of New York for completing twenty-five miles of railway construction out of Otter. As a matter of fact an announcement was realistically made that railroad train service for the Charleston, Clendennin, and Sutton would be valiantly increased in order to proficiently run two locomotive trains each way on a daily basis.

Both Davis and Bower had earnestly concluded to make a worthwhile trip over this newly proposed route of the Coal and Coke Railway between Elkins and Charleston in May of 1903. Moreover Davis had preferably traveled by locomotive train to Tunnel No. 1, and then moved on by way of Grassy Run to Sago for a distance of thirty miles from Elkins. Next, they continued at Sago on horseback to Copen, and went over these streaming waters of Otter Creek and Elk River onto Frametown before arriving at Otter—end of track at present for the Charleston, Clendennin, and Sutton line—and finally onto Charleston by rail for a distance of sixty-four miles. On the contrary Henry G. Davis had been fairly pleased with that route, however the average cost of building a road between Elkins and Charleston for a distance of 175 miles was absorbingly costing about $25,000 per mile.

While back along its south end of this new route, Bower advisedly reported to Davis by August of 1903 that the first five miles of tracks would not be ready before September 1st, and also that not much railway construction work had comparatively appeared to have been rather accomplished. However some progress was being made for upgrading its existing line, and actual work had again purposely started along the southern end of this road. More importantly, during an annual meeting of their stockholders and directors of the Charleston, Clendennin, and Sutton Railroad an imperative resolution was reached, approved, and subsequently passed in deliberately providing for an essential purchase of that railroad by the Coal and Coke Railway. Furthermore in August of 1903 the Charleston, Clendennin, and Sutton Railroad was then officially dissolved of, and it was henceforth coincidently operated by the Coal and Coke Railway as its Charleston Division.

On the contrary within this next year Davis was to undeniably recommend shutting down railway work due to severely extreme weather conditions, and also because of its inadequate as well as poor financial outlook of this country at that time. However, trackage was continuously laid to reach Groves Tunnel while these headings at Shipmans Tunnel were being fortunately completed as this tunnel had utterly been expected to be totally finished by March 1st. In addition there were also spontaneous and compulsive discussions about its potential importance of running their rail line over to French Creek which had advantageously passed through these prosperous coal lands that were prestigiously owned by Davis. Most of all and worth mentioning were that two new Baldwin steam locomotives (2-8-0) had been approvingly ordered during February of 1904 at an apparent cost of $12,000 each, and they were properly named as C. & C. No. 11 and No. 12.

An important and firm decision had been resolutely made to advisably relocate their Coal and Coke repair shops and train offices by 1903 to a more suitable site near its mouth of Otter Creek that runs alongside the Elk River. Moreover that location of this place was perpetually situated roughly halfway between Elkins and Charleston which then eventually became known as Gassaway. In August of 1904 Davis was ingeniously determined to intentionally acquire and purchase these right-of-way privileges from the Little Kanawha Railroad at Copen which actively had been running to Confluence at this time. Valuable to note was that on February 26, *Railway Age* had articulately published an emphatic announcement requesting for sealed bids to be submitted in acquiring thirty miles of railway construction work between Frenchton and Copen Run would be initially opened on March 10th.

Special attention should be made to the fact that a mutual accompanying contract for obtaining labor and materials to construct fifteen miles of railroad tracks starting at Frenchton and moving onto Chapman which had been some of its most toughest work along this new line was being vitally issued to E.E. Smith Construction Company of Philadelphia. In addition enforceable contracts were also given out to Joseph Fuccy for readily building six miles of trackage, and to J.P. Thompson for another three miles of rail work performance during July of 1904. However, six miles of that roadway had not yet been under contract, but which was later necessarily relinquished to Armstrong & Guthrie for them to build four miles of railway construction, and also to Hoover & Kinnear for its final connecting two miles of tracks along this route. Last of all a relevant contract to extensively build a two-arch bridge stretching across Two Mile Creek at Charleston was inevitably released and consequently received by Nance & McFall.

In May of 1905 locomotive train service was substantially traveling between Elkins and Sand Run for a total distance of twenty-three miles, and which had taken one hour and fifteen minutes to jubilantly achieve this one-way trip. Likewise, Bower was being reasonably informed that along its Charleston Division a bridge crossing over at Birch River some twelve and a half miles away from Gassaway had been under immediate construction during July of that year. Moreover at Copen a railway passage tunnel was fully finished by August, and trackage had amply been able to reach this town of Adrian near the end of December. Furthermore, Bower had additionally requested considerable and rightful permission to affluently purchase 750 tons of rails for workable construction and had also intelligently reported that railway work at Frenchton was smoothly moving ahead.

It was purely indicative that Davis and Bower were prudently under consideration for a new train station to be built at Gassaway, and consequently a wooden structural building was chiefly erected during 1905. Also digging and tunnel excavation work at Otter was nearing its final completion by August, and rail track construction could be constantly pushed along in both directions for an anticipated attempt and desirably undertaking of virtuously being concluded. On November 17th, Bower was wisely able to insistently confirm that only 5.3 miles of roadway track had still inadvertently remained to be built for this railway. Most importantly it was not until December 2nd of 1905 before their railway line was competently accomplished, and Davis had taken his first locomotive train ride over this newly prepared route from Elkins to Charleston on December 28, 1905.

Passenger service along the Coal and Coke Railway was officially started on January 21, 1906 as a timetable had distinctively indicated that two locomotive trains were finally in operation, one in each direction between Elkins and Charleston. Likewise there had been four other local trains running which were fluently providing railroad services from Charleston to Gassaway, and also between Gassaway and Elkins. Especially significant was the West Virginia legislature rationally passed a bill in boldly requiring that railroads had to charge all boarding passengers no more than two cents per mile of roadway train services, and this abiding law definitely became effective on May 21, 1907. Near its end of January in 1908, reluctant news was hastily reported that E.W. Bower had voluntarily resigned from the Coal and Coke, and as a result his brother Edwin Bower had been amply appointed to relatively serve as acting general manager. However during October of 1907, the Coal and Coke Railway had deliberately brought intimidating action against the Circuit Court of Kanawha County to absolutely restrain this State of legally enforcing this two-cent law towards its railroad company. To conclude with on June 8, 1908, Judge S.C. Burdett had accordingly ruled in favor that this two cents fare was ambiguously unconstitutional while his decision strictly applied only to the Coal and Coke Railway. Furthermore, Davis was firmly advised not to initiate that newly rail rate increase immediately, and it was currently delayed until June 24, 1909 when a three cent charge was formally introduced.

By the end of 1909, Davis fervidly wanted to capably reduce these present salaries of all his employees by ten percent while at this time monthly income for an engineer and foreman had been $100. Davis also peculiarly became quite concerned about those vastly large expenses of operating the Coal and Coke, and had solely written to Daniel Willard of the Baltimore and Ohio Railroad whereby potentially indicating to him about desirably selling their railway during January of 1911. In early February, Willard had beneficially made an inspiring effort to valuably inspect that line which had temperamentally brought about an emotional panic of newspaper published reports involving a probable sale of the Coal and Coke. Nevertheless, the incidence had disturbingly stirred up some great excitement among many storekeepers of Gassaway who spitefully assumed that their railway shops would be closed down if this Baltimore and Ohio were able to gain a takeover although nothing had ever profusely transpired by its arousing occurrence.

On the other hand by 1912 this provoking and amazing news was about its curious discovery of oil productively existing along the Elk River Valley which had long time been suspected within that area. As a matter of fact a major oil field was permanently in position at a site location by the mouth of Blue Creek with one oil well consistently in operation and producing 500 barrels per day during January. Also, oil wells were being sensitively drilled along its rail line of the Coal and Coke from a point of within seven miles north from Charleston to about two miles northwards of Blue Creek. Furthermore tanker cars which were holding between 100 to 250 barrels of oil had been conveniently added on for the Coal and Coke in order for them to sufficiently serve its majority of these oil fields, and their train fares from Charleston to Blue Creek a distance of thirteen miles was easily costing forty cents each way.

More importantly the legislature of West Virginia had licitly passed an act to be principally enforced on May 21, 1913 which had severely prohibited its liable issuance or presumable usage of a train pass; or even any other acceptable forms of free locomotive transportation except only to railway officers, employees, or their families. A key factor had been that numerous coach car derailments and train accidents were beginning to abundantly surface, and Davis was drastically complaining in February of 1914 that he had to repulsively spend $190,000 over these past few months just to keep this railroad profitably in productive operation. However several technical improvements were urgently made during 1914, and Davis had given his prior authorized permission to incessantly begin work on relining some dilapidated tunnels with concrete instead of wood as they were visibly beginning to rot away much faster than normally anticipated. Likewise by the end of December 1915, an inspection report had further vitally exhibited that these 60-lb. rails along its southern end of this route were showing considerable wear, and also a section of railroad tracks between Charleston and Blue Creek was being suitably replaced with 85-lb. rails. On the contrary, a major concernment of John T. Davis, the son of Henry G. Davis had been about adequately providing enough train cars for their coal mines of the Davis Colliery Company where he was officially its president during January of 1916. Even though Henry G. Davis soon became seriously ill on March 10, 1916 and had disappointingly passed away at an age of ninety-three on that next day while in its last entry of Henry's diary he recorded, "Railway and coal mines doing fairly well".

After this apparent death of Henry G. Davis there was volatile activity taking place among their company so as a result crucial proceedings had been cautiously taken in order to outright sell the Coal and Coke Railway, and accordingly enough Charles D. Norton who was vice-president of its First National Bank had deviously arranged for a business syndicate to influentially and financially purchase this expeditious railroad. Valuable to note was that a final accountable asset report assuredly manifested on January 8, 1917 had extremely indicated that this railroad owed $1,700,000 to about twenty-five different banks, and there was no possible way of paying off those outstanding debts unless by radically and rationally selling its acquired coal lands. On January 20, 1917 a special meeting among these prominent board members was officially held, and at which time it had been reputably decided upon to substantially and indisputably sell the evident Davis Colliery Company. Additionally a second board of directors meeting was appropriately in session on January 31st, and an inclusively earnest and intensive proposal was wholly given by Norton to expressively purchase both the railroad and colliery companies. That convincingly submitted offer had totally been in compliance upon an agreeable amount to all equally involved parties of its respectable action. Moreover this associational syndicate formally organized the West Virginia Coal and Coke Company to which it then had legally transferred all of their pertinent and mutual coal mining properties that had been recently incurred. Furthermore, the Coal and Coke Railway was entirely and considerably responsible for this rapidly growing development of lumber mills, coal mines, and oil fields within an encompassing region which impelling existed along that Elk River placidly located in West Virginia.

CHAPTER SIX

By the early 19th century both these regions of southern and central Illinois had largely grown while expanding in size so as to profitably become its more heavily established settlements within this State. Once the Erie Canal was initially opened during 1825 it had conceivably contributed to those Midwest states and Great Lakes which amazingly resulted about bringing on its western movement towards the Ohio River along some vital areas of Chicago. Valuable to note that before 1837 its population of Chicago was nearly 4,200 once this place had crucially been incorporated as an important city, and by 1856 it was magnificently developed into a supreme capital railroad center. Moreover much of their valuable and richer trading commodities of Chicago with other leading European markets had mainly consisted of wheat, grain, and furs.

The National Road which was built between 1811 to 1837 stretching westwards from Maryland to Vandalia had been explicitly responsible for carrying a large number of pioneers as well as settlers onto Illinois, while several nearby local towns were becoming extremely prosperous. Special attention should be noted that waterway transportation in addition to barge traffic was efficiently increasing when Lake Michigan had fundamentally been connected up with the Mississippi River during 1848 by expedient means of the Illinois and Michigan Canal so it could eagerly join together those major rivers of Chicago and Illinois. Specifically the Illinois and Michigan Canal had totally been completed in 1848 which then was able to substantially link places alongside this Illinois River with other sites located on both sides of the Mississippi and Lake Michigan watersheds. Furthermore that term Middle West has been relatively associated with those newly flourishing communities of its Far West and was often sometimes frequently referred to by this phrase "Heartland of America".

In the Midwest geographically situated at a position northwesterly of Illinois lies Chicago which had fortunately satisfied these necessary requirements as being an ultimate alternative for many eastern railroads, and was soon to respectably assume its considerable role of becoming a Great Junction. Nevertheless by 1850, four out of ever ten miles of railways in this world were assuredly allocated within the United States. The State of Illinois had seen and noticeably observed some construction of sequential branch lines from its water hub at Chicago, going westward towards some river ports which had been strategically devised alongside that Mississippi River. Essentially those railroads usefully brought about farming products from the west and south as well as in hauling cattle, hogs, and sheep to Chicago for slaughtering and packing.

Before the year 1850 had suitably arrived many vastly expanding territories of both East and South alertly built and bearably operated nearly 5,000 miles of railroads. During 1837 this State of Illinois had conveniently set aside $11 million dollars as an assurance and contingent source of central railway transportation for traveling through Illinois, and then down to Ohio while it stretched westerly to reach the Mississippi Valley. Also, an indulgent and lenient effort was being made for by that State to build and construct a worthy railroad throughout Illinois which ran its first locomotive train called the Northern Cross Railroad on November 8, 1838. Additionally that State of Illinois had spent over one million dollars for this railroad, however it was sold at an auction and later became part of the Wabash System.

By the month of January during 1836 this Illinois Central Railroad was permissibly granted a charter from its State for building a north and south mainline with an extension branch starting at Centralia (south-central Illinois) to arrive at that city of Chicago. More importantly, Stephen A. Douglas an elected U.S. Senator representing Illinois in 1847 was consentaneously favorable about approving railroads, and inceptively had prominent intentions for planning and constructing a State-owned railroad to adequately run through the middle of this State. As a result after almost a three-year contentious struggle with Congress, Stephen Douglas had approvingly won a federal land grant of 2,595,000 acres of public land before 1850. On the contrary a beneficial advantage was that instead of paying land taxes to the government this railroad would only have to actual compensate seven percent of its total gross earnings which were being accrued from their charter lines.

Land surveying work over these flat and rolling prairies had been incidentally started during 1851 to plan out a possible route for the Illinois Central Railroad. Likewise its road grading and construction project for laying down rail tracks and wooden crossties was precisely set to begin at Chicago, and also along a designated site known as Cairo by two separately individual companies. In fact, the Illinois Central train station was readily erected between Randolph Street and Michigan Avenue just eastward of this Chicago River. On May 21, 1852 its first passenger locomotive train running from Detroit had encouragingly entered into that city of Chicago, utilizing the Illinois Central railroad tracks as a temporary route in traveling over those prairie lands to east of Michigan Avenue.

Roswell Mason of Connecticut was selectively appointed to be chief engineer for the Illinois Central, and roadbed grading as well as trackage construction south of Chicago had been repetitiously progressing ahead at a comparatively steady pace while being eventually finished in order to enter upon Kankakee by July of 1854. Additionally this extension branch line traveling through the center of Illinois was triumphantly open for railroad train operations in December of 1855; and for that entire 705 miles of railways—from Dunlieth to Cairo along their southern terminus, and for its northern station from Chicago to Centralia had been proficiently achieved which was finally accomplished on September 25, 1856. Likewise this Illinois Central had significantly moved forward with extending its railway routes into New Orleans and also to the Mississippi by either purchasing other inert rail lines or taking over extinct lines. It was furthermore understood that the Illinois Central had been built as a farmer's road, and which was expeditiously completed within a moderately short time period.

Salary wages of the Illinois Central Railroad had prudently ranged from $200 a month for construction engineers to sixty-five dollars for locomotive engineers and fifty dollars to train conductors. More important was that in less than one decade there relevantly had been reliable, dependable, and through service connections with other railways which were steadily extended further, and were capably available all the way from Chicago towards the East Coast. Also, the Illinois Central had been expanding downwards into southern Illinois where it had particularly drawn a keen awareness of this increasingly growing commerce situated within that lower Mississippi Valley.

During 1848, many of these dynamically involved and participating grain dealers had built the first steam operating grain elevator in this State alongside Chicago's lakefront, and as a result were seriously gaining control of its lavishly plentiful eastern trade. Consequently by 1852, that city of Chicago was consistently receiving more grain shipments via railway line than by turnpike wagon road and canal waterway combined together. In addition, the Illinois Central viably constructed grain elevators of enormous and extensive sizes while a majority of those grain dealers were keeping them filled to capacity in 1860. Evidentially railroad rates were sharply declining by 1873, and long before this century was over the steam locomotive had strictly acclaimed much of its productive grain activity going to the East. Worth mentioning was the Illinois Central had to presently move their main passenger terminal within a mile southward to an appropriate new location which was being built at East Eleventh Place and Michigan Avenue in order to easily accommodate these ever anticipated and predictable crowds for its World's Fair of 1893.

* * * * * * * * *

George Forquer who was a State Senator from Illinois had firmly supported state-sponsored internal improvements during 1834, as these Southern states generously offers abundant and ideal workable conditions which covers an almost level surface of terrain across those open prairies. Before March of 1835 an estimated group of 1,000 citizens had collectively gathered and were utterly assembled together at Springfield so as to imperatively discuss advantageous plans of building a railway originating from Springfield to arrive upon Alton, and then to cautiously proceed ahead for this line in reaching the Mississippi River. As a result a land survey of its proposed route was being fastidiously performed in May 1835 by W.B. Mitchell who was a civil engineer from Pennsylvania. Mitchell along with his helpful associates initially began their surveying work at Alton while continuing north towards Springfield for a distance of seventy-two miles. A key feature was that certain committed delegates to publicly represent the Tenth General Assembly legitimately had approved spending expenditures of $10 million dollars for a waterway canal, a network of railroads, and also river and road improvements within this immediate area by December 1836.

Over these next few years several public meetings were being sufficiently conducted at Alton and Springfield for gracious measures to start with rigorous negotiations about having a rail line serve their indigent aspirations along those adjacent vicinities. In fact during the 1840-41 legislative sessions, Abraham Lincoln had proudly introduced and efficiently presented a bill which positively made that State an individual partner of this Alton and Springfield railroad project. More important was Lincoln's bill voluntarily provided that in substitution for stock subscriptions with this new company, the State would exchange supplies and provide land to apparently permit construction for a railway route to be built. Furthermore, this governor of Illinois at the time whose name was Thomas Carlin had been in compliable agreement of granting a corporate charter to the Springfield and Alton Turnpike Company on February 27, 1841.

While in the meantime four years had gradually passed before another robust attempt was to fully resurface for initiating consideration of building a railroad at Alton as prosperity was beginning to rapidly return once again to this country. In its spring of 1845, a group of highly powered politicians exclusively met at the U.S. District Court House at Springfield to willfully propose an Alton-Springfield rail line to be put under construction. However, it was not until February of 1848 when a new land survey had to be thoroughly conducted and was methodically carried out by William Crocker who had been an engineer from Boston. Moreover stock subscription revenue sales had quickly improved during March of

1849, and by October there were expressive reports which formally indicated that its much needed capital had been expediently accomplished. In addition it had taken over two and one-half years to affluently raise enough available funding expenditures for incorporation, and during February of 1850 pertinent documents were officially filed with the State at that time.

An engineering survey for construction work of a terminus at Alton was currently under vital contemplation, and had been absolutely completed during that summer of 1850. Stone and timber building materials were tolerantly planned to be used for erecting this depot and engine house. As a matter of fact a railway builder by the name of Joseph Gilmore from Dayton, Ohio was handily hired as a subcontractor and his workforce principally prepared these first four miles of trackage from their main train terminal location on Seventh Street to realistically arrive at Coal Branch. Additionally iron rails of 56-lb. which had been solely manufactured by Bailey Brothers and Company of Liverpool were brought up from New Orleans for finishing up this necessary roadbed groundwork. By late autumn there were more than 150 men being steadily employed, while another 200 laborers were working about ten miles north of Brighton, and some of those grading crews had actually started with rail construction at Coups Creek and Carlinville.

The Seventeenth General Assembly was insistently associated and extremely involved with active railroad affairs while sixty-two railroad bills or amendments were considerably being enacted during its 1851-52 session. Valuable to note that in January of 1851, these roadway graders and construction crews for this Alton and Springfield line uniformly continued along at variable increments, and some incisive reports were accurately indicating that 779 men and sixty-four horses had been heartily working near Alton. Although a major concernment among them was this right-of-way passage in place between Alton and Carlinville which had been divided into thirty-six subsections, that were all either under partial preparation or elementary construction with about fourteen miles of trackage being moderately near fulfillment. Likewise skillful masons were anxiously kept busy digging culverts while structural engineers strenuously built bridges at various places along this railway line, and twenty-three miles of roadbed had been smoothly graded while another ten miles were almost halfway finished. Last of all locomotive train facility foundations and supporting walls for building an engine house, train depot, and machine shops at Alton had capably been approaching their eventual accomplishments.

John Shipman who had been primarily appointed as chief engineer on the Alton and Springfield Railroad was wisely exploring this countryside for a practical and suitable route of an extension link to be built into Bloomington. In his potential findings, Shipman had carefully concluded that an adjacent railway line traveling to Bloomington could be laid to essentially run from Springfield. In fact during August of 1851, their working crewmen were eagerly grading a route along these rather evenly flat prairies almost within near sight of Carlinville. Also additional train crews were laying railroad tracks along a stretch of six miles, just north of Carlinville in an arousing attempt of pushing its way towards Springfield. Likewise, bridges were being constructed with spans up to forty feet wide while a 100-foot long trestle was structurally built across Macoupin Creek.

By April of 1852 roadway grading was further being developed to Virden which was located about fifty-one miles north of Alton, and bridges at Lick Creek and Sugar Creek were nearing its final completion. Railroad equipment such as crossties, spikes, and rails had been brought up through the Illinois and Mississippi rivers before being basically unloaded at Naples, then had continued moving onwards to arrive at Iles just two miles south of Springfield. More importantly had been the reassuring news that this steam locomotive B. Godfrey an intended passenger engine was running 12-mile trips from Alton to Brighton which certainly had drawn some considerable interest and special attention among many presumptuous railroad supporters. Consequently, by mid-May railway trackage extensively proceeded along this route from Alton to Coups Creek, and notable announcements had been appearing in some local newspapers which were seeking proficiently qualified excavation contractors for purposes of digging water wells at Carlinville, Auburn, Chatham, and Springfield.

On the other hand, Senator Ashley Gridley of Bloomington inevitably returned back to the Illinois Senate for its presentable introduction of an integral part of legislation for this Alton and Springfield Railroad. In early June, Gridley had reasonably initiated a bill to the Seventeenth General Assembly which was favorably passed on June 19, 1852. As a result that bill had effectively doubled the projected length of their railroad by allowing this company to literally bring its line from Bloomington so as to enter into the city of Chicago. Also, the Illinois legislation had intuitively provided for a proper name changeover of its ever present Alton and Springfield to their indivisibly acceptable Chicago and Mississippi Railroad. Furthermore, Gridley's legislative amendment had reservedly broaden their route to St. Louis, and on the contrary this Chicago and Mississippi Railroad was permissively able to operate steamboats between Alton and St. Louis for possible conveyances.

In June of 1852 Oliver Lee was aspiringly hired by Henry Dwight Jr. to act as chief engineer of the Bloomington and Springfield branch. Oliver Lee was well experienced in railroad engineering, and he had spent five of his past years working for the Hudson River Railroad. Except for an intimidating rise of about twenty miles south of Bloomington, Lee found those rolling prairie lands considerate enough for a rather straight right-of-way route. While these land surveys for this extension line were being swiftly planned out for its roadway, construction crews situated to the south of Springfield moved ahead, and also a bridge was being constructed for crossing over the Sangamon River.

Meanwhile railway constructional work resumed again and some moderate progress improvements were further advanced while train crews had fortunately laid thirty-five miles of trackage running out of the Alton Bluffs to virtually extend over those open prairies before reaching that town of Carlinville on July 1, 1852. On July 5, a great proclamation took place with an estimated crowd of among 6,000 to 7,000 persons in attendance which had been abundantly gathered for officially celebrating its elaborate evolution of that new railway line. Also, there were publicized notices which were commonly appearing in both Alton and Springfield newspapers of announcing their operational train services between Alton and

Carlinville. However until final attainment of its roadway, this railroad company had been operating a passenger train in mutual conjunction with its building materials car between Alton and Carlinville. Most of all only nine miles of rails had still remained to be laid and simultaneously connected before joining together the mainline from Alton with that which was being built southward from Springfield. In late summer of 1852, the route line was commendably consummated at Alton to Springfield as these prominent citizens were sequentially lining up outside of those single rail tracks just along Third Street when that first locomotive train from Alton sharply approached and bringing with it this promise of an indispensable and consentaneous railroad.

During October of 1852 regular passenger service and freight transportation between Alton and Springfield initially began providing locomotive operations on an everyday basis except on Sunday. Also, passenger trains were being scheduled to leave Alton at eleven o'clock with a stopover at Virden for meals before arriving at Springfield. In addition, these passengers had been departing from Springfield at ten o'clock in the morning with an apparent meal stop at Carlinville contrary to their arrival at Alton. Worth mentioning was that this railroad train ride from Alton to Springfield had been occasionally described as a comfortable trip of about four to five hours at an average speed of fifteen miles per hour including all stops along its way. Last of all its railway train services which were stupendously offered by the Chicago and Mississippi Railroad was vastly by far a substantial improvement over other trips which had formerly taken much longer sometimes even days by either stagecoach or horseback.

* * * * * * * *

Valuable to note railroad promotion within this State of Illinois had become an important factor of controversial and debatable conversation among most citizens for better transportation long before steamboats dominantly ran throughout many of those canals and rivers. When the State legislation appropriately met for their winter session of 1836-37 at Vandalia, the capital of Illinois, an act in creating to establish and maintain a positive general system of internal improvements had been overwhelmingly supported and eventually approved. While these lawmakers intently decided upon decent and respectable funding for river improvements, there was more than ninety percent of its revenue set aside for about 1,300 miles of railroad construction. Likewise, the legislature of this State dignifiedly had allowably permitted a $3.5 million allotment for a north-south rail line which would evidently link together Galena, a booming lead mining camp—with Cairo, a village perpetually situated near its mouth of the Ohio River. More important a corporate charter had legibly been granted to the Galena and Chicago Union Railroad on January 10, 1836 for their specific purposes and meaningful intentions of reaching some lead mines at Galena which were located along this northwestern corner of Illinois.

On the contrary those influential directors of that Galena and Chicago Union Railroad had promptly sent out a party of surveyors into its immediate area for planning out a feasible line to build a railway. In fact James Seymour was exceptionally hired by this railroad company to actually perform a land survey of an intended roadway route, and he ultimately finished his work by April of 1837. Moreover Seymour's detailed report findings were readily acceptable by these railroad directors because it had particularly offered a rather straight route between Galena and the Des Plaines River for a total distance of ten miles westerly of Chicago. Additionally the most notable aspect was that financial costs involved for constructing a roadbed with double tracks for a single line would equivalently amount to about $7,500 per mile which also conclusively included that risky expensive of excessive pile driving work throughout portions of its slightly grassy prairie lands.

The Rockford Railroad Convention of 1846 was an indicative event which stupendously brought with it a great deal of strength and stability amongst many railroad promoters. Likewise a group of individuals who collectively assembled together at Rockford on January 7, 1846 were under this prevalent impression that railroads prosperously created wealth which would be certainly crucial to their beneficial progress of the State. Also, an overall common purpose of that convention gathering had been to advantageously take clearer measures for commencing with railway construction of this Galena and Chicago Union in order to begin work at its most earliest possible time. As a result several intensive meetings for the proposed line were being confidently held among some land grazing farmers and local merchants so as to privately promote raising sufficient funds for building its railroad. Moreover those exclusive results of its Rockford Railroad Convention assembly which was thoroughly encouraged by public support had been extremely tenacious of an urgent need for a railway, and desired to principally acquire their necessary available security funds while vigorously pushing along stock subscriptions for this company.

William B. Ogden from New York became especially concerned about the Illinois and Michigan Canal project, and by his political and resourceful contribution had brilliantly produced its consistent organization. Additionally, Odgen and his business associates desperately needed capital before any railway construction work could preferably originate for the Galena and Chicago Union, and thus had splendidly enough sought to constitute financial arrangements. On the contrary these inspiring directors of this company had imperatively won an indispensable approval during February of 1847 for an allowable increase of their capital stock up to $3 million dollars. Furthermore, Ogden soon became president of its Galena and Chicago Union Railroad while soliciting his earnest and avowed encouragement in absolute conquest of obtaining stock subscriptions for undergoing the fundamental rail work.

Although it was obviously understood that another major step would have to be necessarily required towards development of the Galena route as a concise summary report was being inevitably prepared for preliminary preparation of their proposed line. Favorably this board of directors had diligently chosen to wisely procure its reputable services of civil engineer Richard P. Morgan along with his esteem associates to carefully examine and reliably consider the surrounding terrain of these areas intervening between Chicago and Galena during 1847. In his conclusive survey report, Morgan had effectively estimated that its lavish expenses of roadway construction for building a 182-mile rail line of standardized single-track gauge along with connecting bridges which were being explicitly designed for double train tracks at an approximate cost of $14,550 per mile. Furthermore when the board members had initially received Morgan's 18-page report of factual and precise survey findings those expectable building costs were neither unreasonable nor excessively high by indubitable comparison.

While many of these distinguishable and perceptive railroad investors had precarious desires for arriving at this lead mining town of Galena they eminently focused their inspiring efforts towards an area of land some forty-one miles away situated between Chicago and Elgin. Basically its construction work for that Galena and Chicago route to be built was considerably started within June of 1848, near a corner of Kinzie and Halsted Streets located just along the outskirts of Chicago. Moreover road grading and track lying had eagerly moved ahead, and by late fall, skilled laborers had stably accomplished ten miles of trackage from Chicago to Elgin alongside the Fox River. In addition that Galena and Chicago Union Railroad had conceivably established and adequately erected a train depot westerly of this Chicago River by 1848.

At the time their chief engineer for that Galena and Chicago Union was John Van Nortwick who had been using strap iron rail along its line. Essentially these twenty to twenty-five foot strips of iron were solidly bolted onto wooden beams for rigid support, but had sometimes often worked loose thus causing snakeheads. Valuable to note Galena's first steam engine was the 10-ton Pioneer, and it had been utterly assembled by this prominent locomotive manufacturer Mathias Baldwin at his shop in Philadelphia. Special attention should be made that this steam locomotive vigorously began to productively pull some train cars which were burden with supplies and workers at a steady speed of sixteen miles per hour, and by November of 1848 its Galena road had prudently been able to finally reach the Des Plaines River.

More importantly a formal opening along its first section of Galena's railway attentively demonstrated that this railroad operation was a remarkable and valuable source of dependable transportation which drastically had been reducing their shipping costs as well as transit time. During April of 1849 roadbed construction was stringently extended twelve more miles, and by July, passenger service was customarily increased eighteen miles westerly of Chicago to enter upon Cottage Hill. Throughout that year of 1849 railway construction work along this Galena and Chicago Union line had splendidly continued, and by the time Cottage Hill was gainfully attained, continuous train receipts were practically averaging about sixty dollars daily. In late November of 1849 these railroad workers were able to accomplish another thirty miles, while the rail line for reaching Elgin was undoubtedly connected together on January 22, 1850. A key feature of its firm's third annual report which was relatively issued during May of 1850 had inflexibly signified that this railroad company dependently owned four steam locomotives, sixty-seven freight cars, and eight passenger coaches.

The most notable aspect was that this first phase for Galena's mainline had been vitally fulfilled at an average cost of $9,000 per mile while many of their cheerfully proficient directors took pride over these achievable accomplishments, and immediately were beginning to properly concentrate within its next ensuing segment. On the contrary this latter phase which was strategically being planned out for the Galena and Chicago Union Railroad had incisively involved railway work to fully advance that route line at Elgin in expanding over to Rockford for a total distance of fifty miles. As a result its constructional crews strenuously continued along rather sluggishly at their original onset although the first twelve miles northwest of Elgin were immediately accessible and open for train passenger services on September 15, 1851. Likewise another twelve miles of trackage construction were uniquely in functional operation on October 18th, and to conclude with an additional twelve more miles of this route had been affluently finished on December 3, 1851.

For a while the Galena line had temporarily remained inactive because of severe winter weather conditions which obviously delayed laying tracks onto Cherry Valley until March of 1852. However in great anticipation, the Iron Horse had conclusively arrived at Rockford which was seven miles west of Cherry Valley, and ninety-two miles away from Chicago on August 2, 1852. Consequently, the Galena and Chicago Union was rather significantly drawing a potentially considerable amount of westward traffic, and exceptional profits were beginning to sizably surmount within much greater quantities. In fact a major concernment was that the second phase of this indicative railway had assertively cost these railroad directors more than their first segment as its overall bill was in excess of about $16,000 per mile of roadway construction.

By now that Galena and Chicago Union Railroad could easily afford better improvements of its roadbed, and sensibly enough opted for standard T-rail which came from Welsh mills weighting fifty-six pounds to the yard. On the other hand their board of directors, and president William B. Ogden amply wanted to realistically reach the Missouri as its third and final phase of these liberal proceedings for this Galena line were currently being staged in final preparation. Likewise Ogden's original plans were mainly destined to broaden its new route for a distance of twenty-nine miles westward onto Freeport, and once at that site they could mutually connect up with the projected Illinois Central Railroad. Valuable to note the railway construction work cautiously endured along its east bank of Rock River, and laying trackage further continued until arriving at Freeport, just 121 miles out of Chicago which was stupendously attained on September 1, 1853. Last of all this added supplementary extension branch had crucially crossed over some of the most roughest terrain which necessitated in building a bridge over Rock River, and conclusively resulted for an approximate estimation cost of nearly $20,000 per mile of roadway.

As being powerful investors of railroad advancement that Galena and Chicago Union critically grew, and had moderately been able to accrue creditable banking assets which would be actually available for absorbing weaker lines if this were those evident circumstances at that time. However its Galena and Chicago route was pushing westward, and confidently encompassed rather two new additional lines which traveled northward to reach the Wisconsin boundary line. In late 1853, a railroad company had built an extension line east from Fulton along the Mississippi River to virtually connect up with this Illinois Central at Dixon. More importantly, the Galena and Chicago was unavoidably prospering and had rightfully incorporated that new railway line before entirely completing it through to the Mississippi on December 16, 1855.

Even though the Galena and Chicago Union Railroad had never theoretically arrived at these plentiful mines in Galena as much more useful resources of lead and zinc were later found in Missouri. On the contrary it soon became recognizably visible that during fall of 1854, this originator who initially began construction and built those fifty-one miles of railway tracks between Freeport and Galena had legitimately and legally belonged to the Illinois Central Railroad. Likewise a major decision by their board members of the Galena and Chicago had been that they absolutely needed its own route to advantageously reach this Mississippi River rather than trackage to Galena. Special attention should be noted that this Galena and Chicago Union had considerably been the first railroad to be fortunate enough in realistically obtaining an agreeable contract with the Union Pacific Railroad. Furthermore during the mid-1840's, an intriguing plan to construct and build an acceptable railway line from Lake Michigan going to Oregon had willingly provoked some widespread discussion among many railroad developers in the Midwest.

During April 1853, the board of directors especially announced its predicable determination for building a direct route to the Mississippi River at Savanna which was approximately located forty miles south of Galena. As a result surveying teams promptly went to work and their report findings had largely indicated an attainable route could be possibly constructed within thirty miles west of Chicago from Junction; formally where the Aurora Branch Railroad had met up with that Galena and Chicago in September of 1850. Moreover this newly proposed line had apparently passed through Dixon before it virtuously terminated at Fulton about twenty-five miles south of Savanna. Speculatively their Dixon extension branch line would be 125-miles in length thus being its shortest practicable railway line traveling between Chicago and the Mississippi River.

Meanwhile work progression was frequently moving ahead for building its route as road graders and track crews were able to consummate forty-five miles of railway construction by January of 1854. However, this trackage was not yet in running condition to regularly permit allowable passenger service operations until about

May 1, 1854. Nevertheless those construction gangs exceedingly reached that town of Dixon on December 4, 1854 which was sixty-eight miles away from Junction. And during the summer of 1855, railroad tracks were being mainly concluded to Sterling and also at Morrison in Illinois. More important this Galena and Chicago Union reputably took over its failing assets of the Mississippi and Rock River Junction Railroad during February of 1855 which had partially finished some roadbed excavation work between Dixon and Fulton. As a matter of fact these constructional crews accurately constructed its railway line to efficiently reach Fulton on December 16, 1855.

In this State of Wisconsin the Galena's northern section of its railway which primarily started out as the Madison and Beloit had been formally organized on July 3, 1849. However, that line reluctantly was taken over by the Galena and Chicago Union Railroad under another name. On the contrary this recently acquired company built their railway line from Janesville northwards to adequately arrive at a place called Fond du Lac, and then had actively proceeded southeast in order to meet up with another rail line which was subsequently started northwest of Chicago. As a result, these modest railway lines were essentially able to consume smaller idle ones which had meagerly gone almost bankrupt in 1857, and then resiliently formed together a bountiful reorganization which then became known as the Chicago and North Western Railway. The Galena and Chicago Union was also clearly sensing their utmost possibilities of strong and forceful competition within southern Wisconsin, and some of those rail lines were beginning to quickly fall into troublesome difficulties which had pungently caused the Galena and Chicago to wisely merge together with this Chicago and North Western Railway on June 3, 1864. Rather significant was that the Chicago, Milwaukee, and St. Paul Railroad had tenaciously started to build northward, while a Milwaukee and Chicago Railroad began its strenuous track construction work southward, and those two rail lines utterly met within accordance during June of 1855, before being wholly combined in assimilation with the North Western Railway by an infinite lease of 1866.

Before the Civil War had spitefully begun this Illinois Central Railroad was currently stretching outwards while railroad train service was being aptly carried westward to reach Waterloo situated in eastern Iowa. Additionally by using its trackage rights on that Galena and Chicago Union Railroad, this northwestern branch of the Illinois Central had distinctly secured a feasible route which was almost instantly accessible to Chicago. Moreover the Galena road notably stretched forward and expanded onto Fulton, and had even crossed over into Clinton located in Iowa before being perpetually pushed west to as far as Cedar Rapids. In conclusion the Chicago and North Western Railway successfully entered into northern Illinois, southern Wisconsin, and other railroad junctions before conveniently finding its prewar terminus at Appleton in this State of Wisconsin.

* * * * * * * * *

A corporate railroad charter was being affluently granted on February 12, 1849 for the Aurora Branch Railroad which formerly ran their first steam locomotive train before November of 1850. This line had been gradually prospering which exclusively resulted for them in gaining allowable credit with eastern bankers, and as a result that fearless investor whose name was John M. Forbes of Boston had then contentiously decided on changing its name over to the Chicago and Aurora Railroad. Additionally, their advantage of this particular available banking support had been extremely helpful when lending out any money to various other local lines which clearly were in near bankruptcy. Moreover, Forbes and his associates also began some effortless attempts to reliably establish a railway system by heavily investing in a Michigan Central Railroad.

That Chicago and Aurora Railroad had the financial strength it eagerly needed to build connecting stretches of track as they further extended a rail line through from Aurora to Galesburg within western Illinois. Also, two other railway lines were under scrupulous construction from Galesburg out to the Mississippi—with one of them terminating opposite at Burlington in Iowa, while its other route had thusly ended at Quincy, Illinois just eighty-two miles away from

Burlington. In fact that Mississippi River was vehemently attained once the Chicago and Aurora had solely accomplished a railway merging conjunction with their Burlington line in March of 1855. After all of this having been consequently produced, the Chicago and Aurora had proudly renamed itself the Chicago, Burlington, and Quincy. Furthermore that Chicago, Burlington, and Quincy Railroad had finally arrived at Chicago by 1852 along these North Western railroad tracks, and later had uniquely built its own line into Chicago before 1864.

During 1847 a group of respectable business associates were gathered together at Hannibal in Missouri only nineteen miles below Quincy. John Clemens (father of Mark Twain) strongly stimulated his recommendable efforts to begin building tracks for a rail line along the Missouri River at St. Joseph's. However for a period of ten years Clemens had only constructed thirty-five miles of trackage even though they originally received a land grant of 600,000 acres; and as a result the Chicago, Burlington, and Quincy was to have fashionably stepped forward in order to finish up this necessary work by 1859. More importantly, it's Hannibal and St. Joseph rail line was expeditiously carrying the U.S. mail which had intimately started America's first railroad mail car train service between West Quincy and St. Joseph on July 28, 1862. Valuable to note was that the Chicago, Burlington, and Quincy line had probable intentions to advertently juncture up with its Omaha connection, and by earnestly working along with this Burlington and Missouri River Railroad they were bearably able of making it through to the Missouri River on New Year's Day of 1870.

On the contrary this Chicago, Burlington, and Quincy Railroad was extensively growing and had voluntarily used some of its yearly surplus to necessarily replace those old rotten out wooden tracks with iron rails and later on with steel tracks. In addition, more powerful steam engines were also being purchased which could produce faster speeds of forty to fifty miles an hour on level ground, and train coaches were substantially increased to conveniently provide seating capacity for up to sixty passengers. Chiefly that Chicago, Burlington, and Quincy Railroad had been made up of 203 links along its roadway which were prudently purchased as possible bankrupts when prices sharply fell after the Civil War. Of these notorious and resilient Midwestern railroads only it's Chicago, Burlington, and Quincy had sold out at a premium price to James J. Hill who had been consistently busy for enabling to create a new railroad empire of his own with a railway which was operating within the State of Minnesota.

Although during a thirty year period there had been more than four hundred railroad charters perpetually being issued and were conceivably released for railway lines to be built throughout the Middle West from 1830 to 1860. Originally those initial twelve miles of the Chicago, Burlington, and Quincy had been greatly advanced which fluently resulted to over nine thousand miles, and easily covered as many as eleven States that were indeed located around this Midwest vicinity. Likewise the Chicago, Burlington, and Quincy Railroad can be truly described as one of its first great diagonal route lines in copiously and plentifully stretching across this escalating North American continent moving from northwest to southeast. Furthermore several new roads were constantly branching out from that city of Chicago, and had been well organized by 1870 which authentically made them a dependable and responsible systematic mode of rail transportation for agricultural products, freight carriers, and passenger service accommodations.

* * * * * * * * *

This awesome race of reaching Chicago which had alertly and informatively been started was prosperously carried on by respectable railroad companies who curiously consumed local lines, and building whenever necessary to insistently achieve a through route for a worthwhile railway to applicable function. In 1851, the Chicago and Rock Island Railroad earnestly began their railway construction work to tolerably build a roadway route which would run parallel with that Illinois and Michigan Canal, and then could stretch westwards so as to reach this Mississippi River at a place called Rock Island located within the state of Illinois approximately seventy-five miles south of Galena. Moreover the Chicago and Rock Island Railroad had courageously executed its further determination and purposeful plans of railroad building between Chicago and Joilet which were proficiently operating their own locomotive train service by October of 1852. During the following spring of 1853, road excavation and track lying had been amply built to Peru just alongside its northern bank of this Illinois River, and by late February 1854 these constructional crews had appropriately arrived at Rock Island. At first locomotive freight trains were not properly allowed to actually run through train service into Chicago because merely an expectably cooperative agreement with that Chicago and Rock Island Railroad of allowably permitting "through freight service" had not been readily reached yet in conformance as those trains were being promptly terminated at Joilet upon its arrival.

In 1854 an eastern terminus was being constructed for the Chicago and Rock Island Railroad at a site along Van Buren and La Salle Streets following this compelling and skillful construction work which immensely concluded after their Joilet branch line was suitably completed. Worth mentioning the Chicago and Rock Island was principally involved for constructing its first bridge to crossover the Mississippi River during 1856, after that brilliant attorney Abraham Lincoln had deviously defeated some compulsive efforts of river boatmen to elusively divert away from their constructional project for thoroughly being reasonably consummated. Coincidentally, John B. Jervis had helpfully supported for advantageously broadening the Chicago and Rock Island onto Davenport in Iowa; and he also favorably aided Lincoln by deviating to justly defend its right of bridging this navigable stream, certainly a major victory for a lawyer from Springfield. Nevertheless many river steamer men totally fought that bridge construction work across the Mississippi legally in court, and thus apparently failed which resulted in them deliberately burning it to the water line before those diligent expeditious railroad crewmen were competently able to reconstruct it back again.

Significantly enough the Chicago and Rock Island Railroad enduringly passed across these rolling grassy valleys and level prairie lands between the Great Lakes and its mighty Mississippi-Missouri regions hauling locomotive train cars loaded with boxcars of coal, lumber, and ores traveling towards the West, while farming products abundantly filled them up moving out to the East. Essentially during

1854 their operational railway connections with Chicago going to the southwest propelling through St. Louis was primarily obtainable, and that Chicago and Alton Railroad exceptionally made it across from East St. Louis and Springfield to a branching line route at Joilet over its Chicago and Rock Island's trackage stretching into Chicago. On the contrary becoming it's first through line running from Chicago to this customary eastern terminus of the Pacific Railroad, and then after concisely sensing that fundamental success, this Chicago and Rock Island was then renamed to the Chicago, Rock Island, and Pacific Railroad. Also as an occurring consequence the newly organized Chicago, Rock Island, and Pacific Railroad had closely been able to form relevant links with another expanding Midwestern road of this North Western Railway.

Special attention should be noted that this railway gauge being used for the Chicago and Rock Island as well as all its other railroads of Illinois except only on the Ohio and Mississippi Railroad had been utilizing the standard size of 4 feet 8-1/2 inches. More importantly was that the Chicago, Rock Island, and Pacific Railroad had been able to accessibly reach a site located at Council Bluffs where this eventually became its eastern segment for an overland route extending across to the Pacific Coast once the Union Pacific conventionally connected up with that Central Pacific during June of 1869 at a place known as Ogden situated within the state of Utah. Furthermore these reputable and infinite Midwest railroads were constantly and repeatedly being terribly annoyed about lowering their freight rates for shipping costs mainly because they were widely becoming flamboyantly fortunate throughout railway development. In fact during the early period of railroad operations passenger business was of somewhat greater importance than that of freight while many rail routes urgently became more flexible with their established railways. Although solely traveling along by railroad in comparison with other modes so as to strategically provide for an utmost effective means of self-assured transportation quickly had acquired those worthwhile train passengers of riding to its particular scheduled destination within a rather considerably swift and expedient time frame.

CHAPTER SEVEN

Much of these surrounding lands westerly of the Mississippi River over which many miles of railway lines were to be built for this Santa Fe had been part of that Louisiana Purchase of 1803 resourcefully costing our nation less than three cents an acre. In fact those first white canvas covered Conestoga wagons departing out from Missouri actually started rolling westward during 1821 which had been commendably led by Captain William H. Becknell, and were spending almost six months before arriving at Santa Fe in New Mexico. Although by 1850 that stagecoach journey coming out to Santa Fe from Independence, Missouri had been taking about two weeks and which was literally costing $250 for this intensive trip. Moreover these wagon trains had suitably traveled along by forming parallel columns, and bringing with them products of calico, hardware, and trade goods while traveling back lighter and faster with wool, furs, and buffalo hides. Most importantly the Santa Fe Trail an extinct Indian pathway which stretches across from Missouri to New Mexico was approximately 850 miles long and in many places 250 feet wide.

Colonel Cyrus K. Holliday who was a notorious lawyer from Pennsylvania and member of that Kansas legislature had effectively written an appropriate charter for the Santa Fe Railroad in 1859. His essential granting agreement had obviously began their proposed route at Atchison, and thoroughly passed through Topeka over an area up to a point along its southern boundary of Kansas Territory leading into this adjacent direction of Santa Fe, and then continuing outwards towards the Gulf of Mexico. Likewise after making a distant trip to Atchison these prominent and perpetual railroad promoters for the Santa Fe were able to adequately raise its needful requirable capital, and during that month of September 1860 had officially organized their own railway company. Furthermore at the first annual board of directors meeting Colonel Holliday was preferably elected to be president of this Santa Fe Railroad by its original thirteen responsive and influential members.

Senator James H. Lane of Kansas was proficiently favorable to introduce and enact a bill during 1863 by which the federal government had permissively granted this State certain tolerable lands for a projected railway. As a result on November 24, 1863 some of these elite railroad stockholders strategically met together at the Chase House that was located in Topeka, and compulsively officiated of changing its name over to the Atchison, Topeka, and Santa Fe Railroad which was wisely suggested by Senator Samuel C. Pomeroy. On the other hand more than 150,000 people had subsequently moved out from the Missouri across those deserted plains during 1864. Valuable to note was that Colonel Holliday along with his associates had been able to advantageously purchase 3,000 tons of 56-lb. iron rails at an ultimate cost of $100 per ton and which were being imported from England in August of 1865.

The first authentic and accountable land surveys accurately prepared for a feasible railway between Topeka and Atchison had been relevantly planned upon by Otis Gunn within 1865. Also Gunn was able to further proceed ahead with his surveying work, and by January of 1866 he had precisely outlined an acceptable route to as far as Emporia just sixty-two miles southwest of Topeka, and 111 miles away from Atchison. In addition an experience and well-qualified contractor was considerably hired by this railroad company, and he had spent several weeks studying over much of its scarce terrain before giving it up as desperately hopeless. More important was that at Topeka the capital of Kansas, help wanted ads relatively appeared in some local newspapers which were skillfully asking for 500 railroad surface graders at a reasonable pay rate of $1.75 per day during this month of October 1868.

On the contrary an established contracting firm by its name of Dodge, Lord, and Company had been frugally selected on June 20, 1868 to intentionally perform their roadway grading and trackage construction work for the Atchison, Topeka, and Santa Fe railway line to officially begin at that time. This new railway route was directly aimed at heading up to Shunganunga Creek, and not Atchison because there were vast amounts of black coal deposits being fatefully found near Carbondale. Also, these capable men on the construction crews began its treacherous work near the end of October 1868 as this roadway was being built in order to arrive at that Kaw River just located within a few hundred yards from their actual starting point along Washington Street. Among its building materials being used timber lumber was abundantly hauled in by ox teams to this Kaw Bridge site, and two 150-foot trusses were scrupulously under construction by some active workmen. Furthermore by March of 1869 its roadbed was smoothly graded upwards towards a small hill which was boldly situated near this town of Pauline, and soon afterwards those rail tracks were being laid across that bridge only five miles from Topeka.

By its end of April during 1869, two more miles of railway construction had been entirely completed as these iron rails were being cautiously spiked to either walnut or oak crossties. Most of all it was taking approximately thirty minutes by steam locomotive to engagingly embark upon a totally finished section of railroad tracks extending seven miles in length at a careful speed of twenty-five miles per hour. In fact those construction gangs steadily continued along with grading its roadbed while laying rail tracks, and after a few weeks their route was in running condition to Carbondale. Additionally by mid-September of 1869 this sequential route was broadly extended to reach Burlingame which was just twenty-six miles away from Topeka. The most notably aspect was that a round trip train ride departing out of Topeka to Burlingame had efficiently taken two hours, thirty-five minutes by locomotive with four or five train cars although it had to regularly make an apparent stop over for water at Wakarusa Creek.

Meanwhile at Carbondale this roadway had exceedingly passed over its boundary of Shawnee County as their new line was being built across these western territories of Kansas. Worth mentioning were that near those adjacent towns alongside its roadway many substantial business operations began to rapidly develop, and some people conveniently living close by had immensely profited from sharp penetrating increases of real estate land values. Evidently within the summer of 1870 inferential reports indicated that working teams were finally able to enter upon this town of Emporia, and locomotive train services were being promptly started out from Topeka. As an imperative result the Atchison, Topeka, and Santa Fe had been graciously running two of their daily passenger trains in each direction at a compulsory speed of eighteen miles an hour. More specifically this railway line moving across that Kansas prairie was consummately constructed by vigorous strong labor as there was little or no machinery available; and picks, shovels, and horse-drawn scrapers were mainly being put to use for cutting and filling these surrounding land areas. Also many of its railroad crewmen were either Irish or Italians, and those working teams easily had bearably sheltered themselves among other laborious groups of workers who were staying in some accommodating accessible camps which was suitably headed by a boarding contractor.

Much of this railway construction and roadway grading work frequently was progressing for the railroad while its line proceeded ahead through Doyle Creek before eventually arriving at Newton during April of 1871. Although in order for them to respectfully earn their provisional land grant that rail line had to be fully completed at its Kansas-Colorado state line before March 2, 1873. In the meantime a steam locomotive was reliably operating over this route and was providing passenger service between Topeka and Newton for a total distance of 134 miles which commonly made that trip in seven hours and twenty minutes. Valuable to note the Atchison, Topeka, and Santa Fe had occasionally transported migrating settlers westward in either boxcars or coaches, and also that railroad company partially depended upon a great deal of cattle business from many of those places around its plentiful areas.

Principally the construction building for its Santa Fe line had begun northwards from Topeka to reach Atchison and which was moderately advancing in late 1871. Additionally these construction teams steadily built towards each other, and had jointly met within two miles west of Valley Falls, Kansas. As a matter of fact its first Santa Fe locomotive train proudly ran along this route from Topeka into Atchison on April 24, 1872. Special attention should be noted that those Santa Fe trains crews often kept Winchester rifles handy which sometimes were used to exchange gunshots with town drunks as well as would be train robbers when it was traveling throughout these rolling prairies.

More importantly Captain John Ellinwood and his associate Albert A. Robinson necessarily conducted a land survey within an immediate area just west of Newton alongside the Arkansas River. Also, a routine survey was accurately being prepared for a stretch of section which was located exactly twenty-seven miles southward to this village of Wichita. Likewise J.D. Criley who had compellingly helped build much of the Kansas Pacific line to Denver was quickly appointed to be officially in charge of roadway construction work by 1872. In addition he usefully had exhaustively managed to lay down a mile of iron track per day while further extending this route from Newton to essentially reach that Colorado boundary line.

In May of 1872 with only about ten months left to go before wholly and concisely fulfilling their incentive land grant, its surveying teams warily calculated that only 271 miles of trackage had to be indeed finished. By June of that year, both grading crews and track gangs initially began work again and were soon able to enter upon Hutchinson near this Arkansas River. As much of the construction work progressively endured notable developments along that railway line were conclusively extended to reach Great Bend by July of 1872. Furthermore those rigorous working crews of J.D. Criley had relatively laid down sixty-five miles of rail tracks in thirty days and obviously were able to safely arrive at Pawnee Creek.

One significant aspect was that three miles of iron track a day had been pretentiously constructed during October of 1872, and more than 300 miles of rail trackage were undeniably achieved in 230 days. Ultimately this Kansas-Colorado boundary line was incredibly attained on Thanksgiving Day of 1872 once its roadway graders had intensely arrived, and their railway tracks were fundamentally accomplished on December 22nd. As a result within a few hours after these railroad tracks were laid into Colorado, the first steam locomotive train ran along this line with its chief engineer whose name was Peter Tellin. Last of all that railway route stretching from Atchison over to the Colorado state line was 470.5 miles in length, and its governor of Kansas rode out for final approval and inspection of the line before officially approving their land grant which had been formerly given to the railroad company.

* * * * * * * * *

During this treacherous and sudden panic of 1873 these roadway graders were able to inevitably approach upon reaching Dodge City along its western end for the Atchison, Topeka, and Santa Fe Railroad. However, there were not enough adequate and available finances to be needfully obtained for beginning with new construction work although tracking crews had exceptionally managed to amply lad down thirty-three miles of rails to that town of Granada. As a matter of fact at the time an engineer working for this railroad could make up to $3.25 a day while steam engines were comparatively costing its company about $7,000 each. On the contrary there were no lavatories aboard those coaches, and coal stoves had to be reluctantly supplied for heating up its locomotive cars during colder weather conditions.

Unlike its more common places such as Topeka, Hutchinson, Emporia and other Kansas towns, Dodge had been laid out with rather narrow roadways for a potential route. Morcover that town of Dodge located alongside the Arkansas River had exceptionally begun to gradually develop, and which sufficiently grew as buffalo hunters could possibly earn up to $100 dollars a day. Especially crucial was that by 1874 this rail line had extensively been in running condition from Atchison and Topeka out to Granada, and even with some of their branch lines advancing onto Wichita and El Dorado. During the spring of 1875 that Atchison, Topeka, and Santa Fe Railroad had astutely acquired a Kansas Midland line which was basically started out of Kansas City, and then extended onto De Soto for a distance of twenty-four miles in length. In addition this Kansas Midland Railroad had bearably used these Missouri Pacific railway tracks so as to reach Lawrence for a distance of fifteen miles, and continuously built twenty-six more miles of trackage onto Topeka.

Special attention should be made that the Atchison, Topeka, and Santa Fe as well as other similar customary railroads which were responsible for this initiative and primary development of the West definitely had a tremendous effect upon creating an advantageous transcontinental route. Yet many of its wealthy eastern investors had become extremely doubtful to confidently anticipate a railroad which would travel across that remote desert, and they were unwillingly putting their gold coins away in safe-deposit boxes. On the other hand these railroad crewmen had persistently worked between twelve and fourteen hours a day with no Sundays off, and a great number of families were being raised on either twelve or fifteen dollars a week. Exclusively it was normal practice for the Atchison, Topeka, and Santa Fe to voluntarily transport desolate settlers free of charge as out on those lonely isolated prairies were noticeable signs which explicitly read: Railroad station, five miles—food and water.

In compliance with their permissive land grant which was generously attained much of its railway construction for crossing over to the Colorado line had sizably entitled this roadway to procure about 3,000,000 acres of accessible land. Consequently the land incurred along that railway had to incisively commence paying local taxes while it also was carrying government freight in addition to soldiers and officials for half rates, and mail was often purposely hauled by this railroad at morally reduced charges. Valuable to note that the usual rate for stagecoach travel was around twenty cents per mile while this railroad company might be charging anywhere between five or seven cents, and some nearby farmers would be able to economically prosper within a few miles of a railway. Slowly the panic of 1873 had densely dissipated and many seeking prospectors were moving ahead into these Colorado canyons where they had been able to profitably begin to start opening up silver and gold mines.

Meanwhile trackage construction starting from Dodge City and going out to Granada was thoroughly concluded by May of 1875 over a 133-mile stretch of land. Imperatively an important election was being creditably held during March of 1875 to gainfully vote on subscription bonds to be diligently dispersed for the Atchison, Topeka, and Santa Fe of further extending their line onto Pueblo, and in effect a considerable bond amount of $150,000 was eventually allocated and subsequently passed. As a result a precise land survey was being concisely prepared along a section of land for building an efficient rail line beginning at West Las Animas to arrive at Pueblo, Colorado. Also grading crews and track gangs primarily began constructing a railway line along its north bank of the Arkansas River. Likewise that extension link covering an area from West Las Animas to Pueblo was about seventy miles in length and which had been totally finished near its end of 1875. Furthermore, once this Pueblo branch line began to significantly operate these constructional crews had to suitably replace and change over their railroad tracks with heavier steel while many improvements were being properly conducted on several of its dilapidated bridges.

Valuable to note were that railway train service operations departing from Atchison as well as Kansas City to this State capital situated at Topeka had officially been started on March 1, 1874. Additionally Kansas City was decisively selected in becoming its utmost place of where to build a riverside terminal for its railroad company. Once being solely situated along this river and with their facilities well secured the Atchison, Topeka, and Santa Fe would not have to venture upon building eastward for years to come. More importantly a steam locomotive could make that run from the Missouri River to Pueblo in about thirty-one hours. In spite of the fact that even though some Indians had often torn up these tracks, burned bridges, and looted way stations, those railroad crewmen determinedly continued building its rail lines westward.

Formerly William B. Strong of Vermont had been its general superintendent for the Burlington when that Atchison, Topeka, and Santa Fe had voluptuously acquired him on November 1, 1877 as their general manager. Moreover one of his first assignments were to pertinently proceed ahead westward for laying out its necessary groundwork going up through these mountain passes, and then down into the Gulf of Mexico. When William had firmly joined forces up with this Atchison, Topeka, and Santa Fe it was presently operating 786 miles of trackage with 618 miles of rails running from Topeka to Pueblo. Another important railroad builder for the Atchison, Topeka, and Santa Fe was Albert A. Robinson who consistently supported in extending this railway line over the Raton Pass down towards New Mexico, and then pushing westwards to Arizona. However, Albert Robinson perpetually left the Santa Fe so he could infinitely take over construction work of the Mexican Central Railroad when that Atchison, Topeka, and Santa Fe had been its most superlative system in this world.

The Atchison, Topeka, and Santa Fe had especially continued to lay tracks along its roadway and finally were able to reach La Junta located in Colorado. Also, road construction work just east from Pueblo had simultaneously met up with those working crews who were building west from Granada by February of 1876 at a site known as Trinidad. Fundamentally from Dodge City westerly to Pueblo was a total distance of 265 miles, and there were only eight towns existing along this railway route. During September of 1878 the Atchison, Topeka, and Santa Fe had worthwhile constituted reliable passenger service with four daily locomotive trains that were purposely running in each direction. As a matter of fact Dodge City inevitably became a plentiful booming cattle town which would conventionally send their foremost shipments by railways along to many Eastern markets.

In 1877 an appropriate charter had been written by the State legislation of New Mexico and which was earnestly issued to the Atchison, Topeka, and Santa Fe for constructing a route over this Raton Mountain range. More important William Strong and these dedicated loyal promoters were able to initially organize the New Mexico and Southern Pacific Railroad, and also for them to fully commence with building a rail line from Raton Pass to arrive at its Arizona boundary line. Nevertheless some land surveying work was being scrupulously accomplished by Strong and his surveyors from La Junta across an area of terrain towards Raton, New Mexico. Additionally both Albert Robinson and William Strong had infallibly decided upon creating a mainline divisional point at Bernalillo just situated within sixteen miles northward of Albuquerque. Last of all it had been utterly determined to build east from Albuquerque towards the direction of Raton, then west to Santa Fe, and from there out to El Paso.

Likewise constructional crews began grading work and laying rails westward from La Junta during May of 1878, and their tracks were formatively laid to Trinidad by September of that year. Around this site at Trinidad these level plains were beginning to end, and its rugged mountains looked ahead as 600 miles of iron railways had been eloquently stretched out over those Kansas prairies. In the meantime, railway trackage was entirely completed to reach its Colorado-New Mexico boarder line on November 1, 1878 with 56-lb. rails which were being aptly spiked onto wooden crossties. Although before December 3, 1878 its last spike was being driven down and the first steam locomotive engine majestically began rolling into New Mexico along these Santa Fe railroad tracks.

By 1878 the Atchison, Topeka, and Santa Fe line wholly departed from Pueblo while swinging southwest along its route through Trinidad, then it enduringly headed up to the Raton Pass. However much of this difficulty along its way was not the pass itself, but an incidental fact that another railroad builder called Denver and Rio Grande had prudently wanted to obtain the same route for building their own line. Most importantly was that under the law relating to public lands, this area of uncertainty fittingly went to its railway company which was first to file an original surveyed map of a probable line, or if in case of any doubtful skepticism on that point, it would go to the first one putting in construction work. So while both of these railroads simultaneously pushed ahead for Raton Pass the Atchison, Topeka, and Santa Fe had been first, and they also arrived at Albuquerque along its mainline on April 15, 1880.

* * * * * * * * *

During the fall of 1877 there were affluent silver strikes occurring at this time mainly within the Leadville country which travels alongside its Arkansas River near these Rocky Mountains regional area running north and west of Pueblo. Likewise some newly existing settlements were desperately in desirable intentions of having a tolerable road to be integrally built so as to proficiently move their ore cheaply out, and only a rather narrow passageway stretching over those mountains at Royal Gorge in Colorado could be its only advantageous route for railway construction. In June of 1877 the Atchison, Topeka, and Santa Fe had particularly laid out a land survey going across a section of land which passes through this gorge, and ideally filed a plat that was noticeably acceptable with the land grant office. Furthermore the Atchison, Topeka, and Santa Fe had boldly announced that they would continue building its route west from Pueblo in order to enter into Leadville and Canon City.

Many of these railroad crewmen were kept rather busy with evenly grading its roadbed from Pueblo leading up to Canon City by mid-April of 1878. Also, Albert Robinson along with his qualified team of surveyors planned out a route line up along this Arkansas River, and Leadville was tangibly approached on June 18, 1878. Meanwhile those railroad builders and financial promoters of the Atchison, Topeka, and Santa Fe had chiefly agreed to valuably release constructional bidding contracts for trackage work so that it could be able to reach Leadville by April of 1879. On the contrary much of that road grading and track lying continuously advanced ahead and prevalently proceeded up towards this gorge, while on May 7, 1879 their first locomotive train jubilantly began traveling along these railroad tracks.

Within late summer of 1879 the Atchison, Topeka, and Santa Fe had instantaneously constructed twenty-three miles of rail line from Canon City, and adherently promised its road would soon be built to Leadville by October of that year. However, the Denver and Rio Grande Railroad had effectively brought a court injunction against the Santa Fe to perpetually cease from any grading or building workable achievements westerly of this canyon. Worth mentioning was that inside the courtroom there were numerous flurries of appeals, denials, charges, and countercharges among these two railroads. And as a result, during March of 1880 an approvable agreement was severely announced by both of those railway companies which ultimately concluded for immediately allowing that Denver and Rio Grande to principally pay this Santa Fe a rationally required sum in the amount of $1,400,000 for all work construction west of Canon City, and the Santa Fe highly pledged of totally abolishing any further plans on extending their route out to Leadville and Denver. So ended its courageous discrepancies which were pertinently involved with between these two prestigious companies about railway conflicts; and afterwards the Denver and Rio Grande went directly back into this canyon while the Atchison,

Topeka, and Santa Fe further continued to move forward in pushing its line south and west through New Mexico.

While those Royal Gorge unruly disagreements and persistent squabbles were still enduring the Atchison, Topeka, and Santa Fe steadily progressed westward in a general direction for the city of which it was named. During April of 1878 the Atchison, Topeka, and Santa Fe as well as the Southern Pacific Railroad were both land surveying possible routes along southwestern New Mexico, southern Arizona, and northern Mexico. Valuable to note was that the Southern Pacific had started building eastwards from this Pacific Coast, and had justly arrived at Yuma in Arizona on April 29, 1877. Additionally this Atchison, Topeka, and Santa Fe had virtuously developed some alternate and dependable routes while linking up with that Southern Pacific by which passengers and freight could intently reach its West Coast from the Midwest.

Chiefly these Santa Fe railway crews had feasibly initiated building their trackage in order to reach Las Vegas and also New Mexico as its first passenger train conservatively ran to that area on July 1, 1879. In addition a land survey was being ideally prepared for a rail line to crossover Glorietta Pass, and then descending downwards through Bernalillo, which further would be extended onto Albuquerque. Specifically this planned route had wound down into a valley near Galisteo Creek where it had relatively met up with the Rio Grande River at Santo Domingo. Its roadway then consecutively sustained by following this river southward towards Albuquerque and Isleta, and later out to the Mexican border at El Paso. As a beneficial impact that railway was utterly prosperous in its locomotive operations of 1,168 miles of tracks while their total gross earnings for 1879 were significantly reported to be slightly over $6 million dollars.

As a matter of fact railroad tracks for the Atchison, Topeka, and Santa Fe were being sensibly built over this crest of Glorietta Pass while at Canon City only five miles beyond that pass their railway line was back again on its original old trail. Moreover only twelve miles away to the northwest stood this town of Santa Fe and railroad construction had expectantly arrived there on February 9, 1880. As an effect the inevitable steam locomotive train had considerably wiped out this Santa Fe Trail, and no more would these mule wagons have to necessarily make that long tedious trip over those mountains and across its Missouri plains. Furthermore this last dusty Barlow & Sanderson stagecoach had promptly arrived out from the East, and at Kansas City to Santa Fe there had instantaneously been 860 miles of railway trackage in running condition for the Atchison, Topeka, and Santa Fe Railroad.

One notably aspect of concernment was that their western branch of the Atchison, Topeka, and Santa Fe which had been situated at Deming in New Mexico presumably met at this juncture place along with the Southern Pacific for its first time and their rails were simultaneously connected together on March 8, 1881. Special attention should be noted that the engineer aboard this Santa Fe train diligently drove his steam locomotive over those railroad tracks, and at the same time there was a steel trail extending from Kansas City to the Pacific Coast which eagerly existed in full operation. Additionally that Atchison, Topeka, and Santa Fe also built an extension line for appropriately arriving at this Colorado River as construction work steadily followed ahead, and by mid-February of 1881 these railway tracks were able to reach Fort Wingate just 128 miles west of Albuquerque. However once uniquely in position at that Colorado River the Atchison, Topeka, and Santa Fe still was short some 630 miles from San Francisco, and also 340 miles away from Los Angeles. More importantly, William Strong who had been their general manager of this railroad primarily became president on August 1, 1881 thereby formally succeeding President T. Jefferson Coolidge. Consequently at the time its track layers as well as railroad graders were being adequately paid $2.25 for one shift of work while spike workers and iron men were modestly receiving $2.50 per day.

* * * * * * * * *

The Atchison, Topeka, and Santa Fe had prudently purchased a Kansas City, Lawrence, and South Kansas Railroad which extensively permitted them to admissibly acquire an additional 365 miles of trackage between Lawrence, Coffeyville, Vellington, and

Harper during 1880. In July of 1881 its roadbed was being graded while these rail tracks were amply laid from Rincon in New Mexico to within fifty-eight miles of the Texas border, and then concurrently continued onwards twenty more miles to reach El Paso. On the contrary those working crews were expeditiously being tenaciously occupied with building and constructing more trunk lines along its swiftly developing Kansas vicinity. Valuable to note was that this railroad company had cumulatively incurred 348 steam locomotives and around 10,000 freight and passenger cars.

By 1882 the Atlantic and Pacific railway line was under rigorous control by this Atchison, Topeka, and Santa Fe, and which had evidently elapsed westward from Vinita to Tulsa in Oklahoma for a comparative distance of sixty-four miles of roadway that aptly consisted of steel track mainlines. In fact during 1883 the Santa Fe was reasonably operating about 2,620 miles of trackage in which 1,700 miles were actually steel railways. Nevertheless it had rightfully owned and firmly operated under its own name only 470 miles of rail tracks. Although by its end of 1884, this Atlantic and Pacific line was being inferably linked up with the Santa Fe at Emporia, and some newer branching lines further increased their overall total length to 506 miles. Furthermore within two years later these railway tracks were invariably running south throughout Indian territory, and gainfully had been dependently stretching ahead onto Fort Worth in Texas as that Atchison, Topeka, and Santa Fe was definitely well along its way out to arrive at the Gulf of Mexico.

During 1884 the Atchison, Topeka, and Santa Fe had resolutely worked out an admissible acknowledgement on paper with this Southern Pacific Railroad for building a rail line to vastly arrive at these Western Coastal regions. In addition a practicable route was earnestly established for the Atchison, Topeka, and Santa Fe via Albuquerque in New Mexico to reach that Colorado River which was located at Needles in California. Moreover the Santa Fe was able to willingly lease this Needles line along with trackage rights into San Francisco as an option to purchase its route was also under very serious contemplation. Preferably with their essential approved admirable lease that Atchison, Topeka, and Santa Fe was adherently allowed to run 170 miles west of Needles to Waterman, and then further built a rail line of seventy-eight miles in length to thoroughly reach San Bernardino over the Cajon Pass.

Joseph O. Osgood was their chief engineer of the Atchison, Topeka, and Santa Fe when he especially had traveled to San Diego for strong possibilities of negotiating a tenure lease so as to shrewdly rent a waterfront office in attempting to formally set up business for this railroad during October of 1880. Likewise he quickly organized together a surveying party, and by March of 1881 these construction gangs were put back to work again at a place known as National City, California. Also a section of rail tracks were being virtuously laid along a wharf side in which this Atchison, Topeka, and Santa Fe had basically constructed as its first locomotive cars were being unloaded there to usefully haul mostly all of its building and constructional materials which were going to be reliantly used. In fact much of these crude new construction elements for their crucial and necessary roadway development north towards Colton were bearably carried ashore by towboats which were conveniently situated out along the bay. Valuable to note that this nearest railroad was approximately 132 miles away located at a site called Colton which had been under prominent operation by the Southern Pacific Railroad.

In January of 1882 this railway line was fortunately running to Fallbrook and tracking crews were rapidly moving forward into Temecula Canyon while crossing over these Santa Ana Mountains. Moreover road grading as well as construction work regularly continued along while that route was safely operating locomotive trains to Temecula on March 22nd, and also to East Riverside on August 12, 1882. Nevertheless within only nine days later the Atchison, Topeka, and Santa Fe had incidentally made it into this town of Colton where a joining connection was wholly possible with the Southern Pacific Railroad. More importantly that link along their railway tentatively made a veracious transcontinental route going West out from Kansas City to San Diego but still was not Atchison, Topeka, and Santa Fe all the way.

Spring and summer of 1883 were beginning to slip past while these two contentious railroads had been terribly fighting over condemnation of right-of-way. Meanwhile there was a rail rate war going on in Colton as those merchants were shipping their valuable goods from San Diego to its city at a cost of forty cents per hundred pounds while on the other hand Southern Pacific was comparatively charging forty-two cents. As a matter of fact just four miles of trackage between Colton and San Bernardino were being consistently constructed, and its only missing link was crossing over those railway tracks of the Southern Pacific. At this time another rail line had been near completion so as to safely reach San Bernardino while the first passenger train began running there on September 16, 1883. Furthermore according to the *San Bernardino Index* a new train depot for the Atchison, Topeka, and Santa Fe was being prestigiously placed under initial construction at San Bernardino.

However because of extreme and severe weather conditions which had reluctantly caused some water flooding during February of 1884, many miles of railway trackage extending across Temecula Canyon had been vitally wiped out. Also, bridges and crossties were being swept away out to sea while ships had relatively reported seeing pieces of debris floating within 100 miles offshore. Valuable to note there were no train tracks in functional service between Oceanside and Temecula, while also San Diego was without any rail service for nearly nine months. Special attention should be noted that this canyon route was brutally abandoned, and subsequently a new line had been built up along the coast way going through San Juan Capistrano and Santa Ana.

On the other hand these uncertain problems still had presently existed for this Atchison, Topeka, and Santa Fe Railroad of permanently obtaining passageway from San Bernardino over an ascending route to arrive at the end of its westbound trackage in Needles located 248 miles away. Moreover the Santa Fe had no such authority over this Southern Pacific line going from Needles to Mojave where indispensable business ventures were sometimes forced to stringently travel. Although the Atchison, Topeka, and Santa Fe had been able to favorably gain access to this railway line by imperceptibly signing a binding lease agreement with that Southern Pacific Railroad in August, and on September 29, 1884 its first steam locomotive had proudly rolled over those tracks. As a striking result this remarkably had given the Santa Fe one more linkage of controllable line out to the Pacific Coast except was unfortunately not its through route customarily needed.

Once this Needles-Mojave line was assuredly under control the Atchison, Topeka, and Santa Fe had explicitly planned on building a route from Waterman (later renamed Barstow) seventy-eight miles in length departing over the Cajon Pass leading into San Bernardino. In effect that would at last beneficially give the Atchison, Topeka, and Santa Fe a key through route from Kansas City out to the West Coast continuing along on their own railways. Moreover by 1881 an appropriate land survey was being precisely prepared for building a canyon route, and during the winter some clearing and grading work had been partially started. However for a period of three years nothing much had keenly emerged until 1885 when railway construction work was efficiently resumed again under its supervisory direction of Frederick T. Perris who helpfully supported in aiding to build this line.

Especially significant these first true land surveys being primarily provided for a railway route over the Cajon Pass were tolerably made in 1853 by Lieutenant R.S. Williamson who was a government engineer at this time. Special attention should be specifically noted that his extensive findings report had competently indicated that its only definite approach of arriving down into a valley from this sandy desert would be through a 3.4-mile length tunnel. However, Frederick Perris presumably insisted that there was a potential route through East Cajon where just a simple cut could be properly made along the roadway through its desert rim, and thus tunneling excavation would be unnecessary as this route was the one eventually chosen by these railroad developers. Cajon Pass was unique because it had not been a passage through a mountain, but between two mountain ranges and also travels across an earthquake fault. As those rails were being laid out over that roadway its last spike was driven into the ground, and on November 14, 1885 their railway line had been officially open to the public for traveling and transportational purposes.

Its most notably aspect was that this Atchison, Topeka, and Santa Fe had finally achieved an independent regulation of having a transcontinental railway out from the Midwest as their first through steam locomotive train had deservedly departed at San Diego heading for the East Coast on November 16, 1885. Moreover the highest rate for purchasing a railroad ticket between California and some Missouri river points was regularly costing fifteen dollars in 1886. Although the Santa Fe had been cutting its train fares down to ten dollars while the Southern Pacific further reduced their rates to five dollars. In fact that for only one day of service at its peak of these railroad rates this substantial cost was actually one dollar. Conclusively by fall of 1887 the Atchison, Topeka, and Santa Fe was able to offer complete locomotive train services between Los Angeles and San Bernardino as there were an accumulative combined total of twenty-five cities spanning throughout a distance of thirty-six miles along this railway.

On the contrary there were eleven approachable roads also being abundantly built among these nearby communities which were located within that San Bernardino area with its coming of the Atchison, Topeka, and Santa Fe Railroad in order to fluently arrive at the Pacific Coast. One of these accessible roads had been this Los Angeles and San Gabriel line which was readily opened for locomotive train services to Pasadena on September 17, 1885; while it had clearly approached on towards San Gabriel, and they had mutually connected up with a rail line from San Bernardino. Nevertheless its sensible directors and financial promoters of the Santa Fe alarmingly showed a great deal of consistent interest to advantageously purchase that railway line which was currently headed by J.F. Crank, and president William Strong had successfully acquired ownership of its rail line after a decently reasonable offer was absolutely in compliable acceptance. As a result these construction crews immediately went to work, and were quickly building another route so as to jointly connect together San Bernardino with Los Angeles, and once they thoroughly secured rightful obtainment of this Los Angeles and San Gabriel railway accomplishment it had put the Atchison, Topeka, and Santa Fe into Los Angeles on May 31, 1887. A key feature was that a new direct line had been briskly completed via Riverside, and Redondo was later obviously finished on August 12, 1888; while chiefly providing through railway locomotive train services out of San Diego into Los Angeles which indeed had prodigiously given this Santa Fe the available and influential accommodations of neutrally consummating two West Coast railroad terminals.

* * * * * * * * *

It had become apparently perceptible that the Atchison, Topeka, and Santa Fe would have to build a railway line sufficiently enough to reach Chicago from their mainline terminal facilities at Kansas City as an organizational plan was considerably taken into logical expectation. Consequently once after all of its pertinent arrangements were practically made a route was carefully being surveyed by a team of Santa Fe engineers, and construction work began to move ahead by March of 1887 at Knoxville situated just a few miles outside of Galesburg. At that time more than 7,000 men were working for this railroad company, and soon after construction work began a train depot was also being built at Galesburg in Illinois. Furthermore within only nine months after the Santa Fe train crewmen had affluently located, surveyed, graded, and spiked over 350 miles of new trackage for a rail line.

In fact it was utterly determined that five essential bridges stretching across some of those major rivers had to be built and structurally erected to say nothing about smaller ones totaling in all almost nine miles of strenuous bridge work. Moreover this Mississippi Bridge being 2,963 feet long had skillfully been completed by its working crews, and their last spike was hammered down along these new tracks on December 31, 1887. In addition at that big Missouri Bridge (4,053 feet) work efforts were to be temporarily delayed because of icy weather conditions, but prevalently had been finally finished on February 11, 1888. During April of 1888 steam locomotive trains began to broadly run each day in the morning and evening, which were taking thirteen hours and forty-five minutes for a trip departing from Chicago to arrive at Kansas City. More important for its first time the Atchison, Topeka, and Santa Fe entirely possessed and were solely occupying their own railroad tracks extending from these Great Lakes out to the Pacific, and had productively been able enough to offer through rates as well as dependable locomotive services for its available train passengers.

At the time William Strong had possibly decided to voluntarily resign from his prominent position as president on September 6, 1889 and he was prudently succeeded by Allen Manvel although most Santa Fe men would have mostly preferred Albert Robinson. William had fought bravely for that road which he amazedly built expanding across mountains, through canyons, over rivers flowing past remote desert areas, and down into its lush valley of this Pacific Coast. By May of 1890, Allen Manvel had gainfully purchased the St. Louis and San Francisco Railway which was a 1,329-mile line for over $22 million thus vastly giving its Atchison, Topeka, and Santa Fe instant accessibility into Missouri. Also a Colorado Midland Railroad was courageously bought during September of 1890, and regularly permitted the Santa Fe with a new line out of Colorado Springs to Glenwood Springs, which had gradually conceived a railway connection with this Rio Grande line going into Salt Lake City.

Although after the Civil War had brutally ended that city of Houston soon then became its railway center of Texas with four famous railroads existing in full operation but there had been no such direct railway connections with any other of its adjacent States. Especially significant was that on May 28, 1873 a corporate charter was accordingly granted for developing a rail route starting out from Galveston to arrive at Houston, and with this consent of land privileges had partially aided and potentially helped in moving their plans along the way. Special attention should be made that in a public speech which was intentionally given by Senator Guy M. Bryan on May 1, 1875 at Galveston, he had particularly ended it with an amendable prediction that "the Texas-Santa Fe will be a highway for the grain of the west, the wealth of the Pacific, and the minerals of the far off mountains of Colorado". Principally, General Braxton Bragg along with his competent associates were accurately making suitable land surveys for building a rail line proceeding across Galveston to reach its mainland since July of 1874.

By June of 1875 roadway grading work for constructing a new route had initially began at this mainland in Houston, and it almost nearly took two years to effectively bring forty miles of railway trackage into running condition. Nevertheless financial resources were becoming rather harshly difficult to extremely incur except by 1878 their rail line was promptly extended for twenty more miles so as to reach that town of Richmond. Meanwhile construction work continuously moved ahead again, and within August of 1878 these tracking crewmen were able to lay down sixty-three miles of new line from Richmond to Brenham, and by the next year 100 miles of rails were confidently being built to Belton. In fact Fort Worth was adequately tracked with rails in late 1881, and by May of 1882 this westerly route had been productively carried out into Lampasas for a considerable distance of 361 miles of railway. Also that Lampasas line went down through Ballinger and then exceedingly continued onwards to San Angelo while expedient arrival of the Atchison, Topeka, and Santa Fe at San Angelo was authentically commenced on October 1, 1888 which had excitably touched off a festive parade and cheerful celebration. Additionally another rail line was being constructed from Alvin going directly into Houston for a total distance of twenty-five miles during 1883.

On the contrary this Atchison, Topeka, and Santa Fe would be able to further increase their railway by building a route southward to Purcell located in Oklahoma while its Gulf line had earnestly managed to build northeast at Paris, Texas with a branching line from Cleburne to Weatherford. By April of 1886, an evident roadway survey was being concisely conducted along an area of land so as to basically reach Purcell, and then continuing to Paris and Weatherford in all 300 miles. Valuable to note these constructional crews of the Santa Fe were aptly laying down trackage in Texas faster than it had ever been probably achieved before, and once they fastidiously spiked two miles of rail tracks those tiresome workers were temporarily finished for the day. Also, road graders and track layers were moving south from Arkansas City, Kansas as another route was fundamentally being built for connecting up with its Gulf line which was coming north from Galveston so that they could both mutually meet together at Purcell in Oklahoma.

During 1886 the Atchison, Topeka, and Santa Fe crewmen had relatively started road grading and railway construction again and by December of that year this Salt Fork River was being radically bridged at White Eagle, Oklahoma. Specifically on November 29, 1886 steam locomotive trains were beginning to imperially run between Arkansas City and White Eagle which was a distance of thirty-one miles. Likewise its roadway graders and tracking crews were able to enter upon Cimarron, and a bridge was being liberally built at Lawrie in Oklahoma on February 5, 1887. On the whole by February 8th that rail line was rigorously constructed to Deer Creek (later Guthrie) and through locomotive trains had eventually started operating with passenger services being discreetly offered between Galveston and Arkansas City on June 18, 1887. Furthermore this railway route was finally completed to Paris in spring of 1887, and Weatherford was fully consummated during its fall while approachable arrival of the Atchison, Topeka, and Santa Fe for reaching Texas definitely brought about some enticing enthusiasm among these prominent and influential railroad builders.

Special attention should be noted that a one-way train trip in traveling across this country from San Francisco to Chicago for an incredible distance of 2,577 miles of railway tracks had incidentally taken sixty-nine hours at an average speed of thirty-seven miles per hour on January 21, 1890. Exceptionally out along the flat prairies where these operating locomotive engineers could let those steam engines run, rolling short bursts of speeds had been recorded at eighty, eighty-five, and ninety miles per hour. Valiantly just within a little more than twenty years from 1869 to 1890 the Atchison, Topeka, and Santa Fe had marvelously grown to be its most dignified and impressive railroad system in this world. More important it had either owned or controlled trackage from Chicago stretching out to the Gulf of Mexico, and also along this Pacific Coast at both San Diego and Los Angeles as well as to Denver in Colorado.

After its resourceful and sole acquirement of the Colorado Midland Railroad another rail line was being built westward over these Rocky Mountains from their railway tracks at Colorado Springs through Leadville and Aspen. As a matter of fact that Colorado Midland had chiefly made a joint connection with the Denver and Rio Grande at a place called Grand Junction therefore allowing its Santa Fe line an immediate and available entry into Denver. Moreover during 1887 this Atchison, Topeka, and Santa Fe had conveniently purchased 157 steam engines, 198 passenger coaches, and 3,108 freight cars; then during 1888 it also added 115 newer locomotives, 97 passenger coaches and 5,664 freight cars while still even more equipment was additionally bought in 1889. On the contrary J.W. Reinhart was apparently chosen as president during 1893 in order to physically succeed Allen Manvel, and he had been strictly assigned to be put in charge of its railway lines financial situations.

Unfortunately at this time railway rate slashing started up again within 1893 and the Atchison, Topeka, and Santa Fe had been drastically reducing their train fares departing out of Chicago going to its West Coast on a round trip ticket from $88.50 down to $55.50 so as to possibly expand and realistically accumulate more railroad business opportunities. In the meantime, Reinhart had internally prepared an indicative statement during May of 1893 understandably announcing that "it will be the policy of the road absolutely to maintain rates". However an important examination among their balance sheets was prudently being conducted during that Reinhart management period, and this president was indeed later reluctantly prosecuted by the Interstate Commerce Commission for intentional reasons of granting illegal rebates. Although J.W. Reinhart was readily freed because at the time of when these actual revenue returns supposedly occurred he had not actively been in charge of its railway lines operation.

Consequently with this sort of deviant and delinquent activity bitterly surfacing within its workplace a crucial reorganization plan for the Atchison, Topeka, and Santa Fe Railroad was being desperately developed amongst an official appointed committee mainly composed of selective individuals; and as a residual result on December 10, 1895 their entire system had been tolerably sold during an auction to Edward King at a compelling bid of $60,000,000 which prominently included the property and all of its franchises. Then subsequently within two days later that newly formed company was originally granted their own charter, and its complete assets were essentially turned over to the uniquely established corporation of Atchison, Topeka, and Santa Fe Railway Company. In addition this recently attained organization had imperatively appointed a person by the name of Edward P. Ripley from Dorchester of Massachusetts to be their initial president for its railroad. Although after that substantial change within its recognizable structure the Atchison, Topeka, and Santa Fe had remorsefully lost both the Colorado Midland as well as the St. Louis and San Francisco railways. Therefore with all of this sort of critical and skeptical movement currently taking effect at that present time the palpable Atchison, Topeka, and Santa Fe was graciously left with about 9,000 miles of its own through line services from Chicago to Denver, Los Angeles, San Diego, El Paso and Galveston.

Meanwhile a vicious railroad battle had been spitefully commencing out in the West which was beginning to eminently involve about having that Atchison, Topeka, and Santa Fe being righteously exposed out towards the Golden Gate along its own railway tracks. And exclusively on January 22, 1895 an emphatic and important meeting was strategically held in San Francisco at the Chamber of Commerce on formal discussions and plans to be taken for constructing a railway route into the San Joaquin Valley. In fact some of these nearby valley towns which were constantly subscribing for railroad stock had incidentally included Fresno, Stockton, Bakersfield, Santa Clara, and San Jose. In a meaningful effort the San Francisco and San Joaquin Valley Railroad had been officially organized on February 20, 1895. Valuable to note was that William Storey who had been an assistant engineer for the Southern Pacific Railroad was amply hired on to be their chief engineer of that new line, and at once he simultaneously went to work preparing land surveys along this flourishing valley towards Bakersfield for its route.

Important attention should be significantly made that the first shovelful of dirt was promptly turned over in Stockton, California for new construction work to begin on July 22, 1895 and which would customarily stretch southwards as some proposed towns were already conceivably beginning to be built ahead of the rail line. Once this railway constructional activity began at that site twenty-two miles of tracks were solidly being laid with 62-lb. rails to reach Escalon where an irrigation project was also being inevitably started. Meanwhile these roadway graders and tracking crews cautiously proceeded ahead constructing their line steadily southwards to Fresno, where it had officially opened for services on October 5, 1896. In addition another thirty miles down that line from Fresno lays this town of Hanford which was triumphantly consummated, and its first locomotive train ran there on May 21, 1897. Furthermore it was on September 9, 1897 when these freshly built rail tracks were soundly put down in place at Visalia, and on May 27, 1898 this railway line was efficiently running locomotives which provided regular passenger train operations to Bakersfield.

In the meantime Storey was insistently preparing some land surveying for several routes to adequately crossover these Tehachapi Mountains although most of them would have meant terribly expensive constructional costs. Worth mentioning was that the Southern Pacific Railroad had its only shortest and most practical rail line at this time. Moreover the Valley Road had conceivably extended from Bakersfield over to Kern Junction where it appropriately met together, and at this juncture point it continuously connected up with that Southern Pacific railway line. Under favorable consideration an agreement was elementally reached to permanently assure having general usage of a fifty-eight mile route between Kern and Mojave, thereby rejoining those separate lines of the Southern Pacific and Santa Fe at Mojave. Once it's Kern Junction and Mojave link had been justly made this potentially gave the Valley Road rightful passageway for advantageously creating a more frugal and through route from Chicago to Stockton.

A beneficial engineering survey had accurately indicated that there were ten miles of tulle swamps and two mountainous ranges to cross intervening along a seventy-seven mile route from Stockton leading out towards the East Bay in California. Specifically a section of these tracks had been built by steam shovels which were skillfully able to allowably throw up an embankment for building a secure and stable foundation so as to productively run steam locomotive trains. Even though the Franklin Tunnel which was regionally located on unsteady coastal hills had aptly caused some rather minor problems most of its apparent difficulties had been firmly resolved, and by summer of 1900 this railway line was principally accomplished to a mainline train terminal at their Richmond site location. Moreover, that Santa Fe line had virtuously procured a narrow-gauge railroad which was relevantly named the California and Nevada in order to capably assume ultimate access into reaching Oakland. As an enduring consequence this railroad was then later renamed to the Oakland and East Side which prestigiously ran their first locomotive train service into its city on May 16, 1904.

The ferryboat *Ocean Wave* had evidently departed from a docking slip on July 6, 1900 situated at its foot of Market Street so as to basically and resolutely start its first localized direct Atchison, Topeka, and Santa Fe train service between San Francisco and Chicago. On the average it had particularly taken nearly forty minutes for that ferry to intently arrive at their Santa Fe terminal in Richmond, and once there those awaiting passengers instantly climbed aboard a Dixon locomotive which was suitably heading east into Stockton. As a result, within only two hours later the first transit locomotive train ever had expectantly pulled in from Stockton with fifty passengers which where then expediently taken to San Francisco aboard the *Ocean Wave*. In fact to further conclude with these train passengers leaving out of Chicago going to San Francisco over the Santa Fe's own railway system had encouragingly embarked upon its Ferry Building at Market Street primarily located in San Francisco. Last of all this Valley Road which was originally organized during February of 1895, and after thusly having moderately served and remarkably achieved its bearable purposes had been vastly sold to the Atchison, Topeka, and Santa Fe once they impulsively began and dependably started their own operations of that line in early July of 1900.

* * * * * * * * *

The Atchison, Topeka, and Santa Fe had courageously moved forth with its struggling battles and competing rivals into these scare deserts of Arizona as early attempts of having a railroad built there had feverously been started which was beginning to center around that countryside. During the 1880's this Atlantic and Pacific Railroad was jointly owned by the Santa Fe and San Francisco, while much discussion for constructing a railway line at either Seligman or Ash

Fork in Arizona leading out to its territorial capital of Prescott was meticulously under sensible, useful, and considerable investigation. Additionally the governor of this territory F.A. Tritle had largely supported its determinable project, and was anxiously trying to eagerly persuade Colonel H.C. Nutt president of the Atlantic and Pacific to diligently prepare a land survey route into that adjacent mining country except his desperate scheme had affluently lost mostly all of its vitality. Remarkably enough Governor Tritle was able to competently render creation of the Central Arizona Railroad on May 10, 1884 while an application had been gainfully made to the State legislature for granting a corporate charter for this line. However that probable charter had mischievously disappeared and a member of the legislation was distrustfully accused of possibly having improperly stolen it.

On the contrary during June of 1885 an influentially determined Minnesota Syndicate actively made another attempting effort, and which had currently concluded in an intentional organization fortuitously known as the Arizona Central Railroad subsequently just a reversal of its original name. Moreover that Arizona Central was practically planning to build a narrow-gauge line from Prescott going north to meet up with a joining connection of the Atlantic and Pacific mainline which was situated at Seligman. Nevertheless within a week later another dependable association from New York had confidently taken over, and therefore had reorganized this Central Arizona to inevitably initiate constructing a standardized gauge track line traveling along this same route and then trouble furiously started. As a result, these reputable competitor rivals urgently met together, and on July 16, 1885 both the Arizona Central and the Central Arizona were accordingly merged in combination under this newly acquired name of Prescott and Arizona Central Railroad. In fact a former adventurous railroad promoter of that Arizona Central by the name of T.S. Bullock had begun land surveying a route, and he instantly went ahead with railway construction of its line. Likewise Bullock held stringent control of this line while fortunately obtaining some old 40-lb. iron rails from the Atlantic and Pacific, and had been finally able to satisfactorily have these tracks abundantly finished. Furthermore its first locomotive train being put into operation from Seligman to Prescott ran on January 2, 1887 and their passenger fare was costing ten cents a mile while freight rates were mostly excessive by actual comparison.

Although after five years later perceivable entry of this Atchison, Topeka, and Santa Fe into Arizona was strongly capable merely because of these disputable services and exorbitant rates which were solely in effect during the time under Bullock, and had strictly been morally imposed upon by that Prescott and Arizona Central Railroad. Especially noteworthy was its first spike for the Santa Fe, Prescott, and Phoenix rail line was soundly driven down at Ash Fork on August 17, 1892 and this route had inevitably started to ornately extend south over a land survey that had been originally prepared by their chief engineer whose name was Major G.W. Vaughn. While at the time when those road graders were making a sizable cut along its roadbed near Iron Springs, gold was obviously discovered there during 1893 which presumably reflected in an overall anticipated work stoppage of all further railway construction. On the contrary rails for this line were being built up to Prescott, and on April 26, 1893 their first passenger train was eloquently running along that route. Most of all its final link which readily stood between Ash Fork and Prescott was a total length of fifty-seven miles.

Major Vaughn and William A. Drake were both from New York and had been its two supportive men who were partially involved with on assisting to build an extensive road within Northern Arizona. Also, Drake had built that Denver line for the Santa Fe from Pueblo, and he insistently took over this Santa Fe, Prescott, and Phoenix Railroad by 1895. In addition Vaughn and Drake had dynamically pushed ahead for a railway southward as it was advertently a rather costly proposition of constructing through elevated mountains, and realistically some of those miles impelling ranged up to $40,000. More importantly their railway tracks at Prescott were amply finished so as to pertinently reach Phoenix on March 13, 1895 which had delightfully been traveling over some of its fabulous and spectacular scenery while efficiently running along these mining branches for a distance of 136 miles.

Valuable to note was this Atchison, Topeka, and Santa Fe had wisely invested in building a rail line from Deming northwest to Phoenix, and then from there eastward to Colorado which would promptly meet up with its mainlines between Mojave and Needles. Likewise these Santa Fe railroad promoters were able to prosperously organize the Phoenix and Eastern Railroad on August 31, 1901 while essential land surveying plans were immediately being started easterly for this route. Soon after its roadway grading initially began trackage crews had exceptionally completed a section of that line to arrive at Winkleman on September 28, 1904. Furthermore the railway line was appropriately extended onwards to Salome and Wickenburg as this route had finally reached Parker alongside its Colorado River on June 17, 1907; however, it was not until 1908 before these first Santa Fe locomotive trains were imperiously running between Phoenix and also out to the West Coast.

In 1906 there were several scanty railroads running within California and this Atchison, Topeka, and Santa Fe was virtuously worthwhile in formally purchasing a 38-mile line which ran south from Eureka to Shiveley. One vital aspect was that the Southern Pacific Railroad had eventually started to begin performing some land surveying work in order to feasibly build a route north through Willits, and also onto this Eel River suitably located within Northern California. Moreover crucial studies of this land terrain as well as expressive written reports had indicatively shown that two roads passing through these richly majestic hills and long narrow canyons of this timberland country would not necessarily supplement enough latent commerce opportunities for potential possibilities of acquiring new business relationships. So at last these two contending railroad companies courageously met together, and on January 8, 1907 they had significantly formed the Northwestern Pacific Railroad on a fifty-fifty basis. Also as an imperative and vigorous result this Northwestern Pacific had utterly taken over many of those smaller rail lines within California while construction work sluggishly continued forward rather slowly. Furthermore the Northwestern Pacific had only built thirty-nine miles of track line by 1912; twenty-four more miles in 1913, and additionally twenty-nine miles during

1914 before inceptively opening their railway for passenger service from Sausalito to Trinidad on July 1, 1915.

As a matter of fact a famous train depot which was being explicitly built for that railroad had been well known around the world and it was advantageously opened by the Atchison, Topeka, and Santa Fe at Los Angeles on July 29, 1893. Likewise this train station had customarily cost their railroad company only $50,000 and it was called "La Grande" which had faithfully stood at Santa Fe Avenue and First Street for over forty years. Additionally some of its authentic features of that terminal had uniformly included an interior trim of Oregon pine and California redwood, and also there were even separate lunchrooms for both ladies and gentlemen. Most importantly had been that fifty-two steam locomotive trains were entirely able to modestly arrive at and thusly depart from its train station on a daily basis, while especially situated in each one of their waiting rooms an apparent sign visibly appeared which was inspirationally carved in Flagstaff sandstone with this expressive motto "East or West, Santa Fe Is Best".

Special attention should be made that its very first ever steam locomotive in passenger operation for this Atchison, Topeka, and Santa Fe was traditionally called the C.K. Holliday and it was absolutely assembled at their shop in Topeka, Kansas. Worth mentioning was the steam engine had reasonably been weighting thirty-nine tons, and which also was generally provided with air pumps, driver brakes, and coal burning equipment. It should be noted that some of their older types of earlier steam engine locomotives were adequately able to reliably provide endurable and sufficient services to its railroad company for more than sixty years. Even though many of these water cars running along its railway were simply just two wooden tanks which had been solidly bolted down to one of the flat cars and evidently was being supplied with a flexible rubber hose. Last of all those railroad working crews of the Santa Fe occasionally hung out in wooden boxcars, and were usually seated on burlap sacks of beans, flour or coffee.

CHAPTER EIGHT

The United States had been less than one hundred years old when its first transcontinental railroad was beginning to be built across North America. Significantly this elemental and fundamental understanding of a transcontinental railroad was presumably considered to be these rail lines which incipiently begun building usually from the Missouri, and enduringly continued for its duration to eventually reach that Pacific Coast. Chiefly the conceptual purpose and beneficial factor of solely creating a transcontinental railroad from Iowa to California was perhaps one of America's most intensive and sensational achievements before this earlier part of its nineteenth century until completion of the Panama Canal in 1914. Moreover during August of 1859, Abraham Lincoln had amply met together with Grenville M. Dodge at a place known as Council Bluffs which was located in the State of Iowa so as to imperatively discuss pertinent strategies and useful plans to construct a potential future railway route for a Pacific Railroad which would ultimately reach that Far West. Furthermore, Lincoln relevantly wanted the federal government to lucratively have those States use their sale of public lands in order to rationally raise its much needed capital investment for promoting and constituting railroads within our country at this time.

Grenville Dodge was from Massachusetts and he had earnestly worked on his first railroad at the age of fourteen in planning out roads as a land surveyor for Frederick Lander. During 1848 Grenville competently entered for acceptable enrollment into Norwich University at Vermont to affluently take up principal courses of relative study to impelling become a capably qualified Civil Engineer. He also diligently served attendance within Durham Academy situated at New Hampshire, and had proficiently graduated as a military engineer by 1851 just about the exact time when railroad building was beginning on a large scale along some populated regions. Additionally Grenville was deeply determinable and strongly in approval of running steam power locomotives, while in his diary of 1850 wrote; "Forty-three years ago today on October 12, 1807, Fulton made his first steamboat trip up the Hudson River". Consequently within about two months later Dodge obligingly moved out to Illinois, and soon he went to work conducting land surveys for the Rock Island Railroad as well as other primary railroads which were currently being established in that State.

Henry Farnam and Joseph Sheffield were both land surveyors working for the Mississippi and Missouri Railroad during 1852 while making some routine progressive accomplishments which were evidently organized by Peter A. Day. Likewise Peter Day had promptly hired Greenville Dodge for probable work before June of 1853, and he integrally assisted with a construction project, after subsequently acquiring him on as a surveyor in developing roads to run across the State of Iowa for this Mississippi and Missouri Railroad. More importantly, Iowa was rapidly becoming an intermediate link for any railway lines that were being inceptively generated westwards out of Chicago, and this site had critically became an indispensably required bridge in which to crossover from the Midwest and Far West. In 1853, Dodge carefully guided and incidentally led a surveying team west of Iowa City with the Missouri River being his apparent destination, and after cautiously crossing over that river in a flatboat, he immediately went ahead to vigorously examine its countryside of this Platte Valley in addition to much of their natural embankments. As a final result he instantly knew then at first sight that here was an impeccable place to start with building and constructing an eastern terminal for its coming of the first transcontinental railroad.

Especially important was that Dodge had accurately made an efficient routine land survey over the Platte Valley in 1856, and even beyond up until these Rocky Mountains. Specifically based upon his conclusive results of this report, Council Bluffs was appropriately chosen for the Rock Island road to end, and rationally an ideal place to begin building tracks for a Pacific Railroad, once the government had astutely been assured to possibly proceed ahead with railway construction. Dodge had advantageously pointed out that this route would remain flatly along ground water by productively following the Platte Valley, and he quickly went to work while preparing a sufficient surface grade for a roadbed just located east outside of Council Bluffs. Distinctly it was in 1858 when Dodge persistently decided to make his permanent residence at Council Bluffs, where he also ventured into real estate and was even buying land for the Mississippi and Missouri Railroad. Most of all Dodge's own conceivable intention for a rail line extending towards the West would be on a road running almost straight out of Omaha, alongside this Platte Valley until arriving at the Rockies, then over these mountains in order to mutually connect up with another railroad coming East out from California.

Valuable to note that during 1852 a group of prosperous, reputable, and prestigious men residing within California were eminently gathered together so as to strategically formulate major plans for a railroad to run north and east out of Sacramento which would presumably arrive at some richly mining areas of its lower Sierra Nevada slopes. In fact its name of this rail line was desirably organized as the Sacramento Valley Railroad, and formally Captain William T. Sherman became vice-president of it by 1853. While in the spring of 1854, Theodore D. Judah from Bridgeport, Connecticut had obligingly spoken with these prominent owners of this Sacramento Valley Railroad, and consequently he was at once overwhelmingly selected to be their chief engineer. Meanwhile that State legislation of California had resiliently passed a firm resolution asking for urgent demands to the federal government which would allowably permit those courageous and obvious possibilities of having a meaningful railway connection with the East.

On May 30, 1854 Theodore Judah had adherently reported his first truly prepared land survey findings to its responsible directors of the Sacramento Valley Railroad, and fortunately proclaiming that a road originating from Sacramento to Folsom running along this western edge of these Sierra Nevada Mountains would be best suitable for constructing a railway. Nevertheless during June of that year his team of surveyors had been able to adequately reach Folsom, and as a result by November of 1854, the Sacramento Valley Railroad had responsibly signed a constructional contract with Robinson, Seymour, and Company. A key feature was that together with over a 100 men workforce their roadway grading work for this unique route had resolutely commenced on February 12, 1855. More importantly on August 9, 1855 its first rails west of the Missouri, and also within California were being soundly laid to officially set off trackage construction. By February of 1856 that line was successfully completed to arrive at this mining town of Folsom for a considerable distance of twenty-one miles, and the Sacramento Valley Railroad was plentifully bringing in over $200 dollars a day. Special attention should be noted that when Judah actually arrived at Washington during 1856, he ambitiously wrote a rather short pamphlet (published January 1, 1857) which was equally distributed to every representative member of Congress and had been entitled A Practical Plan for Building the Pacific Railroad.

Since 1852 there were many incentive Pacific Railroad bills intimately introduced to Congress in auspiciously proposing for land grants, and massive sums of dollars for construction work although none of them had ever satisfactorily passed. On the contrary, Congressional debates enticingly ensued at Washington as these more crucial and decisive issues of slavery had to be benevolently resolved, and which became of greater importance than railroads at this time. Moreover in another trip to Washington, Theodore Judah had essentially met together with Congressman John C. Burch of California who agreeably promised to help in drafting of a transcontinental railroad bill, and deliberately introduced it on this floor of the House. Even though Judah had accordingly managed to make an appointment with President James Buchanan on December 6, 1859 while in an anticipated effort of outlining his capable ideas except the President had gone on record earlier in his administration with an endorsement for a railroad to its Pacific Coast. One notable aspect was only the federal government would have that largest capacity of prudently performing a rather difficult task like this, and also the lengthy amount of time amply required to firmly deal with building a transcontinental railroad solely because of available funding resources to finance expendable construction expenses of such an extreme project. Furthermore its proposed line had nearly two thousand miles of rugged terrain to crossover which ran through stretches of desert and over mountainous ranges.

As a matter of fact Theodore Judah was permissively given a spacious room at the Capitol for devotedly promoting his railroad affairs after which he graciously turned it into the Pacific Railroad Museum. Largely contained inside of this room were particularly displayed items such as maps, diagrams, surveys, reports, and other such relevant data. However for six entire months, Judah had constantly been engaged in favoring to promote its practical passage of a Pacific Railroad Bill before returning back to California during July of 1860. Moreover many members of both Houses and departmental officials had quite often frequently visited this museum as Judah's intuitive knowledge of its subject was so though and his revealable conversations expressively entertaining that few resisted their revocable appeals.

By early October of 1860, Judah conformably met up with Dr. Daniel W. Strong who was a drugstore proprietor living near Dutch Flat some seventy miles northwest of Sacramento. In addition Dr. Strong had intelligently heard about Judah's exploring and surveying, and deviously wanted to show him an old emigrant road which runs across Donner Pass. Chiefly this Emigrant Trail had been worthily traveled by its Donner Party during 1846, and which was still in existence as a predicable road leading up over these mountains, and then further extending downwards into Nevada although it was not a terribly busy traversed route. At that time Theodore Judah sought out in meeting up with Dr. Strong at Dutch Flat, and the two men rode off on horseback over to a ridge above Donner Pass. Generally its only obstinate engineering problem was to pretentiously uncover a favorable passageway going down through a 1,000-foot rocky crest past Donner Lake, and next to follow alongside Donner Creek which leads out to this canyon heading into Utah formed by the Truckee River. Moreover Judah had purposefully decided to readily devise upon making his land survey across Dutch Flat and even over Donner Pass, then onward to this Truckee River and also into Nevada Territory. In fact Judah had once feasibly estimated that this Pacific Railroad would eventually cost $200,000 for just surveys alone, plus an additional $75,000 per mile of railway track construction.

Furthermore Judah then officially drawn up what he called "Articles of Association" for the Central Pacific Railroad of California as he and Dr. Strong were among its first ones to sign up for an amount of capital in this way of railroad stock subscriptions.

A certain factor by this time was that Theodore Judah had held several important meetings in Sacramento at the St. Charles Hotel during 1860 with such immortal and distinguishable individuals such as Leland Stanford, Mark Hopkins, Charles Crocker, and Collis Huntington. Likewise these enterprising men and noble storekeepers with goods and supplies to handily sell among prospective miners within this area were utterly anxious of having a roadway built to Sacramento from its Nevada boundary line which was located about 115 miles away. Also, Judah spontaneously explained to them that he had currently crossed over its crest of the Sierra Nevada, and he completely seemed to be assuredly convinced that this Donner Pass road beyond Dutch Flat was their best potential route for constructing a railway. However, he substantially needed to have enough financial aid for his customary practice of making an accurate and thorough examination of its proposed line, and conservatively after aptly presented a tenacious offer to these Sacramento merchants about making them a partnership of this Central Pacific Railroad.

Theodore Judah was heedfully accompanied with Dr. Strong during the spring of 1861 for approaching their way towards Dutch Flat sequentially to perform an expedient land survey of reaching its Nevada state line which almost took nearly all summer before finally accomplishing this enduring task. Even though at various times Stanford, Huntington, and Crocker would often join Judah who was busy surveying within the Sierra Nevada, and also to pretty much acquaint themselves with these adjacent surrounding areas. On June 28, 1861 the Central Pacific Railroad originally came into its radical existence at California, and by August of that year those curiously searching problems of crossing over its Sierra Nevada had been conceivably solved. Furthermore the Central Pacific Railroad was fully incorporated along with Stanford as president, Huntington vice-president, Hopkins treasurer, Judah chief engineer, and with Dr. Strong and Crocker as their directors.

Obviously their Central Pacific boards of directors were absolutely convinced that Judah knew more about the Sierra Nevada as well as building railroads than anyone else in this country. During September of 1861, Judah had physically prepared some survey maps and gathered together pertinent data, strictly for use with Congress upon his returning arrival. On October 11, 1861 Judah had tactfully proceeded ahead onto Washington as an Accredited Agent, and he was wisely representing the Central Pacific Railroad of California. Also, Judah was delicately seeking both land appropriations and financial bonds from the government to encouragingly produce probable subsidies for its possible construction of a roadway. Moreover Judah was well known among these Congressmen, and had been lobbying in the past for acquiring land grants when he earnestly appeared again in December of 1861. On January 21, 1862 Representative Aaron A. Sargent of California had the House floor while publicly speaking at length on many creditable developments and exceptional elaborations of Judah's work, while coherently pointing out that the Pacific Railroad would be useful, and additionally could even serve as a military necessity for our nation if this situation should arise. However despite these civil war and slavery issues, the House had effectively appointed a special subcommittee of their Pacific Railroad Committee to especially assist with helping work on Judah's bill.

Meanwhile the much controversial deliberations and opposing debates over this Pacific Railroad Bill were literately continuing into spring of 1862, and which evidently focused on these immense amounts of plentiful revenue to properly allocate its presentable corporations of building a conceptual road at an approximate projected cost of $150 million dollars. As a matter of fact Representative Thaddeus Stevens of Pennsylvania had rigorously insisted upon a stringent requirement that all of their rails and other ironwork be of an American manufacturer. Most importantly, President Lincoln had affluently taken an enlighten interest at the time, and explicitly made it accordingly clear to Congress that he justly advocated this bill's passage in addition to construction of its road. On May 6, 1862 the House by a majority vote of seventy-nine to forty-nine had convincingly approved this Pacific Railroad Bill, and initially the Senate then subsequently passed the bill on June 20, by an overwhelming vote of thirty-five to five before Lincoln had authoritatively signed it on July 1st. Specifically, under that Pacific Railroad Act of 1862 which had fortuitously made it terrifically latent to fundamentally permit creation of this Union Pacific Railroad, while on the other hand its Central Pacific was partially required to scrupulously complete fifty miles of track laying within two years, and fifty more miles each year thereafter as the fulfilling roadway had to be finished by July 1, 1876. Furthermore it should be mentioned that the Union Pacific would indicatively build west from its Missouri River while the Central Pacific was duly directed to start their railway construction east from Sacramento.

* * * * * * * * *

That enhancing magnetic enforcement of the Pacific Railroad Act of 1862 impact had compulsively permitted political justification for its Union Pacific Railroad, and their first board of directors meeting collectively had taken place at Chicago on September 2, 1862 amongst an elite group of prominent railroad men, local bankers, and tactless politicians. Significantly at this time there were only sixty-seven of these railroad directors in total attendance, and Samuel R. Curtis was preferably selected to be chairman while Mayor William B. Ogden of Chicago was solely made president of its company. Many of those directors were in considerable agreement that one of their biggest problems with this Pacific Railroad Act had been about the first mortgage of government bonds, thus rather making it nearly impossible for the Union Pacific of selling its own bonds. Also, by faultlessly setting the stock issue at 100,000 shares with a par value of $1,000 each severely had limited any eager participation of other smaller investors. Most of all, that public statue reluctantly required demanding encouragement, and endurable fearless individuals who were tough and practical men which would have the ability to compatible lobby in Congress for a more lenient and supportive bill. Valuable to note was that Brigham Young its inspirational leader of these Mormons was the Union Pacific's first stockholder and he had easily paid in full for five shares.

Grenville Dodge had inevitably enlisted in joining up with the Union Army during 1861, and by spring of 1863 he compellingly received an urgent dispatch from General Grant of ordering him to actually proceed immediately onto Washington, and officially report to President Lincoln upon his instant arrival. Then once at Washington, Dodge had soon attentively realized that Lincoln conscientiously wanted to speak with him about railroads—thus recalling his 1859 discussion with Dodge. Moreover this President had pretentiously fixed its eastern terminus of the Union Pacific, and particularly deemed to further consult with Dodge for his confirmable confident decision. Furthermore almost every village located alongside the Missouri River mindfully possessed a definite interest and excitable desire to have a transcontinental railroad start at its site, and Lincoln had intelligently shown Dodge actual pleas from some nearby towns which were relatively located within fifty miles above and below Council Bluffs.

On the contrary Dodge again had to expectantly recur of his firmest belief in this Platte Valley route with Omaha being its best practical place for building an eastern terminus. Likewise a great advantage of utilizing the Platte Valley was it had reasonably extended from its basin of these Rocky Mountains within just one continuous reach for six hundred miles east of this Missouri River as Lincoln was wholly in full agreement with Dodge's decisive selection. Also, Dodge had remorsefully explained to Lincoln about that Railroad Act of 1862 in necessarily having many unkind deficient clauses which crucially made it somewhat difficult in order to sufficiently raise its required capital for hiring private enterprises to beneficially permit any further construction of it. However, Lincoln was mainly in allegiance of having an influential road built, and would critically give this project all attainable support although the federal government could not feasibly build its entire road alone. Nevertheless Lincoln then repeatedly reiterated to Dodge that the government would make any conceivable changes under the law or tolerably give some type of logical assistance to obliging ensue with its constructional building for a railway.

When an emphatic meeting amongst its Union Pacific stockholders had taken place on October 29, 1863 these original number of their commissioners were erroneously being disposed while reliantly enough a firsthand board member of thirty directors were newly elected. On that next day, its active and responsible members easily appointed General John A. Dix who had been readily associated with the Mississippi and Missouri Railroad to be their first president. Thomas "Doc" Durant a railroad promoter who gainfully developed similar interests with this Rock Island Railroad had vitally been chosen and aptly was given the title of vice-president, with Henry Poor editor of the *Railroad Journal* serving as secretary. More importantly, the Union Pacific was sensibly established and prodigiously brought forth after more than a year until Congress had concisely passed its Pacific Railroad Bill of 1862 with Lincoln's satisfactory approval and authentic signature.

Meanwhile John A. Dix its recently official president for this Union Pacific Railroad had presumptuously signed an abiding document on January 1, 1864 formally appointing Peter A. Dey who recently served on the Chicago and Rock Island Railroad as well as the Mississippi and Missouri Railroad to that respectable position of chief engineer. Principally "Doc" Durant pragmatically knew its building materials and labor costs for constructing such an extensive new road like this one would realistically require an enormous amount of capital, and that a contracting company would only allure and attract excessive profitable investments. In March of 1864, vice-president Thomas Durant along with George F. Train an eccentric supporter who virtuously earned a valuable fortune within the shipping trade industry had strategically purchased and rightfully secured control of a Pennsylvania Fiscal Agency which had not yet transpired nor conducted any business transactions until both Durant and Train were legitimately made directors of this recently acquired company. Also during May of that year the Union Pacific board of directors had pertinently been expanding, and they supposedly needed to bring in more men for building their railroad, at which time George Train then renamed this company "Credit Mobilier of America" and whereby making it legally into a construction business. An initial aspect which should be pointed out is that as both tenure stockholders of its railroad investment and constructional company, these deep-hearted investors would justly procure in seeking lucrative and infinite amounts of rational expenses for undertaking such an immense project.

Almost everyone in Congress evidently knew that this Railroad Act of 1862 would either have to be repealed or modified so as to certainly provide for better provisions to productively make its joint connection, and also for other resourceful reasons which were under probable consideration. During May of 1864 an affiliated bill to immeasurably stipulate abundant capital investment had been earnestly introduced into Congress which was finally passed by June, and on July 2, 1864 President Lincoln had radically signed the newly created bill into law. Primarily this Pacific Railroad Act of 1864 had permissibly allocated these directors of both the Union Pacific and Central Pacific to substantially issue their own first mortgage bonds in an equally fair amount with government bonds. Moreover its par value of stock subscription was sternly reduced from $1,000 to $100 each, and exact limitations for an amount held by any one individual person had been instantaneously removed. Additionally that currently amended Railroad Act had morally obligated the Central Pacific to build up to 150 miles east of its California-Nevada border, and also positively restricted the Union Pacific of building no more than three hundred miles west of Salt Lake City. In conclusion President Lincoln perpetually authorized these first one hundred miles of railways from Omaha going out to the west, and he exactly set their track gauge at its standard size of four feet eight and a half inches.

By fall of 1864 the Union Pacific had agreeably accepted a moderately decent and respectable building proposal from Herbert Hoxie an Iowa politician who was selected by "Doc" Durant to construct their road for about $50,000 to $60,000 per mile for its first 247 miles. Consequently this implicit contract was legitimately signed on September 23, and almost immediately had quickly been turned over to its Credit Mobilier whereby Durant then cautiously instructed Dey to perceptively resubmit his own proposal and duly make it $60,000 per mile. However upon disdainful efforts, chief engineer Dey had regrettably tendered his resignation on December 7th, stating that he simply did not wholly approve of this apparent contract with Mr. Hoxie, and voluntarily left the Union Pacific on its last day of 1864. Near the end of December 1864, grading work on the roadbed had been thoroughly accomplished along a twenty-three mile section of land from Omaha stretching westerly to the Platte Valley. In fact on December 6, 1864 this freshly re-elected President Lincoln faithfully delivered his Annual Message to his members of Congress while mentioning that its transcontinental railroad was proceeding ahead with admirable anticipation.

For that Union Pacific Railroad their general route traveling north alongside the Platte River had been customarily under discussion although its exact boundary line was still under favorable contemplation. During 1865 only forty miles of railway tracks were being satisfactorily laid up to a point just beyond the Elkhorn River with all of their indispensable and required sidings, station houses, and water stations in position. By mid-October of 1865 the *Omaha Weekly Herald* had especially reported that roadway grading crews were able to reach this Loup River, and advance teams were already making their way across its next hundred miles. Also preliminary preparations were in progress for building some foundation work at Loup Fork Bridge (fifteen hundred feet in length) and which was adequately scheduled to be put into place and erected during spring of 1866. Valuable to note that at this time railroad graders were significantly paid as much as $2 or even $3 a day while they physically lived out in the open air, worked hard, ate and slept well.

At Omaha on July 10, 1865 these railway tracks for the Union Pacific were being responsibly built and by September of that year track lying was rapidly continuing forward at an energetic pace along its way. Moreover trackage work was frugally started in Omaha to inevitably build a machine shop and roundhouse for its railroad by amply using genuine solid bricks for their raw materials. Likewise the town of Omaha was suddenly growing in size and new buildings were being numerously constructed within its adjacent area. More importantly was that by November of 1865 this Union Pacific Railroad along with vice-president Thomas Durant and a group of local leading citizens ran its first excursion locomotive train to Salings Grove which was only fifteen miles away. One notable aspect was that the Union Pacific adamantly demanded a stronger hand to financially manage their Credit Mobilier which had been nearly approaching deflation, and Oakes Ames a member of Congress since 1862 had mutually joined up with this railroad, and attentively brought about a great deal of beneficial supporting strength to these many occurring problems. Furthermore, Oakes Ames along with his brother Oliver Ames had advisedly purchased $1 million worth of Credit Mobilier stock and they proficiently lent the Union Pacific $600,000 dollars.

* * * * * * * * *

In this electoral delegation of 1860 its Central Pacific president Leland Stanford was diligently swept away into the state house as California's first Republican Governor. Henceforth Theodore Judah had principally submitted his first actual survey findings report since returning back from Washington during October of 1862, and consistently urged that these land surveys be further pushed beyond Nevada, and also efficient plans should be made available for railway construction as far east as Salt Lake City. In the meantime Charles Crocker had a compelling conversation among his board members of its Central Pacific, and was fully received conformable assurance by them with their consenting cooperation to set himself up as Charles Crocker and Company, while competently doing business as a railroad contractor builder. Likewise Crocker intentionally drew up an exclusive contract for advantageously awarding to this Charles Crocker and Company along with several other minor companies its potential right to appropriately build and construct the first eighteen miles of roadway work which also included grading, masonry, bridges, and rail tracks departing out of Sacramento. Moreover the Charles Crocker and Company was being dependably awarded a special contract for supplying all crucial equipment, materials, supplies, and rolling stock to be absolutely necessary in constructing this inclusive project. As a result its Charles Crocker and Company had then immediately filed an affirmative acceptance of those provisional terms and agreement which were adherently demanded upon by that Railroad Act of 1862 with the United States Department of Interior on November 1, 1862.

On January 8, 1863 an advertisement tacitly appeared in this *Sacramento Daily Union* newspaper for the Central Pacific Railroad affluently indicating that pertinent building proposals would be timely received at their office for its fundamental construction work of the American River Bridge. More importantly, Charlie Crocker was trying to severely avoid conflict of interest charges as well as any other sort of unethical practices, so consequently he had gravely submitted his resolute resignation to its board of directors. On the other hand, while acting as master of ceremonies Crocker formally introduced Leland Stanford to a large group of spectators which were publicly gathered together at an event on January 9, 1862 to uniquely shovel its first spade of earth for the Central Pacific Railroad as some intense crowds carried on before slowly dispersing away from this joyous celebration of that day in Sacramento. During February of 1863 this grading work for its route had purposely started up again, and their western end of the Central Pacific line was underway to build a truss bridge across its American River.

Within early April of 1863 construction work for that Central Pacific Railroad slowly proceeded onward, and in the meantime Judah was already laying out this surveyed road through Dutch Flat and even over its Donner summit. Near the end of that month, grading work for their roadbed was basically completed from this American River along a seven-mile stretch of land. And on October 26, 1863 these railway tracks for the Central Pacific were being spiked to their crossties, but there still were many miles of trackage work ahead, while on November 10th, the first Central Pacific steam locomotive Governor Stanford ran along a two-mile section of railroad tracks. In fact a pile driver was specifically being used for its foundation work to construct building a bridge, and wooden piles were deeply driven down to twenty feet before they had finally reached solid footing. In addition another newspaper advertisement for the *Sacramento Daily Union* notably appeared which had promptly announced to all building contractors that sealed bids would be particularly received until June 1, 1863 for its entire remaining portion of this route. Much of its invoking work mainly consisted of grading, masonry, and bridges within a section of that roadway located between Placer County to Clipper Gap for a considerable distance of thirty miles.

Meanwhile Theodore Judah was kept extremely busy during early May of 1863 for the Central Pacific where he was carefully planning out his concise surveys of this Sierra Nevada region, and soon afterwards withdrew from those mountains in order to officially attend a board of directors meeting that was stringently held at Sacramento. Valuable to note the Big Four (Stanford, Huntington, Crocker, and Hopkins) as they were beginning to be known confidently affirmed that it had been awfully tiresome of constantly having to bear all of their tremendous costs of construction, and inevitably wanted every director to be somewhat equally responsible for its accountable expenditures which would be merely required in building and constructing this railway. Judah then anxiously became bitterly unwilling over its obvious situation, and he relevantly felt that the Big Four were defiantly being dishonest with him. Also in the matter of where this Sierra Nevada route had originally started, and even on its Dutch Flat wagon road wrongly accusing them of mishandling and distortion of the public's trust and their monies. Realistically, Judah had predictable determinations of buying out these Big Four, and dynamically enough had reliantly made communicable contact with Cornelius Vanderbilt from the east who evidently told him, that he would be vitally interested in virtuously purchasing the Central Pacific, but clearly wanted to have more definite details about this railroad and all of its current activities.

Nevertheless an abrupt dispute had regrettably arisen within California about who would own the Central Pacific Railroad, and therefore Judah obtrusively was excitedly influenced in bringing about a changeover. Moreover on October 3, 1863 Judah along with his wife Anna had taken off on a steamship in order to especially meet up with Vanderbilt at New York. However during this exhausting trip he was caught up in a violent rainstorm while also suffering a terrible headache that night, and mortally contracted yellow fever where he had fallen victim to its critical epidemic in less than one week. After his apparent death Judah's wife Anna visibly erected a memorable monument for him when he was peacefully buried on November 4, 1863 at a very quiet cemetery just outside of Greenfield in Massachusetts.

Special attention should be noted that this board of directors for the Central Pacific had resiliently appointed a New Hampshire man by the name of Samuel S. Montague who had been lured away from its Sacramento Valley Railroad to intensely act as their new chief engineer. As a matter of fact his first responsible assignment was to begin preparing a land survey for a practical route going to Big Bend that runs alongside the Truckee River, and which was situated more than forty miles east of this California-Nevada boundary line. Likewise Montague along with a small group of his surveyors had wholly developed their land surveying to reach Big Bend during December of 1863, while many of these reputable loaded cargo ships usefully contained with rolling stock, and cut lumber had been fittingly arriving at those shipping docks at Sacramento. By February 1864 railway tracks were being solidly laid down just outside of Sacramento to a place called Junction (Roseville) and there awaiting passengers would be able to take horse-drawn carriages in order to travel seven miles beyond Newcastle to come upon Bloomer Cut. At this time, constructional workers were being paid $3 a day or so plus board, and sometimes there were certain instances of drunkenness, strikes, and slowdowns.

Chiefly on March 19, 1864 its Central Pacific Railroad had encouragingly exercised an excursion trip for some members of this California legislature along with their families which was expeditiously led by Governor Leland Stanford over to some newly opened granite quarries just outside of Sacramento. On the contrary, that Central Pacific began running their regular passenger service into Roseville located only twenty-two miles east of Sacramento, and operated three locomotive trains daily in each direction. Worth mentioning were these train crews had to use black powder charges for blasting away this rocky hard gravel at Bloomer Cut, and picks and shovels substantially filled many wheelbarrows to capacity in order to move out any scattered remains. By the end of its first week of June, Crocker's men had consistently laid trackage to reach Newcastle, and passenger trains sufficiently started operating from Sacramento to Newcastle. At its beginning of July 1864, the Big Four were urgently sent an emphatic wired telegram message from Huntington who was in Washington, which accordingly informed his partners that this Pacific Railroad Bill of 1862 had been moderately redrafted.

In January of 1865 the construction crews were able to lay down five miles of trackage from Newcastle to Auburn and by April, Bloomer Cut was also readily road graded and had later been completely tracked. On May 13, 1865 their first train began carrying passengers and freight to Auburn as this railway was closely approaching these Sierra foothills. By June its working crews had further pushed forward to arrive at Clipper Gap which was situated about forty-three miles east of Sacramento. And in August its railway tracks at Clipper Gap were feasibly extended eastward eleven miles to reach Illinois Town (renamed Colfax) which was fifty-four miles away from Sacramento. In essence three regular scheduled locomotive trains a day were traveling each way between Sacramento and Colfax, and the Central Pacific Railroad usually had set their passenger fares at ten cents a mile while in addition these freight rates were costing fifteen cents a ton per mile—payable in gold only. Before its end of 1865 there were more than seven thousand Chinese at work for the Central Pacific and with just under two thousand whites.

During mid-October of 1865 there was a granite sloping ridge which ran three miles long located alongside of this American River thus nicknamed "Cape Horn" which had to severely require regular blasting with continual usage of black powder explosives. Distinctly no road grade could ever be built going through that crest or even over it as optimally thirteen tunnels had to be dug and bored along this stretch, and while just situated at the other side of it stood Dutch Flat. Although it had taken until August of 1866 to extensively reach Dutch Flat from Colfax for a proportional distance of fifty miles which were some of the toughest, hardest, and rather expensive to sequentially construct. Last of all on November 29, 1865 some designated government inspectors thoroughly examined this railway track from Newcastle to Colfax and safely pronounced it to be vigorously tolerable.

* * * * * * * * *

For its most part a major concernment at the time were that these Union Pacific rails had fastidiously been increased to arrive at Fremont in Nebraska just located forty miles west of Omaha while their first terminal supply center was also being exclusively constructed at this site. By the end of January 1866, three appointed government commissioners were gainfully accompanied by vice-president Thomas "Doc" Durant, and they rode out together so as to prudently make an accurate inspection of this route which already was laid to its end of track at Fremont. Likewise their return trip back to Omaha was ordinarily accomplished at an average speed of thirty-five miles per hour, and these official commissioners were in mutual approval to accept on behalf of the government its first actual forty miles of railroad trackage. Moreover during February of 1866, two brothers by the names of John Casement and Daniel Casement both from Ohio had meticulously submitted their prepared building bid proposal to this Union Pacific Railroad, directly through its Credit Mobilier as track laying contractors for performing that intensive purpose of constructional work. Additionally between them these two brothers had valiantly formed their own construction firm of J.S. and D.T. Casement which had been conceivably hired by Durant, and they were mostly assigned to be solely in charge of supervision for laying those railroad tracks.

Meanwhile some variable land surveys which were sensibly guided under its direction of James Evans and Samuel Reed were being satisfactorily conducted which ran clear to this Humboldt River located in Nevada approximately two hundred miles west of Salt Lake City. More important at Washington the war department prevalently granted indefinite leave to Major General Grenville M. Dodge at his tentative request, and thus taking off he properly proceeded ahead to Omaha in resuming his competent duties with its Union Pacific Railroad as chief engineer during May of 1866. Nevertheless Dodge had at once met up with these land surveyor parties while they were out on a close inspection for a projected route going alongside a southern fork of this Platte River in Colorado. Valuable to note it had been positively assumed that this railroad company would build their mainline through Denver City into Colorado Territory nearby these prosperous gold fields of its encircling area.

It was during early June of 1866 when railroad crewmen were able to efficiently move ahead with rail construction of its roadway so that they could reach Columbus in Nebraska which was ninety miles away from Omaha. At Columbus both the Loup River and Platte River gently flow into each other, and railway tracks had to be built over a 1,500-foot trestle bridge at this site. Also, its roadway graders and track gangs again continued working along the route and intently arrived at a small German settlement of Grand Island by late July, and at that place had securely created its first divisional point which was 153 miles away from their initial source of origin. Additionally by August of that year its end of trackage had been further increased to a thirty-seven mile section of land west of Fort Kearney, and also onto a stagecoach and emigrant station situated alongside the Oregon Trail.

On September 21, 1866 the *Omaha Weekly Herald* had been viably announcing that this Union Pacific Railroad was able to permissibly print a timetable schedule which clearly indicated their daily routes as they were running two locomotive trains a day from Omaha into Kearney for a distance of over two hundred miles. As of October 6, 1866 its end of track had temporarily reached the one hundredth meridian line in Nebraska at this 247th milepost marker which had been written into that Railroad Act of 1862. On the other hand a victorious celebration known as the Great Pacific Railway Excursion was being publicly advertised beforehand in New York and Chicago which then became an epochal occasion on October 16, 1866. Moreover this Union Pacific delegation was indicatively led by Thomas "Doc" Durant, and in its evening of that night an excursion locomotive train especially pulled into Columbus where a campsite had been amply setup while supper was waiting for them. Shortly after these joyous festivities had taken place the Union Pacific Railroad was beginning to operate daily locomotive train services along this line up until Grand Island, and additionally by late August it was able to reliably extend their train operations for proficiently running to Kearney nearby that military post. Special attention should be noted that their total spending expenditures for this railroad construction to be built in reaching its one hundredth meridian position which also included building and equipment costs were relatively less than thirteen million dollars.

By mid-November the roadway graders and track layers were busy building their rails to as far as North Platte. Also, during 1866 Dodge had sent out his land surveyors to logically locate a best possible route for traveling over these Black Hills which directly leads through Wyoming into Salt Lake, and even beyond up to the California state line. Although there were huge mountain ranges along the Rocky Mountains to crossover Dodge could potentially overcome its Black Hills without incurring too many extraordinary expenses, and while still rather keeping their roadway grades comparatively light for a mountainous railroad. In his absolute conclusive report to its board of directors, Dodge was able to plainly achieve a much orderly description of this surrounding terrain from that western part of Nebraska all the way up until it had evidently reached the Sierra Nevada. By end of November 1866, the Union Pacific directors tenaciously met together at New York to heartily discuss pertinent affairs for dealing with this position of a new president, and Oliver Ames was imperatively elected by a majority of votes.

At Omaha during its winter of 1866-67 this Missouri River was frozen over, and twenty miles of railroad tracks were utterly destroyed east of Grand Island due to such extreme weather conditions. Also, Indians were inevitably reported to have been seen out along the North Platte which were hostile and warfare, and they emotionally despised these iron rails. Nevertheless Dodge had supposedly given his confident commanding order that he necessarily wanted every available man armed, and they were to permanently keep their rifles always within easy reach in order for safety and protection. By mid-April of 1867, Jack Casement along with his working crews were starting up again and had handily proceeded to begin laying new tracks. Since their onset of construction during 1867, these Union Pacific workers were tolerably able to push ahead and seventy miles of rails had been continuously laid up through that valley of Lodgepole Creek between its two forks of this Platte River.

During the beginning of May 1867 its track layers for the Union Pacific assiduously advanced forward in commencing to lay down rails quickly, and they were averaging more than one mile per day while moving across western Nebraska towards Julesburg. Additionally the roadway grading parties cautiously worked far beyond these track layers even sometimes as much as one hundred miles, and their land surveyors were always assuredly in front of those graders laying out the final line of its route. Moreover that unkind and unruly weather had sluggishly slowed down their track construction of this railway, and even had tentatively stopped it while some Indians were fervently threatening to improperly put it out of circulation. In fact many of the Union Pacific railway crews greatly had what these Indians readily needed such as hats, jackets, rifles, ammunition and livestock while much of it could be easily captured by a violently raiding party. On May 1, 1867 the Cheyenne's had ultimately eliminated a four-man mail pack just west of Laramie, and on May 18th an Indian war party was obviously reported to have deliberately pulled up one mile of railroad stakes. As the weather conditions began to realistically improve these Indian attacks by both Sioux and Cheyenne furiously increased while striking its rail line along various places, and killing four Union Pacific workers, and even derailing a locomotive train near its end of track.

In July of 1866 a designated surveying party which was partially accompanied by Dodge had been sent out to prepare working along some encompassing land regions just west of this summit near these Sierra Nevada Mountains where it joins the plains to a town known as Cheyenne located at its southeastern edge of Wyoming. Also, Dodge rode off to that summit on horseback and advantageously moved onto Dale Creek which was closely situated by an edge of Laramie Pass where he enticingly studied an overall area of this creek. After going over that pass to thoroughly examine Dale Creek and laying out the town of Laramie, Dodge along with his group of surveyors suddenly pushed west towards its Pacific Coast. Then Dodge becoming tired, overworked, and short-handed strategically went on ahead to further continue with his survey work by projecting a line just easterly of these Rocky Mountains for the Union Pacific Railroad.

What Dodge had mostly observed between Laramie and Utah was an open prairie with reliantly low elevations about seven thousand feet. Likewise surveying work along this parcel of terrain had basically extended across into Wyoming, and also along the Wasatch Mountain Range where Dodge perspectively found a suitable site at Weber Canyon while intentionally marking it down as a probable place to advance onwards through these mountains and continue outwards to arrive at that Salt Lake Valley. While in Weber Canyon near Salt Lake, Dodge had pleasantly met up with its Central Pacific surveying crews which were coming east from the Sierra Nevada across into Utah. Worth mentioning was that Dodge laid out a preliminary route for those land surveyors of the Union Pacific from Julesburg to Salt Lake, and during his routine practical process of it had credibly made its first accountable map of this Great Basin and southern Wyoming.

The Casement brothers along with its significant working crews were almost at Nebraska's borderline near milepost 440 in July of 1867 as their railroad tracks were rapidly advancing to be laid onto wooden crossties. By that month of September, twenty more miles of rails were exceptionally laid to end of track at milepost 460, about halfway between Julesburg and this town of Cheyenne. Also, on October 12th its end of track was neatly in position at Dead Pine Bluffs (now Pine Bluffs) for a reasonable distance of thirty-five miles out of Cheyenne, and by October 29th it was within seventeen miles; while in addition this Union Pacific Railroad was almost nearly five hundred miles away from Omaha. Furthermore on November 16, 1867 the *Chicago Tribune* had plainly published an article which favorably appeared in its newspaper announcing that railway construction for the Union Pacific was physically concluded up to this town of Cheyenne on November 14, 1867.

* * * * * * * * *

On the contrary this Central Pacific Railroad was still rather short of its Sierra Nevada summit as it had to forcefully drive and begin tunneling through severely hard solid granite mountains. However once the Central Pacific had totally emerged out from those

Sierra Nevada Mountains it would be back on that Truckee River, and then their route further traveled until they had distinctly arrived at this Humboldt River. In February of 1866, the Central Pacific was consistently pushing ahead to build their road from Dutch Flat over its Sierra summit and down onto the flowing Truckee River. Although during winter of 1865-66 the supporting embankments along that lower slope near Colfax reluctantly gave way under such immense torrential soaking rains of its climate. Also massive snowdrifts as deep as sixty feet had to be unfortunately shoveled out by hand from below Colfax, and even all the way up to this summit and down into Donner Lake.

By spring of 1866 the Central Pacific promptly hired and amply recruited over ten thousand men working for its railroad company which had been the largest number of employees in America at that time. Nevertheless tunnel digging and excavation work steadily endured ahead slowly at first for building a passageway through this Summit Tunnel until the bottom of it was able to be capably reached before these tedious workers could cautiously begin with drilling and blasting. Valuable to note, there were great amounts of black powder explosives which were being frequently used by Charlie Crocker until he delicately decided to sensible experiment with nitroglycerin. As a result, Crocker soon indeed realized that by drilling several holes of between fifteen to eighteen inches into this solid tough granite, then after carefully pouring in some small amounts of nitroglycerin while capping its hole with a plug, and eventually firing it with a percussion cap—this nitroglycerin definitely displayed in a far better resultant performance than black powder. Additionally their tunneling work was progressing forward at nearly double its speed, and this harden granite had been easily broken up into smaller fragments although these terrible accidents gradually proved much too costly for its present workforce. Considerably enough that nitroglycerin was profitably used only in Tunnel No. 6, and even to a lesser extent at Tunnel No. 8 along its eastern side of this Sierra Nevada slope. Moreover near the vicinity of Cisco, this rock was awfully solid and exceptionally hard that it plainly seemed almost impossible to drill a moderate depth for any type of dangerously explosive purposes.

During 1867 the Central Pacific would not be discreetly patient to allow waiting for its Summit Tunnel to be cut and studiously moved on ahead beyond these Sierra Nevada Mountains. Meanwhile the railroad company sent out three of their exploring parties through Nevada to accurately land survey an area for an accessible route between its Big Bend of this Truckee River located some thirty miles east of the Salt Lake Valley. Explicitly this conceptual route that was traveling in an almost easterly straight line had a series of mountain ranges to crossover for reaching Nevada and Utah which had to be closely inspected. Valuable to note this Humboldt River route was chosen only because it could more practically be built than going into central Nevada, which adequately passes through naturally much better country as opposed to wood, water, and fertility of soil conditions. Superiorly meaningful was that Butler Ives of the Central Pacific Railroad courageously led an original surveying exploration of this Humboldt Valley, and when he aptly arrived at Humboldt Wells had later set off across these Promontory Mountains going around that north shore of the Great Salt Lake, then across Bear River and southward along its western base of this Wasatch Range region to reach Weber Canyon.

In the meantime Charlie Crocker was having several small accommodating cabins being built in order to proficiently provide shelter for his hard-working laborers while large warehouses for holding new raw materials had also been under construction along this Truckee River located about twenty miles below Donner Summit. Moreover Crocker then abundantly sent out his roadway graders and tracking crews to the Truckee, and they immediately proceeded ahead and had started making their way back towards Donner Pass. As a matter of fact loaded freight cars arriving at Dutch Flat, Colfax, and Cisco were actively being unloaded, and these building supplies and other essentials were put into flat wagons going over this Sierra Nevada and down into Nevada. On November 5, the Central Pacific had laid their tracks to Emigrant Gap just situated eight miles west of Cisco, and twenty-one miles westerly of Nevada Summit. Especially of great concern was that its railway construction work along one mile of roadway situated anywhere between Newcastle and Cisco would certainly involve more extensive labor and costly expenses than throughout these level prairies although on November 24, 1866 the first steam locomotive train truly began running at Cisco. Finally on its last day of this year, the Central Pacific had been able to happily announce that their train services were in constant daily operation from Sacramento to Cisco which was a total distance of ninety-two miles, and was within twelve miles of this summit. More importantly the railway traffic traveling between Sacramento and Cisco was occasionally heavy at times as its company's annual operational receipts would fortunately reach close to $1.5 million once these books were conditionally being closed by 1867.

Along this High Sierra region there were forty-four treacherous snowstorms during its winter of 1866-67 as the thermometer rarely was below twenty degrees and usually had risen up to thirty-two degrees. For example one such violent snowstorm occurring within January of 1867 had vitally caused drastic damages to a trestle bridge which was in position one hundred feet high at Cisco. However in less than one month the bridge was rebuilt, and steam locomotives were crossing over this trestle once again bringing rails, supplies, and hardware to these track layers who were working forty miles away alongside the Truckee River. On the contrary a wooden roof covering which graciously extended almost fifty miles in length was assuredly constructed over those railroad tracks to serve its fundamental function of keeping this rail line clear from any such heavy snowstorms.

Approximately there had been some ten thousand men who were heavily engaged at aggressive construction along these railway tracks, and much of their brick masonry work as well as its cumbersome rock excavation had been gainfully completed to arrive at this town of Cisco. Also, twelve tunnels for its productive aspirations of providing passageway were being strenuously bored through around the clock with three shifts of men working together in gangs as an enormous amount of them were mostly Chinese. Except for the Summit Tunnel they would be relatively finished near spring of 1867, and on its Summit Tunnel by November of that year. This Summit Tunnel being 7,042 feet above sea level was sixteen feet wide at the bottom, eleven feet high at the crest of its rise line, and nineteen feet to the top of that archway, thus forming a semicircle of sixteen feet in actual diameter. Moreover there had been a large quantity of railway workers which were mainly situated alongside Truckee Canyon while some roadway graders had been almost three hundred miles beyond the end of track. Although the Central Pacific had utterly estimated that by closure of 1867, these tracks would be able to reach past its California-Nevada border, while this railroad was well into their considerable task of the Sierra Nevada.

One vital aspect should be made that Crocker was becoming intolerably impatient in his relevant driving workforce determinations through the Sierra as rails were being laid from Cisco going up to its mouth at this western heading of the Summit Tunnel during spring of 1867. Also these construction crews were road grading and laying rails on its upper part of the Truckee River moving along in both directions working simultaneously within an eastward and westward location. However there was a sizable gap along this eastern slope of the Sierra which still partially remained without grading or rails, and during late June of 1867 these Chinese laborers had adversely laid down their picks and shovels while reluctantly bringing its manpower to an abrupt halt. Furthermore its railway workers were rationally demanding for forty dollars a month in wages instead of the thirty which was currently being paid, and also were obviously asking for a lesser reduction of their workday to ten hours in its open sunlight as well as eight hours within those darkening vague tunnels. As a result with accordance to the company's own standard policy there was nothing unreasonable about it because normal tunnel shifts were not to supposedly exceed over eight hours anyway, but these Union Pacific directors absolutely had no choice in the matter and angrily agreed to justly pay its agitators, and they liberally convened upon never striking again.

In August of 1867 these diligent railroad workers had cunningly broke through this Summit Tunnel while its headings were properly being met at last, and preferably it was by November of that year before the skillful project was satisfactorily accomplished. Also, rails were solidly laid down for extending this roadway to its east end ultimately breaching the Sierra crest. Nevertheless their end of track had inclusively crossed over this state line on December 13th, and its first Central Pacific construction locomotive steadily steamed into Nevada. However, this was not yet a continuous railway as a stretch of some seven miles still largely remained to be further constructed near Donner Lake. On the contrary its surveyed line of their route had quickly plunged down into a steep slanting descent over such unreliable terrain which was so broken and cut up along the way that even these work mules could barely keep its footing.

More importantly Charles Crocker and Company were almost nearly out of finances while its creditable allowance was all but completely exhausted, and many repeated attempts had been wholeheartedly made to bring about outside capital investment into its firm although without much success. Valuable to note that with this great hurdle of the Sierra passage crucially surmounted, Collis Huntington pretentiously talked over their financial circumstances with some of his influential and wealthy contacts at New York. However, nobody was potentially willing to purchase or even buy Central Pacific stock for its simple reason that they deeply objected refusal of solely going into an unlimited partnership. Consequently as a result the only copious upshot was their strategic development of a Contract and Finance Company which formally became substantially organized during late October of 1867 as a typical construction agency very much like this "Credit Mobilier" of the Union Pacific. Furthermore this newly created company had liberally obligated upon itself to propel building the whole entire remainder of that railway from its California line to Salt Lake at a practical projected cost of $43,000 per mile in definite cash, and including an equal sum of Central Pacific stock subscriptions. Although Crocker still significantly remained to be in charge of construction while this work spontaneously moved ahead without much delay or loss of valuable company time.

Most of all these practical and intelligent land surveyors of this Central Pacific were staying in front of its road graders all the way up until Salt Lake vivaciously planning their route through Weber Canyon and also into Echo Canyon while crossing over the Wasatch Range of mountains. Meanwhile by spring of 1867, its Central Pacific surveying crews were setting up their flags and stakes beside those of the Union Pacific surveyors which were coming out towards the west. Furthermore, during 1867 the Central Pacific had only laid some thirty-nine miles of rail tracks although it was well beyond this Summit Tunnel and had been keenly moving in its direction of the Truckee River. Overall by that year of 1867, those Big Four had conditionally reached out for a monopoly of railroading in California and possessively acquired full ownership of five railroads—the Central Pacific Railroad, the Western Pacific Railroad, the California Central Railroad, the California and Oregon Railroad, and the Yuba Railroad.

* * * * * * * * *

Principally the town of Cheyenne was eventually decided upon to be its winter base and staging center for the Union Pacific Railroad just located along this Black Hills route as switches and sidings were particularly being constructed. Before this year accountably ended Casement along with his construction crews were heading out for Sherman Summit only thirty-two miles away from Cheyenne, and over two thousand feet in elevation. Additionally, just twenty miles beyond past this crest and down its western slope was a place called Fort Sanders which had been their contingently announced goal location of the Union Pacific. Furthermore, the Union Pacific had rightfully owned and continuously maintained fifty-three steam locomotives; nine first-class passenger cars; four second-class passenger cars; and more than eight hundred freight cars while their net earnings for its close of 1867 were $2,061,000 respectively.

The Union Pacific with their grading crews were justly approaching well into Wyoming and these track layers had even past Cheyenne as this much waited eagerness anticipation of a transcontinental railroad studiously mounted with delirious enthusiasm throughout 1868. Likewise almost every newspaper in America was incredibly following the story usually daily or weekly on their front pages, and monthly illustrated magazines also literally featured this intense mania for an impetuous transcontinental railroad. It also soon became a devisable subject of great discussion and mattered importantly among all of these citizens because it was inevitably destined to have an economic affect upon the entire whole population. Moreover there was an attributable article that was written by a Nevada newspaper reporter in summer of 1868 which opened his report saying: "The gap in the great span of iron that shall wed the two oceans is decreasing day by day".

On its last day of 1867, Dodge resolutely expressed to the Union Pacific directors that he expectantly wanted to build this line up to Salt Lake, and then afterwards to accordingly meet up with the Central Pacific at Humboldt Wells which was 219 miles west of Ogden. Outside of Omaha in the east Dodge and his subordinates had sizably shipped an immense amount of rails, spikes, fishplates, crossties, and other supplies to certainly keep these Casements with their extreme workforce busy for quite sometime. Meanwhile in the west Dodge had already prepared some land surveys across Wyoming, Utah, and Nevada even right up until its California state line. Also this route ahead for the Union Pacific moving through Wyoming was comparably easy, and for its next 150 miles from Cheyenne onwards the indispensably contracted company would utterly receive $48,000 of government bonds for each mile of track laid, and which in effect was orderly approved acceptable under final inspection by these decorous authorized commissioners.

By January of 1868 Dodge had spoken with his construction superintendent Sam Reed about their concernments to likely permit its company to road grade three hundred miles in advance for a continuous line of track. Specifically it was that determinable strategy of Dodge for building those railway tracks to within one hundred miles of Ogden, then the Union Pacific could be able to send out its grading crews as far west as Humboldt Wells. Meanwhile Huntington had his distinctive plans and carefully looked over a site map of a preliminary survey where this route ran north of Salt Lake across these Promontory Mountains to Ogden, then which continued eastward into the Wasatch Range, and proceeded ahead up along a northern fork of Echo Creek. On May 15, 1868 this rail line was appropriately ratified by the State, but only as far as Monument Point in Utah as its final conclusion to Promontory and beyond was being seclusively withheld. Last of all a firm decision had not been thoroughly rendered yet about how far this road grading could go so its enthusiast devoted workers went ahead to land survey and road grade as far as possible. Soon enough both of these railroad companies were laying surface grade beside each other at Utah with this Central Pacific going east while that Union Pacific was moving west along parallel roads.

Throughout winter of 1867-68 and much up to and beyond until the beginning of spring some immoderate and violent storms had apparently kept most of their available crews away from working these rails. Although on March 18, Reed had sent out a telegram message to Charlie Crocker providently indicating that his land surveyors had put down their stakes alongside these Humboldt Mountains. By April 5th, those Casement brothers along with its working crews had laid down ten miles of track construction and they nearly reached Sherman Summit. While during the meantime these roadway graders were mainly headed down its western slope towards Dale Creek, just four miles beyond Sherman Summit and thirty-five miles west of Cheyenne.

At Dale Creek both these engineering and constructional workers built a seven hundred foot long pine timber bridge to crossover over this creek which was 126-feet above its bed, thus by far making it the highest bridge for that Union Pacific Railroad. On April 16, 1868 railway trackage to Sherman Summit had been prevalently achieved, and their first steam locomotive earnestly crossed over its Black Hill Mountains. Worth mentioning was that Reed had already composed a land survey of a practical location from Fort Sanders just west of Dale Creek which exceedingly extended all the way to Green River, and on May 6th he had considerately proposed their decisive line for this route. Along the eastern route its road graders were approaching Green River, and Reed had especially planned on going into Salt Lake City where he would fortunately convince Brigham Young in having their Mormons proceed to start on some roadway grading work east towards Weber Canyon.

These Casement crews were really pouring it on racking up one, two, and even three miles of rail tracks a day as that railway was solidly being built over its divide of those Black Hills. On May 5th, this rail line was running down a western slope of its Black Hills well on the way to Laramie with clear objectives in sight of

Ogden, Promontory, Weber Canyon, and Humboldt Wells. Also the route was being graded and ready for rails and crossties up until Green River which was more than halfway through Wyoming as their railroad workers and construction trains were smoothly rolling forward. Additionally, the path of its roadway grade went nearly straight in moving north out of Laramie, then just past Rock Creek, before it again turned straight going westward across the Medicine Bow River up to and even crossing over this North Platte River.

Valuable to note Fort Steele was fittingly situated along its western side of the North Platte River, and located just a bit further west had been a town originally founded by that Union Pacific which was called Benton before moving onto Rawlins Springs. More importantly after this Dale Creek Bridge was stupendously constructed these intelligent engineers had to put the bridge up, and also lay railway tracks over it for locomotive trains to crossover in order to reach that North Platte River. During May of 1868 while erecting the bridge across this river many mules, horses, and men had dangerously drowned in spite of wagons being tipped over into its rushing waters. Furthermore, work along its bridge consistently endured with skillfully putting in pilings, measuring, leveling, and setting these rails in place as the first locomotive effectively crossed over this bridge on July 15, 1868.

Dodge was entirely responsible for planning this route out of Omaha stretching up through Lodgepole Creek and leading onto Cheyenne, then to Sherman Summit and onwards to Laramie, and sequentially to Green River before approaching Salt Lake. In fact there were a large number of wagon teams along with men and women which were increasingly crossing over this North Platte River, and going up as far west as Green River in June of 1868. On July 25, 1868 the end of track for that Union Pacific Railroad was securely positioned at Benton approximately 124 miles past Laramie, and rail tracks were firmly laid in position to Rawlins Springs by late summer. During August of 1868 their railway was thirty miles past this Dale Creek Bridge while traveling over the North Platte River almost within seven hundred miles out of Omaha, and on September 21st end of trackage was just outside of Green River. Moreover from July 21st to October 20th these Casement brothers along with their constructional crews had competently laid 181 miles of rails, and by early November of 1868 this route had felicitously arrived at Bear River City just short of its Wyoming-Utah state boundary line.

* * * * * * * * *

Brigham Young who compelling founded Salt Lake whereby aptly making it into a unique city with his Mormon religion and while during its elementary process of it he exclusively played a major role for its building of the Union and Central Pacific Railroad. Distinctly enough he became head of this Mormon congregational church when their actual founder was cruelly assassinated, and consequently Brigham Young strongly brought forth his faithful members to nearby Council Bluffs during 1846. More importantly, Young had faithfully led the first party of Mormons up through this Platte River Valley, then onwards into Wyoming, and eventually out to Salt Lake City. Furthermore back along in 1863 after the Union Pacific was being effectively established "Doc" Durant had previously spoken with Young about a best feasible route going across America.

Nevertheless from its beginning Brigham Young had been an energetic railroad promoter, and became realistically involved with this route to be followed by the Union Pacific after being one of their first principal stockholders. Also Young was venturesomely eager of having a proficient railroad destined to be at Salt Lake, and he sent out one of his sons Joseph A. Young with a party of Mormons to basically prepare some land surveys. As a result Joseph Young had abundantly reported on a number of primary routes, and the one ultimately chosen by Dodge was up through Weber Canyon and then going over Echo Creek. Although special attention should be made to the fact that when Samuel Reed went out to virtuously inspect that road during 1864, he intently reported it to be much more favorable than had been formerly anticipated.

In 1868 their current situation began for the Central Pacific along this California-Nevada border, and they were some six hundred miles to the Great Salt Lake. On the other hand this Union Pacific

Railroad from Sherman Summit had roughly about five hundred miles to go, and the board of directors virtually ordered Grenville Dodge to have his perspective route line in place from Fort Sanders going up to Green River ready by June 1st, and also to Ogden intervening along Salt Lake by fall of 1868. Meanwhile Brigham Young had mercifully preached a fiery sermon to a fearlessly devoted crowd which was alertly gathered together at Salt Lake, and foretelling them that no railroad could never be built or operated across Utah without their mutual consent and graceful help of these Mormon people. Likewise he also began to think within practical terms for having a railroad of his own by adequately making the best of those existent capable circumstances to abundantly procure that available capacity of connecting Salt Lake City up with its transcontinental railway line at Ogden. Although by spring of 1868, the Union Pacific was absolutely beginning to push forward moving across Wyoming while its land surveyors were well into Utah and beyond.

On May 19, 1868 Samuel Reed had essentially negotiated a constructional contract with Brigham Young for roadway grading and tunnel digging from its head of Echo Canyon situated along this Wasatch Mountain range and extending all the way to Ogden. Additionally these laborious Mormons would precisely receive thirty cents a cubic yard for excavation work, and fifty cents for longer hauls of over two hundred feet while tunneling work was amply being paid at fifteen dollars per yard. Moreover its Union Pacific directors would pay labor costs on a monthly basis, and Young had preferably wanted two dollars and up for one day per worker depending upon their useful skills. A key feature was that Leland Stanford also had been able to coincidentally retain this Mormon contracting firm of Benson, Farr, and West who were in liberal agreement to build one hundred miles of surface road grade starting from Monument Point heading westward. On the contrary, Oakes Ames had chiefly taken it upon himself in totally assuming full responsibility for 667 miles of roadway and rail construction westerly from its one hundredth meridian line at different variable rates of between $42,000 and $96,000 per mile revolving upon contingent of this nature and their surrounding terrain.

Particularly after an initial contract was obligingly signed Young had inspirationally published notices in the *Daily Reporter* and also with this *Desert News* which were asking for all good men who eagerly wanted to willingly work, and some four thousand replies had desperately responded to that actual calling. In the meantime many wheat crops were being terribly destroyed by grasshoppers, and these Mormons confidently showed up in flocking droves as they rationally came from some nearby farms adjacently located around the Salt Lake area. Value to note Young had intuitively sent a wired telegram message to Reed in requesting him to immediately send extra supplies as necessary for putting a large number of available men to begin work at once. Additionally Reed also mainly decided to construct a depot at the mouth of Echo Canyon in which to handle these supplies and materials which were to be necessarily used for its building and construction work.

Fundamentally the binding contract for performing its road grading and railway trackage along an area remotely located just fifty miles east of Echo Canyon towards this vicinity of Wyoming was soundly held by Joseph Nounan and Company. However, there had been some rather deceptive misunderstandings and reluctant miscalculations under that probable contract, and sharp bitterness apparently developed between those building contractors and with the Union Pacific Railroad. A major concernment at this time was that Brigham Young and his three elderly sons were imperatively doing their potential hiring as well as being fully in charge of beneficially directing its men, and two of his sons soon became impetuously involved with a firm known as Sharp and Young. As a matter of fact this newly organized association had primarily started accepting roadway grading contracts, and also its excavation of boring several tunnels, while quickly after these partners were fortunately able to have fourteen hundred men working for them along Echo Canyon.

Early during this summer of 1868 Dodge obligingly arrived at Salt Lake City to sensibly conclude his extensive discussions with Brigham Young for its final route of the railroad. Dodge also vigorously explained to Young that those Union Pacific promoters were aptly planning to build their rail line around its northern end of this lake although Young was in much favor of going south instead.

Nevertheless Dodge's own surveys and those of others had clearly indicated of fully convincing the Union Pacific that north side was its best possible way to go, as this railway would not regrettably run through Salt Lake City, but rather than to Ogden in practical terms. Furthermore Dodge was strongly determined of indicating to Young that its Mormons would have to voluntarily build their own branch line into Salt Lake City.

Brigham Young along with his Mormon subcontractors were road grading and tunnel excavating in both Weber and Echo canyons under the Union Pacific contract while their railway tracks were closely approaching its Utah state boundary line. In addition to the roadway grading and excavation work, those Mormons and other Union Pacific workers had to extensively excavate and bore through four treacherous tunnels along that route. Valuable to note its first tunnel being blasted and dug through was comparatively located in Wyoming at Mary's Creek just 618 miles outside of Omaha. Meanwhile this second tunnel was presently situated at the head of Echo Canyon, but their headings did not properly meet inside of that tunnel until nearly the end of January, and it would be until late spring before any rails could be expediently laid. However these construction crews cleverly built a temporary track of eight miles in length around this second tunnel so that their supplies and materials could briskly move ahead further in a rather much more satisfactory and customary practice for its railroad workers.

Special attention should be made that it was only five miles to tunnel three and about three-quarters of a mile to tunnel four within Echo Canyon and some twenty-five miles to Ogden. In fact tunnel three was relatively on a curvature of 508-feet long while some excavation workers had to tediously burrow through black limestone along a bend in this route which began by September 1868, and was finally concluded during April of 1869. Moreover tunnel four was also on a curve of 297-feet long and which was totally finished before January of 1869. As an inducible result by its middle of January 1869, the first steam locomotive train proudly headed into Weber Canyon just below Echo Canyon, and then afterwards evidently rolled on past milepost 1,000 for this Union Pacific Railroad.

In mid-1868 end of trackage for the Central Pacific Railroad was more than five hundred miles west of Echo Summit as these Big Four were anxiously influenced to begin grading its roadbed into Utah at once. On November 9, 1868 Young readily accepted a perceivable contract with Leland Stanford of this Central Pacific in calling for these Mormons to conventionally build from Ogden going westward until Monument Point just north of Salt Lake. Also that selective subcontractor was the Mormon company of Benson, Farr, and West which had already built one hundred miles westerly from Monument Point. In the meantime that firm of Sharp and Young had actively started road grading west for this Union Pacific, and were practically beside these Benson, Farr, and West workers along its route. Principally up to a particular time both of those two railroad companies were roadway grading exceptionally close towards each other for much of a notable distance especially between its mouth of Weber Canyon and Humboldt Wells.

During November of 1868, Leland Stanford temporarily set up his present headquarters at Salt Lake City and instantly proceeded out to make a close inspection of a preliminary line with his chief engineer Butler Ives. Moreover, Stanford obviously wanted to advantageously persuade these Mormon contractors to initially start their roadway grading work at Ogden then further continue west towards Monument Point. However, Congress had not yet officially decided upon a suitable meeting point for those two railroads as it had been overly ascertained that Ogden would likely be its most conspicuous commonplace. By December 1868, the Central Pacific was in stringent control of a rail line from Monument Point to Ogden, and it also had pertinently finished about two-thirds of roadbed grading at Promontory.

On the contrary Collis Huntington of the Big Four had not been easily convinced to be in consistent approval with its Central Pacific directors, and feverishly decided only to further advance as far east as Echo Summit while reputably meeting these Union Pacific workers there as a central location. Yet the Union Pacific was constantly grading its line from this summit going westward through most of Echo Canyon while their railway tracks were still being obsessively contained in Wyoming. More importantly, Stanford logically saw nothing to be doubtfully achieved by parallel roadway grading along Echo Canyon. Furthermore according to the December 12, 1868 issue of this *Salt Lake Daily Reporter* both its Union Pacific and Central Pacific railroad graders were simultaneously working almost right next to each other. In conclusion end of trackage for the Union Pacific Railroad during December of 1868 was vastly carried onward into Wasatch just 966 miles east of Omaha and sixty-five miles easterly of Ogden.

* * * * * * * * *

By 1868 the Central Pacific Railroad had been under crucial and austere construction for nearly five years while building 131 miles of trackage although they were not absolutely reflected to be in one continuous length. In fact Joseph Graham who was an engineer for its Central Pacific had proportionally staked out a practical route which had been conscientiously surveyed through Nevada before April of 1868. One basic aspect was that in reaching Nevada, Graham widely crossed over country which was already known and had been imperatively mapped out by previous mineral prospectors along this perceptibly established California Trail. During May of 1868, the Central Pacific line from Reno to Truckee was further completed, and by mid-June its remaining distance between Cisco and Truckee was assuredly being closed together. As a result these railway tracks were endurably connected across its Sierra Nevada Mountains while there had been one hundred and sixty-seven continuous miles of trackage laid down in California and also Nevada.

In June of 1868 over three thousand Chinese road graders were being reliantly sent to Palisade Canyon alongside the Humboldt River. Valuable to note was that the Central Pacific began running their first through passenger train on June 18, 1868 from Sacramento to Reno for a total distance of 154 miles. Also, this first steam locomotive ever to crossover these Sierra Nevada Mountains was curiously called the Antelope which had just recently been overhauled and freshly painted. Furthermore this locomotive had bright red wheels with a walnut cab and shinny brassware while a portrait of an antelope was colorfully displayed on its front headlight of that train.

Specifically on July 1, 1868 chief engineer Graham was able to successfully reach the Big Bend of this Truckee River where he set down some marking stakes at Wadsworth. Moreover the town of Wadsworth was significantly located 189 miles away from Sacramento which eventually became their optimal place of storing supplies for its remaining five hundred miles of railway construction. Additionally beyond Wadsworth this route then went northeast across the hot dry desert of sand and sagebrush for nearly one hundred miles before appropriately arriving at Humboldt Valley. The desert an uncultivated region was moderately flat and thus by early August of 1868, these track layers had spiked forty-six miles of iron along the line.

More importantly some of these government appointed commissioners rode out from Sacramento to Reno on September 3, 1868 for justly making their compelling inspection along this railway and found its line to be normally acceptable. Also, survey reports were being concisely prepared for its next two hundred and fifty miles where the Humboldt River plunges down between its rugged mountains through Palisade Canyon. Moreover Butler Ives with a party of twelve men within the far off east had been feasibly making its final preparations for this route from Humboldt Wells to these Wasatch Range Mountains. Special attention should be noted that according to the *Humboldt Register* this railway line was officially open to Winnemucca in Nevada by end of October 1868. Furthermore, Winnemucca was also selected to be a logical terminal and divisional point after Wadsworth before heading up and passing through the lower Winnemucca Mountains.

Specific maps and certain profiles were formally filed with the Interior Department by Huntington during October of 1868 for its Central Pacific's proposed line from Monument Point to Echo Summit. In addition Huntington had virtuously spoken with Stanford about having their rails laid to within 300 miles of Echo Canyon by December of 1868. At the end of November, Stanford along with land surveyor Lewis Clement competently advanced onwards to Promontory where they sufficiently laid out a new line. By December of that year those Central Pacific track layers triumphantly arrived at Elko just 363 miles from Sacramento, and its Mormon subcontractors had their road graders at work from Ogden to Monument Point. The Central Pacific also benevolently built and dependably constructed over 360 miles of trackage during 1868, and they courageously finished as much as two-thirds of its entire road grading.

The Central Pacific route location survey was precisely completed to as far as Great Salt Lake, and predicable lines had been comparatively extended to run further eastward. In mid-January of 1869, these grading crews for the Central Pacific were consummately working at Humboldt Wells in Nevada as well as to its east going into Utah. Although towards the end of this first week during February, the Central Pacific Railroad was suddenly struck by a mighty severe storm which ruthlessly buried that Sierra crest under tremendous amounts of falling snow. For a while there its flow of iron was scarcely reduced to a minimum as this snowstorm fiercely caused their pace of track lying east of Elko to slow down relentlessly. Furthermore the snow slide had vitally carried away a trestle bridge just below Cisco, and also brutally caused an immediate blockage along these railway tracks.

In the meantime Jack Casement along with his construction crews of the Union Pacific promptly arrived at its headway of Echo Canyon by the first week of January 1869. Before the end of February 1869, these track gangs had laid down rails to Devil's Gate as this Weber River runs out of that canyon there, and then flows across sloping terrain to those shores of Great Salt Lake. Once that devastated storm bitterly struck Wyoming it had instantly shut down ninety miles of its Union Pacific line running between Rawlins and Laramie for nearly three solid weeks. Consequently eastbound passengers had been awkwardly stuck at Rawlins and Laramie which were in gallant direction for Washington to be there for its inauguration of President elect Ulysses S. Grant.

While 1868 was rapidly drawing to a near closure these surveying crews had fully accomplished their robust and responsible tasks—for the Union Pacific all the way to Humboldt Wells, and for this Central Pacific to the head of Echo Canyon. Also, during its first month or two of 1869 both the Union Pacific and Central Pacific workforce were diligently working within near sight of each other. In careful consideration these roadway grading lines of the two railroad companies going west from Ogden to Bear River were generally between 500 feet to a quarter mile apart, but at one distinct point along its route they were probably within two hundred feet. Mostly between Bear River and Promontory had been where these Union Pacific workers were particularly close to those Central Pacific crews, redundantly crossing over twice, and with other road grades which were running within a few feet in similar distances.

Mainly along this rocky eastern slope of its Promontory Mountains there had been a large number of Chinese workers which were road grading to the east while Casement and his route graders had been vivaciously working towards the west. At times they frequently were within a few feet of each other while working fast and tenaciously hard all day long. In spite of the fact that those track layers were not within sight of each other, they often were sharply aware of how well each rival line had been advancing ahead. On the contrary, these Union Pacific rail tracks had intensely arrived at Echo City by January of 1869, and had only been within eight miles from its mouth of Echo Canyon. Valuable to note that on January 9th those railway tracks sequentially reached their route which was properly graded at Weber Canyon, and its current trackage was a combined total of one thousand miles away from Omaha.

According to this *Crescent* newspaper a new Central Pacific locomotive readily named the Blue Jay began running trips from Sacramento across its Sierra Nevada to Reno on January 18, 1869. Moreover the Central Pacific had been laying their rails from Elko towards Humboldt Wells during its month of January, and on the 28th these tracks were 150 miles west of Elko. Once out of Humboldt Wells in Nevada, that fixed route would primarily run northeast to its state boundary line at Utah and then onward to Promontory. Inevitably, Humboldt Wells was still 224 miles away from Ogden and which had not been rendered yet by the Central Pacific Railroad.

A key factor was that on January 14, 1869 Secretary Orville Browning who was directly associated with the Department of

Interior had especially given its selective commissioners specific authorization and purposeful instructions to thoroughly make an accurate and essential examination of this route between the two ends of trackage, and also in precisely designating a definitely established point at where these two roads will confidently meet up together. Additionally this chosen special commission would substantially begin with their cautious inspection of that trackage on February 1st, and were observably worthwhile in stipulated conformable agreement to sensibly provide a mutual joining connection at Ogden for both railroad companies. More importantly the Central Pacific Railroad was almost twenty miles east of Humboldt Wells while at the same time this Union Pacific Railroad was nearly twenty miles east of Ogden with its tracks by mid-February of 1869. By end of February, the Central Pacific had further laid another twenty more miles of trackage as their line was being further extended forty miles east of Humboldt Wells and almost into Utah, while yet it still was 144 miles away from Promontory. Meanwhile the Union Pacific had tolerably built and rapidly continued to lay their rails up to Devil's Gate Bridge alongside the Weber River, and were subsequently only six miles from its mouth of Weber Canyon, while still being sixty-six miles away from Promontory although this Central Pacific workforce was prevalently closing its proportional remaining distance between these rails.

* * * * * * * * *

Promontory Summit which stands more than five thousand feet in elevation and some seven hundred feet above its factual levelness of Salt Lake is a reasonably flat even circular basin expanding over a mile in width. Furthermore this summit initially separates these Promontory Mountains that are closely situated at its northern end of the Great Salt Lake, and then gradually a thirty-five mile long rugged peninsula starts to converge. Apparently there were not too many troublesome terrain problems in road grading and laying trackage across this summit basin, however getting up to it on either side was often quite difficult. Likewise along its western side, this joining approach was over sixteen bearably easy miles while on that eastern slope its ascent relevantly required ten harsh miles of uphill climbing, and for the Union Pacific it would be fundamentally their last stretch of roughen country to crossover before arriving at Ogden.

By March of 1869 that Union Pacific had affluently laid their tracks into Ogden while at this same time the Central Pacific rails were 184 miles away from Ogden. Also, its Union Pacific directors had intelligently planned out this new town of Corinne just within five miles of Brigham City along an eastern side of Bear River. Valuable to note the Union Pacific had five pile drivers at work in preliminary preparation of building a bridge over this river while the Central Pacific had only one pile driver at work for them. During early March that terminal town of Corinne was a thriving base for many grading crews of the Union Pacific which had been just twenty-eight miles out of Ogden. Additionally these road graders, tracking crews, and excavation workers were all physically striving along the area vibrantly working that route which was located only twenty-one miles westward of Corinne at where this rising ascent of its Promontory Mountains simultaneously commences to originally embark.

Near the end of March, its Union Pacific roadway graders had their advanced camping site largely setup at Blue Creek which was eighteen miles past Corinne and only ten miles from Promontory. Nevertheless Blue Creek camp was quickly filling up with some idle Union Pacific laborers as a rather scanty grading crew began moving towards its eastern slope of Promontory Ridge. Capably these track layers were working along this route at a leisurely pace although some obstacles still perceptibly had perpetually prevailed, and which resolutely had to be effectively accomplished. For example, a trestle bridge three hundred feet long and thirty feet high was under scrupulous construction while another bridge of five hundred feet long and eighty-seven feet high also had to be potentially built.

The Union Pacific was successful for having their bridge erected first, and on April 7th its first steam locomotive ran across Bear River to keenly arrive at Corinne. Meanwhile the Central Pacific was still almost fifteen miles west of Monument Point. More importantly on April 9, 1869 Dodge exceptionally met up with Huntington at Washington, and these two prestigious men were generally in solid concurrence that both of those roads would conclusively meet together somewhere along its vicinity of Ogden. On the contrary a joint resolution was supremely issued by Congress which said, "The common terminus of the Union Pacific and the Central Pacific railroads shall be at or near Ogden, and the Union Pacific Railroad Company shall build, and the Central Pacific Railroad Company shall pay for and own, the railroad from the terminus aforesaid to Promontory Summit, at which the rails shall meet and connect and form one continuous line".

Ostensibly the selected site at Ogden would be its mainline terminus for this Central Pacific coming east from Sacramento and also for the Union Pacific departing westerly out of Omaha. Likewise with great anticipation the Central Pacific was proceeding forward swiftly and on April 9th their tracks were 690 miles easterly of Sacramento, and by April 17th they had ultimately reached Monument Point in Utah. Especially relevant was that on April 22, 1869 the Central Pacific had been only eighteen miles from Promontory Ridge, while its Union Pacific was just twelve miles away from this summit. Moreover on April 27th the Central Pacific Railroad was fourteen miles short of Promontory Ridge, and realistically this Union Pacific Railroad was within nine miles of its summit approach while laying nearly a mile of railway track per day.

As a matter of fact these Central Pacific working crews earnestly began laying track on April 28, 1869 towards its western slope of those Promontory Mountains. And along this stretch of line there was excessive curvature within its route as each rail had to be meticulously placed between wooden blocks, before being solidly hammered down when it was exactly in the ideal position. Although from sunrise to sunset these courageous and diligently intensive men persistently worked hard continuously lifting iron, and after its spikes were securely driven down into place the next crew would come along to ballast those rails. As a result they were consistently building their rails ahead at a pace of almost a mile an hour, and furthermore there was a total distance of more than ten miles of trackage that had advantageously been completed which absolutely turned out to be a marvelous feat among many railway workers.

More importantly on April 30, 1869 the Central Pacific had remarkably reached its last summit which was more than five hundred miles away—east of the first summit in position above Donner Lake. Meanwhile that Union Pacific route simultaneously continued onwards although they still had to proficiently finish building a trestle bridge which skillfully involved this risky use of rock cutting. On the contrary, its *Alta California* newspaper had conceivably noted that "the last blow has been struck on the Central Pacific Railroad, and the last tie and rail were placed into position today. We are now waiting for the Union Pacific to complete their line". Additionally for the Union Pacific all of their roadway cuts had been made except one, and they were road grading and laying track in both directions while this trestle bridge was nearing its prudent completion.

Once the Union Pacific crewmen began building east from Promontory Summit these two major railroads had decently met unofficially given that its last twenty-five hundred feet were not yet fully constructed. As a matter of fact by mutual consent amongst its Big Four and also with the Union Pacific board of directors, their timely agreed upon date had been graciously set for connecting both of their distinguishable lines together within compliable conformance on May 8, 1869. While on the other hand beginning on May 3rd these reputable railroad companies dynamically began discharging large groups of workers as their boarding camps were chiefly being broken up and abandoned. Also as an impressive result those crews still remaining on the job were significantly busy both day and night in order to justly finish up its road grading and track laying construction work.

Although by end of its first week during May the Union Pacific workers had their iron rails laid over that last trestle bridge along this Promontory approach, and subsequently by May 7th these railway tracks were all but accountably finished. Special attention should be made that on May 6, 1869 the Central Pacific Railroad was running a passenger train which had initially departed from Sacramento with Leland Stanford, the Chief Justice of California, the Governor of Arizona, and other guests aboard its locomotive. Valuable to note the memorable steam locomotive pulling this passenger train was named Jupiter and it imminently arrived at Promontory on May 7, 1869. Also onboard that train had been its last spike made of gold, and their last crosstie made of laurel, along with a silver-headed hammer.

Unmistakably both Sacramento and San Francisco were publicly informed that an expectant joining of the Central Pacific and Union Pacific railroad tracks would surely take place on Saturday, May 8th and this was the date in which they purely intended to positively proceed ahead with their grand celebration. Moreover the first announcement of a traditional ceremony which was going to be held at Sacramento gallantly appeared in the *Union* newspaper just weeks before its impressive commemoration had fittingly taken place. Unfortunately the Union Pacific would not be able to obviously have their locomotive train at this summit site before May 10th because of such extremely constant heavy rainfall throughout Weber Canyon which had reluctantly caused drastic damages to a bridge located above Devil's Gate. Although within these two metropolitan cities this delightful rejoicing steadily went on continuously during Saturday, Sunday, and Monday so as to magnificently signify their enduring development and achievable completion of its transcontinental railroad across North America. Finally the remaining spike was being driven into its last crosstie for connecting their final rails which would sequentially bring together these joining principal route lines from East and West.

At Utah on May 10th a mixed group of Union Pacific and Central Pacific railroad men suitably began to collectively gather among each other while two locomotive trains from the Central Pacific, and also two from the Union Pacific appropriately arrived at this site. Notably there were many glorious speeches eloquently being audibly given and one of them in particular was by a Mormon from England whom had merely rewarded this vital achievement within his own intuitive perception. More importantly Samuel Reed had solely put down its last crosstie—the laurel tie into position, while vice-president Durant partially drove down this last spike into a predrilled hole, and then Leland Stanford officially tapped in the

Golden Spike. Suddenly there had been several champagne bottles which were being cheerfully stricken against each steam locomotive for its desirous fulfillment while Leland Stanford cordially invited some of these Union Pacific delegates over to his private coach for a celebratory occasion. In an instant response across this vigorous nation came the boom of ceremonial cannons, and Chicago had a festive parade four miles long with thousands of people participating, cheering, and watching.

The Union Pacific and Central Pacific railway had officially began with their regular operation of transcontinental passenger services commencing on May 15, 1869. Moreover steam locomotive trains dependably departed daily from Sacramento and Omaha which were gainfully running on timely schedules that necessarily totaled five days between those two independent foremost cities. Valuable to note joint connections east of Omaha could be tolerably made in only six days between Sacramento and Chicago, and it had amply taken just under seven and a half days from Sacramento to New York. However by May of 1870 these patrons who confidently insisted on luxury, comfort, and seclusion could comfortably accomplish their transcontinental railroad trip in about eighty-one hours between Omaha and Oakland aboard the hotel train car which conveniently ran once a week along its railway tracks. As a matter of fact the regular daily passenger train conceivably carried both sleeping cars as well as second-class coaches within its first year of full operation while this overall fare from New York to San Francisco was modestly costing $150 for first-class and $109 riding second-class. Furthermore the Central Pacific railroad traffic uniquely handled over 30,000 through passengers during the year 1869, and in 1870 its Union Pacific had fluently tallied 142,623 passengers with a huge majority of them being through route destinations.

This network of railroads which stretches from these Great Lakes to its Gulf of Mexico and from the Atlantic to its Pacific was the longest strip of iron ever sufficiently built by manpower alone. More importantly only that essential arrival of this early steam locomotive had dimensionally brought about its greatest ominous changeover ever within such a relatively short period of time after it had devotedly crossed over the enormous continent of North

America. Likewise that entire true settlement of three-quarters of America would have been utterly impossible without these steel rails creditably existing within this country, and those useful railways will only attentively succeed while their diverting districts by which they prosperously endure could prospectively serve and eventually become unified. However without railroads, rivers, or canals there would be no such permissible way to easily move tangible products of excessive weight and substantial size coming from its territories within the West to profitable markets subsisting along the East Coast and also in Europe.

Favorably its much accumulative mileage of railroad tracks allocated in the United States are abundantly vast which perspectively ranges from at least two hundred fifty up to two hundred eighty-five thousand while by comparison these quantity of miles for motor freight and public highways far exceeds that of rails. In conclusion no longer will both labor and capital have to valiantly compete against each other in this rail world as they both cautiously must be basically coupled together in an affirmable approval for one responsible team dependably traveling towards a general direction to adequately improve upon its quality of public service for an urgently demanding community. Surely we must not overlook that today the public owns these railways and among those prestigious owners of rails there are potentially tens of thousands of railroad employees who voluntarily purchased rail stock either at par or below. Last of all this prominent steam locomotive conscientiously reflects an aspiring image of a self-contained machine in eloquently pulling forward their rolling stock along a magnitude of railways which were specifically planned and built by such great, enthusiastic, and remarkable railroad builders of our time.

ABOUT THE AUTHOR

Robert Badella lives in Northern California where he grew up and had attended school. Essentially he studied and majored in English at City College under an ethical and superior leadership of influential classroom instructors. Also, Robert enjoys playing guitar and likes to spend his spare time in the garden.

Robert has significantly generated much of his prior work experiences as an Administrative Assistant as well as a Word Processor for supporting well-established companies. Currently he is an active and local member with the Brotherhood of Teamsters Union which is located in San Francisco.

Printed in the United States
56785LVS00004B/60